More Praise for *What They Do in the Dark*

"Amanda Coe's debut novel captures its characters' confusion and disappointments with painful accuracy. . . . [It includes] portraits [that] are both darkly hilarious and powerfully disturbing."
—*Boston Sunday Globe*

"Gripping and disturbing. . . . In masterfully understated prose, Coe explores the way particular adults fail these children, as well as the heartbreaking and horrific effect of violence and ignorance on an entire community." —*O, The Oprah Magazine*

"A fierce, brave, remarkable novel. . . . A long-needled shot that penetrates beyond where we've grown numb; it shocks us, insisting that we feel." —*Pittsburgh Post-Gazette*

"Coe plots these ruined childhoods in a convincing fashion, including everything from drugs to divorce to molestation, without a heavy hand. She has an adept eye for psychological progression." —*Publishers Weekly*

"A brilliant novel. . . . The first half of the book is pure delight. . . . But in the second half, you gradually realize this is not a gentle comedy at all. Indeed, the last 20 pages are among the most horrifying I have ever read." —A. N. Wilson,
Reader's Digest UK

"One of the most masterly, disturbing pieces of fiction I have read in a long while. . . . Will leave you haunted long after you've read the final page." —*Sunday Times* (UK)

"One of the most compelling novels published this year. . . . Its savage wit and transporting eye for detail are the things that keep you along for the ride." —*Times* (UK)

"Despite the undercurrents of violence and sex, this is really a story about character: how childhood innocence is lost, cynicism gained, morality discovered and then, perhaps, lost again. . . . A terrific debut, full of energy and color; as propulsive as a thriller." —*Guardian* (UK)

"[An] impressive debut. . . . A dark, disturbing look at a 1970s childhood, as a tetchy relationship between two schoolgirls culminates in a truly shocking ending." —*Marie Claire UK*

"A rich novel that explores the 'darkness' of social dysfunction both in 10-year-olds and in the adult world." —*Kirkus Reviews*

"Superbly plotted, building, from seemingly disparate elements, with a dread inevitability to a tense and shocking finale."
—*Daily Mail* (UK)

What
They Do
in the Dark

AMANDA COE

W. W. Norton & Company
New York • London

For information about special discounts for bulk purchases, please contact
W. W. Norton Special Sales at specialsales@wwnorton.com or 800-233-4830

Manufacturing by Courier Westford
Production manager: Anna Oler

Library of Congress Cataloging-in-Publication Data

Coe, Amanda, 1965–
What they do in the dark / Amanda Coe. — 1st American ed.
p. cm.
Originally published: London : Virago Press, 2011.
ISBN 978-0-393-08138-1 (hardcover)
1. Girls—England—Yorkshire—Fiction. I. Title.
PR6053.O25W43 2012
823'.914—dc22

2011046038

ISBN 978-0-393-34391-5 pbk.

W. W. Norton & Company, Inc.
500 Fifth Avenue, New York, N.Y. 10110
www.wwnorton.com

W. W. Norton & Company Ltd.
Castle House, 75/76 Wells Street, London W1T 3QT

1 2 3 4 5 6 7 8 9 0

For Andrew

There were terrors, too, of course, but they would have been terrors at any age. I distinguish here between terror and fear. From terror one escapes screaming, but fear has an odd seduction. Fear and the sense of sex are linked in secret conspiracy, but terror is a sickness like hate.

Graham Greene, *A Sort of Life*

The thing about fairy tales is that it's not the spellbound who are free, it's the disenchanted.

John Lahr, on *The Wizard of Oz*

Lallie Paluza

Child star with an uncanny gift for impersonation.

The child star Eulalia 'Lallie' Paluza, who has died two days before her 35th birthday, never attained the profile of her stage school contemporaries Bonnie Langford or Lena Zavaroni. Only eight years old when she won the talent show *New Faces* in 1973, her career was effectively over by the time puberty struck at 13. A precociously pneumatic teenager, Lallie seemed ill at ease with the decision to make her play the nymphet in her LWT show *Me Myself and Her*. Having already endured a brief, fruitless foray to Hollywood, she subsided into a working life of pantos and summer seasons before retiring at the age of eighteen.

Her talent was mimicry. Clive James wrote of her *New Faces* performance that she was 'a phenomenon less entertaining than, frankly, eerie: like watching the product of some mad eugenicist let loose among the chromosomes of Shirley Temple and Mike Yarwood.' Yet there was some evidence that this gift for mimicry was the tip of an iceberg-sized acting ability. Lallie made a memorable straight acting debut in the film *That Summer*, playing a child murder victim. Her portrayal of a troubled child semi-consciously manipulating the paedophile who ultimately kills her, played by Dirk Bogarde, stands out as a performance still remarkable for its unmannered complexity. But Lallie's parents and management were unhappy with the tone of the piece. After cashing in on the short-lived interest from Hollywood, they threw her back into the world of light entertainment, Tommy Cooper impressions and all.

Lallie was married twice: briefly, at eighteen, to actor Steven Garden, who she met in pantomime, and for four years to a property developer, Tim Brian, with whom she had a daughter. Her weight climbed during adulthood, and there were tabloid rumours of problems with drink and drugs. Yet Lallie remained adamant that being famous young hadn't affected her life. 'I was just a little show-off,' she said in a 1993 interview, 'and I loved the attention – every minute of it.'

Lallie (Eulalia May) Paluza. Born April 13th, 1965, died April 11th, 2000.

June, 1975

IT'S NOT EXAGGERATING to say that Lallie Paluza's show is the highlight of my week. Watching her is the perfect end to my perfect Saturdays, which begin with me going swimming with my best friend, Christina. After two hours of splashing and diving but not much actual swimming, we get dressed, shivering and exhausted. Then, hair dripping into the neck of our clothes, we each buy a hot chocolate from the machine at the baths. It's impossible to get warm, so drinking the so-called hot chocolate, with its sweet, powdery bottom layer and topping of tepid purple foam, is the best we can do. We're starving by the time we leave the baths, and each buy a bag of chips with bits from the first chip shop down the road, eating them as we walk.

After that, fingers still greasy, it's a trip to the newsagent, to spend the rest of our pocket money on comics and sweets. The choice of comics is always the same. I pretty much get them all, because I'm spoiled and get 80p a week. There's the *Beano*, *Whizzer and Chips*, the *Beezer* if there's a free gift, and my favourite, *Tammy*, now incorporating *Jinty*, which I used to buy separately. Comics often merge like this, mysteriously. When they do, the week after a surprising announcement, some of the stories you've faithfully followed for weeks fall by the wayside, forever unfinished.

Choosing sweets takes much longer than comics. Although the way we each spend the ten pence for assorted chews, drops and candies doesn't really vary, it's an important part of the ritual, the weighing-up of five milk drops for a penny against the jumbo lolly at two and a half p, the balance between pleasure and value. You want a lot in your bag, the little white paper bag which, within minutes, will have worn wrinkled and slightly grubby, its paper so thin that as soon as the newsagent drops a lolly in it, the stick pokes a hole. The main thing I have learned is that it's never worth buying the chalky imitation chocolate in the penny selection. I'm pretty shrewd, and so is Christina, and if either of us turns out particularly to covet a gum or novelty shape the other has chosen, there's the pleasure of swapsies as we each lay out our spoils on the carpet in her front room.

We always go to Christina's in the afternoon, since my mum and dad both work on a Saturday. Christina's mum doesn't mind us popping in and out. She spends most of the day asleep, either invisibly, upstairs, or stretched out on the settee with the gas fire on, even in summer. She works nights, which makes me a bit frightened of her. Her face always looks puffy when she wakes, and her Glaswegian accent means that Christina has to translate her into Yorkshire for me.

Christina has a little sister, Elaine, who is enormously fat and spends most of the day in front of the telly, watching odd things like racing. We can't persuade her outside very often. Once we cajoled her into Christina's abandoned dolly pram which we had decided to use as a go-cart, and pushed her off on the slightly downhill alley at the back of Christina's house. Elaine, her girth jammed into the tiny chassis, couldn't move as the pram gathered speed, and she hit her head as it smashed into a brick wall. Christina's mum was woken by the wailing and gave us both the same fierce talking to, despite my status as a guest. Christina and I were secretly a bit chuffed about this, since Elaine wasn't badly hurt, and the incident enhanced the image we're keen on as tomboys and scamps. In the books and comics we read and telly we watch and occasional film we see, tomboys and scamps are the only admirable characters, apart from actual boys.

On wet days we shut ourselves in the bathroom and make

cosmetics from talcum powder, bubble bath and unused Christmas-present cologne. We anoint ourselves and Elaine with the resulting paste, which always turns out a disappointing grey in spite of its many pastel ingredients. Or we do gymnastics on the bed until injured or commanded to stop. After tea at Christina's, prepared in zombie fashion by her newly wakened mum, I go home to my mum and dad, who are frying once-a-week steak and chips for their own tea, and establish myself, alone, on the settee. There, with the remaining sweets in their mangled bag, I watch *It's Lallie*. The perfect end to a perfect day.

It starts with the brassy theme music, sung by Lallie in a different outfit each week – usually some kind of sparkly catsuit. During the song she does some of her most famous impressions, with the help of glasses and hats – Harold Wilson, Edward Heath, Frank Spencer – and finishes by tap-dancing down a set of stairs, singing, 'But most of all, I've gotta be me!' The impressions aren't my favourite part, since I don't really know any of the people she's pretending to be, although I can admire the quick way Lallie switches between voices and expressions. I prefer the sketches she does with her guest stars, which are take-offs of famous films, always ending with a song and dance. Most of all, though, I like the glue of the show. Each week, after the theme song, we come upon Lallie in her bedroom – a huge bedroom, stuffed with exotic toys and gadgets, part of the mansion she's supposed to live in which we never see. She lives in this mansion alone, except for a comical butler called Marmaduke, who I adore. He is always trying to escape Lallie's complicated practical jokes, which inevitably end in him wiping some form of cream cake from his face to the unsympathetic farting of a trombone. My dad has told me that Marmaduke is played by an actor who once played a policeman in a famous series.

For me, Marmaduke and Lallie's household lives on in my head long after the programme has finished. It is beyond exciting to see an eleven-year-old girl (Lallie is an important year older than me) on the telly, living a life free of adult interference. For the rest of the week I am Lallie, living in my mansion with my butler and having adventures stolen from Enid Blyton and the comics I read, decorated with bits of the lifestyle my parents' newspapers call jet set. The stories meander, never reaching a conclusion or even a climax. It is the setting, the bright colours and glorious detail, that transfix me.

I wish I looked more like Lallie. I'm pleased that we both have freckles, but her hair is wiry and dark, and mine straight and fair. At the very least I can dress like her, and have nagged my mum into buying me a pair of striped dungarees approximating a pair seen and admired on Lallie in a *TV Times* article. In the mansion scenes, she often sports a pair of polka-dot pyjamas, but I'm resigned to wearing brushed-nylon nighties from British Home Stores. I have mentioned pyjamas, but it seems there are none in the shops. I don't want to harp on about them, as Mum calls it, because I couldn't bear to be teased. Not about the pyjamas, but about Lallie.

The fact is that Lallie, either as herself or as me, is the first thing I think about when I wake and the last thing to leave my head at night. She's more vivid to me than anything else in my life – my parents, or school, or swimming with Christina. And that half an hour feeding on her image is the keenest pleasure of a day spent in pleasure. I'm a lucky girl.

WHEN THE HOUSES on Adelaide Road were built, towards the end of the nineteenth century, they were destined for the newly wealthy, with spacious rooms designed for entertaining and cramped servants' quarters for the staff who made entertaining possible. But after the Second World War, when there were no more servants and much less wealth, bright new suburbs were built away from the centre of town, and the middle classes, eager for the next best thing and poorer than they used to be, abandoned gloomy Victoriana for the all-mod-con estates.

A few elderly householders, the legatees of the nineteenth-century doctors and solicitors, endured. As they died, the rest of the houses on Adelaide Road were sold off cheaply, to anyone who needed the space and couldn't afford to object to rampant damp, ageing wiring and primitive plumbing. Developers divvied the buildings up into bedsits, handy both for the centre of town and the red-light district which was encroaching from the bottom of the road. A couple of unambitious brothels opened. Young couples who couldn't afford the suburbs and were planning on a family ignored the signs of dereliction and spent weekends ripping out original marble fireplaces and oak panelling and replacing them with gas fires and Formica units. Guesthouses were established for the less successful kind of travelling salesmen. And the Brights lived there, among all this improvement and change, with no project other than existence at its most basic.

The Bright household was a shifting population of rabble-rousing adults and their resiliently neglected children, some of whom had children of their own. The family had a dynastic reputation among social services and the local magistrates court;

the Bright name denoted an unworthy expenditure of time, and further signified, at the least, violence and burglary and alcoholism. Bright children truanted and stole and were occasionally sent to Borstal, once Borstal was invented. The adults spent many nights in police cells, and longer periods in jail. The police were the one public body who had a sort of weary affection for the Brights; they could so reliably be traced as the repository of stolen goods or the participants in a bungled break-in. And although individual family members had their moments, there was a Bright attitude born of hopelessness which was the next best thing to affability. No police officer, forced to make an arrest, ever felt that a Bright took it personally.

In the house on Adelaide Road, entertaining as conceived by the original architect had no place, although there were many visitors. Maureen Bright, known universally as Nan although she was only in her mid-forties, kept food on the table for the youngest, even if meals were irregular and usually from the chip shop. She preferred soft textures herself, as most of her teeth were in an agonizing state of decay. Nan was unique among her family in that she drank not to get drunk, but to ease the pain that lived and screamed in her mouth, day and night.

Nan never left the house. This was a fact, not a problem. She gave Pauline or one of the other kids money to get chips or her cigarettes or something from the off-licence if she was flush, and stayed indoors. She wasn't a maternal woman, but she was better than nothing, and Pauline, if anyone had bothered to ask her to choose, would have singled out Nan as her favourite relative apart from her mum. Joanne, Nan's second daughter, divided her time between the house in Adelaide Road and longer periods away with various boyfriends, most of whom were pimps. Pauline knew these times as Joanne's work, and it made her feel important on her mother's behalf when they were mentioned.

Pauline had never met her dad, but next to Nan she was fondest of her mum's brother, Uncle Dave. His unreliability was exotic, as were his tattoos, a new one each time he arrived home from jail. Dave referred to his jail sentences with a mixture of pride at their harshness and formal indignation that he should be punished at all for the various crimes he claimed not to have committed, although he freely recounted his part in them as soon as a drink passed his lips. Uncle Dave called Pauline 'our kid', and had once given her a four-finger Kit Kat on her birthday. He had a son, Gary, who was a bit younger than Pauline. Gary's mum had taken off years ago. Gary wasn't right, couldn't talk much and still pissed and shat himself like a baby. He didn't go to school, and spent most of his days lolled in front of the telly. It was surprisingly difficult to make him cry. Despite his smallness, he was very strong in a fight, and there were plenty of those in the house.

None of the Brights would have noticed if Pauline hadn't gone to school, and so none of them noticed that she did in fact go more often than not. There wasn't a report or a note that made it to any adult member of the family, since Pauline had learned early on the pointlessness of handing these over to Nan, or of asking anyone for money for a special trip or the even more exotic demand for cookery ingredients. At these times she twagged off, then lay in wait for her classmates, ambushing them off the coach for their souvenir bookmarks and keyrings, or knocking their carefully balanced Tupperware boxes from their arms and grinding the clumsily assembled butterfly buns that spilled out into the pavement. In contrast to Gary, it was surprisingly easy to make her classmates cry.

Pauline was quite often hungry, but it never occurred to her to eat the cookery-lesson buns and biscuits instead of vandalizing them. It was their food, and she wanted nothing to do with them. School dinners were another matter. They ate them, but dinners weren't their food in the same way as the Tupperware buns.

Occasionally a teacher would notice the way that Pauline stayed behind at dinnertime to finish every morsel available to her, gobbling gristly mouthfuls rejected by the other children. It was reassuring at such times to know that Pauline, along with the rest of the school's underprivileged children (the preferred official term), received subsidized school meals.

On Monday mornings everyone brought in their dinner-ticket money, except for those children such as Pauline, a few in each class, who were given their dinners free. The teacher dispensed the tickets, blue for the paying customers, pale yellow for the charity cases, from stiff rolls kept in separate recycled tobacco tins. The yellow tickets were always handed out last, with the names called out and ticked off on a special list. So Mrs Maclaren was surprised one Monday to look up and see Pauline offering her fifty pence and demanding a strip of legitimate blue tickets.

'But you're on the other list, Pauline,' she reminded her, leaving the fifty-pence piece where Pauline had placed it, on the register. 'You don't have to pay.'

'Please, Miss, my mum says she'll give me the money from now on, Miss,' maintained Pauline firmly. Mrs Maclaren couldn't be bothered to argue, and handed over the blue tickets, although she recognized something fishy about this transaction. For several weeks Pauline produced her fifty pence on Monday morning, until she was caught by a teacher on playground duty, extorting exactly this sum from a terrified seven-year-old. A letter was sent home, and Pauline's mum invited in to discuss the matter. Joanne had been in Leeds for months, and Nan wasn't about to leave the house, even if she had been informed of the situation, which naturally she had not. Mr Scott, the headmaster, gave Pauline a talking-to, and demanded that she write an essay about why it was wrong for the strong to pick on the weak.

Pauline disappeared from school for nearly two weeks, but when she reappeared, she wrote the essay, covering nearly a side in her chaotically scrawled rough book, then copying it out in good for Mr Scott. No more was said about the dinner tickets, although if Mrs Maclaren had bothered to liaise with any of the dinner ladies, she would have discovered that Pauline had continued to hand in blue tickets. She simply forced the next child in the queue, whether bigger or smaller, to swap a yellow ticket for a blue. It wasn't the first crime she had committed, and it was one of the few that were undeniably victimless.

PAULINE BRIGHT IS trouble. One of the ways you know she's trouble is that grown-ups always call her by her full name. 'Pauline Bright,' Mrs Maclaren, our teacher, says, 'stop that and come and sit next to Gemma.' I am never Gemma Barlow, because I'm not trouble. Quite the opposite, in fact. According to my reports, Gemma is a joy to teach. Pauline Bright isn't. Once Mrs Maclaren said after a test that she shouldn't be called Pauline Bright, but Pauline Thick. Everyone laughed extra loud, because Mrs Maclaren doesn't attempt many jokes, and Pauline got into more trouble because she walloped Neil Johnson who was sitting next to her, guffawing, and the impact she made on the bridge of his blue plastic National Health glasses marked his nose for days.

Pauline Bright can fight. She punches and kicks like a boy. She doesn't care about fighting boys either, or anyone bigger or older than her. Once when she was seven she went for a ten-year-old who had called her little brother a spaz, and knocked out one of his front teeth. He cried to a teacher, who sent Pauline to stand outside Mr Scott's office. Everyone said Mr Scott used the strap on her, but she didn't cry. It didn't stop her either. Whenever they start shouting 'scrap' in the playground, there's a good chance that the excited crowd is clotting around Pauline Bright, or one of her brothers and sisters.

There are loads of Brights, but Pauline's the eldest at junior school. The little one, the spaz one, used to wee on the floor in assemblies, and run around in circles in the hall, shouting, as teachers tried to catch him. Everyone says he got sent to a special school for retards. There's another brother as well, and a sister with a patch over one eye. All of them smell. Pauline Bright

14

smells, and when Mrs Maclaren sends her to sit next to me I try to breathe through my mouth. Dirty clothes. Dirty knickers. The worst is when we have to hold hands, which happens sometimes because we're close in the alphabet, Barlow and Bright. The only other person I can't stand holding hands with is a girl called Ella, whose hand is cool and grey and scaly. She can't help it. I don't say anything with either her or Pauline, but I pull the cuff of my school blouse over my hand so that the skin can't touch. Pauline Bright's hand is small and hot and filthy, with long, black-ringed nails. And the smell. Sometimes Pauline wants to hug up close to you, clamping your hand in both of hers, but sometimes she kicks and tells you to eff off. I'd rather she kicked. If she does, I tell Mrs Maclaren.

'Miss, Pauline Bright's kicking me, Miss.'

'Pauline Bright, do you want me to send you to Mr Scott's office?'

Mr Scott is the Head, with the strap no one's ever seen. I imagine something in lavishly tooled leather, like the saddles I saw for sale when we were on holiday in Spain, specially made and ordered by Mr Scott for the punishment of children as troublesome as Pauline Bright.

Whatever I think of Pauline, I don't ever tell Mrs Maclaren that she has compounded her crime by telling me to eff-word off. 'Pauline said a rude word' always begs the question of whether you yourself will be punished for repeating the word, which is desirable for maximum effect, but I've noticed that saying it at secondhand tends to produce a rebuke for telling tales. Everyone knows that grown-ups swear. You hear it all the time, in the things they watch on TV and switch over once you appear, in conversations on buses they hurry you past, from shouting drunks they drag you into traffic without looking to avoid. And they must know that we swear as well, although we pretend not to. I don't swear, but I know all the words. Pauline Bright says

15

them as well, all of them, even the worst ones. Arse. Git. Bloody. Bugger. Willy. Fanny. Bastard. Fuck. Cunt. Every so often, she throws in a new one.

'Jam rags,' she hisses at me, as I copy words down from the board into my narrow spelling book with the smooth, brick-red cover. My writing sits perfectly on the lines. Pauline carves out the words with her unsharpened pencil lead, tearing the paper; she's lagging words and words behind me. 'Ferocious,' I write.

'Jam rags,' she repeats. 'Your mam sticks jam rags up her.' I ignore her, carefully erasing an imperfect 'u'.

'It's to do with periods,' Christina tells me when I mention it. She's also in Mrs Maclaren's class but we're not allowed to sit together because we giggle too much.

'Oh yeah, that,' I say, quick to be blasé, although I don't know much about periods. Something to do with ladies bleeding and boxes kept in the bathroom cupboard, something which will happen to me, and has already happened to a girl called Danuta in my class, who we stare at when we have PE because, apart from actual bosoms, which are surprising enough and in their way enviable, the poor thing has spidery black hair growing over her privates. She isn't even ten yet. Jam rags. I like the sound of it. I adopt it as my own personal swear word, since it can't be as bad as the really bad ones, and I'm keen on jam. At breakfast when Mum and Dad aren't looking (not that Dad would mind) I prise out the strangely stiff strawberries from the pot of Hartleys and eat them off my knife.

A few days after our spelling test, after school, Mum takes me on the bus to her work. This doesn't happen often. I love visiting the salon and being made a fuss of by the other ladies who work there. I love watching the customers turn into someone else as their hair gets done. As Mum's quick to tell everyone, I've never been any trouble when she's had to take me into work. I sit with the stack of *Woman* and *Woman's Own*s in the waiting area, enjoying the letters pages and the agony aunt and, particularly, the medical column. I also watch the comings and goings through reception. I feel very proud to see my own mum at the centre of this other world, with its unique climate, warm and chemically perfumed.

But that day, even on the bus the atmosphere is different. Mum's dressed up and nervous, and she's put orange make-up on her face which stops at her neck. On the way to the salon, she keeps accusing me of holding her up.

'Gemma, leave that alone – you're holding me up,' she says, when I try to retrieve something interesting, possibly a badge, dropped by the bus stop.

'Gemma, I'm not telling you again,' when I have to stop and pull my socks back up to my knees. It's no good just doing one, as I try to tell her, but she yanks me along without listening.

I can see that her blouse is making her sweat, and the sweat is seeping darkly into the nylon beneath her arms. When we do reach the salon, it turns out that we're not going to stay. Mum is there to meet someone from her work, a man called Ian, and we are going straight out again. I mourn the loss of the *Woman's Owns* and their medical secrets. This is not going to be the day when I finally find out what a rupture is.

'How about the Copper Kettle?' suggests Ian, and I brighten at the prospect of pancakes. Mum explains that Ian does the accounts for her work, and that they need to sort out something important. I know accounts involve sums, but I'm not really listening because I'm trying to decide between the pancake with banana and the pancake with butterscotch sauce, both equally delicious. Ian suggests a combination of the two, and I enjoy the best of both worlds as he and Mum look at boring sheets of paper which they scribble on with biros.

Ian does more talking than Mum. He's quite old and fat with froggish eyes, and his breath smells of mints. I've taken to him immediately because of his pancake suggestion to the waitress. Mum is still on edge, although the patches under her arms have stopped spreading. She has a frothy coffee, although she never drinks coffee at home. As Ian talks she slides her fingers down her biro to the end, then upends it and starts again, over and over. Her nails are always long and painted. Today they're a shiny brownish-pink.

'Don't do that, chick,' she says when I slurp the end of my glass of limeade through the straw.

'That's the best bit, isn't it?' says Ian, winking. He's having two toasted teacakes with his frothy coffee.

'She's old enough to know better,' says Mum, pushing my fringe out of my eyes. She observes me professionally. 'Time for a haircut.'

Ian wants to order me a second limeade, but there isn't time, because we have to be back for Dad's tea.

'Everything seems to be in order,' says Ian, shuffling the papers into a pile. 'We can do the rest next time.'

'I'll make sure about this one,' says Mum, cocking her head over at me, as though I'm deaf, even though I'm sitting next to her. I know she'd rather have got a babysitter for me.

Mum wants to get the bus home but Ian insists on taking us back in his car, which is big and also smells of mints. When he drops us off, Mum turns to me and demands, 'What do you say for the pancakes?' I say thank you, and Ian asks for a kiss, which I give him on his fat, minty cheek. I go to follow Mum out of the car, but the toe of my sandal catches against the door sill and I stumble to the pavement. Although I manage not to fall badly, an exclamation trips from me.

'What did you say?' Mum swivels on me, eyes locking into mine as she pulls me up.

'Nothing.'

'What did you say?'

I whisper it. 'Jam rags.'

She pulls me to the house, gripping my arm hard, and slams the door as Ian drives away. My legs are smacked. According to Mum, at length to my dad over his tea, she's never been so embarrassed in her life. What's worse, she claims that Ian, who she suddenly calls Mr Haskell, was 'disgusted'.

I say sorry, keep saying it, but it makes no difference. She doesn't look at me for the rest of the evening, and even when I go to kiss her goodnight, her own lips don't reply.

Of course I tell her where I've heard it; I'd tell her anything to make her look at me again. To my dread, Mum sends me into school on Monday with a note for Mrs Maclaren, who passes it on to Mr Scott for a full investigation. I am summoned to his office. There is no sign of the strap, although Mr Scott's desk contains many promising drawers. I admire Mr Scott. He has wire-framed aviator glasses and rolls his checked shirts over muscled fore-arms woolly with gingerish hair. Once, during an assembly, he removed a wasp that was distracting us from his version of the Exodus from Egypt by pursuing it to a window pane where he crushed it, oblivious of stings, between finger and thumb.

I can't bear the thought of repeating the guilty words to him now that Mum has left me in no doubt of their weight. 'Disgusting language' is the phrase she's used in her note, signed, as only her notes to school are, 'S Barlow (Mrs)'. The nonchalant authority of that bracketed 'Mrs' sums up for me all Mum's ease with the mysteries of life. While my ignorance has led me here, close to the strap. No threat is needed to get Pauline Bright's name from me. As soon as I say it, Mr Scott's face relaxes into a silent, mournful sigh. I am released, without swearing, and Pauline is sent for. The blame has passed to her, where it traditionally belongs.

She gets me after school. I'm walking home, across the playing fields that divide the school from the subway under the main road, when she comes at me from nowhere and chops me to the ground. I taste dirt, and squeal. She manages to straddle me and uses my own laden bag to clout me across the head with full force.

'I got fucking done 'cause of you, you little cow!'

'I never!' I wail into her face, then the bag wallops me again.

I quickly feel dizzy, but also exhilarated. I'm quite a lot bigger than Pauline Bright. Although my arms are pinned, I wriggle enough to throw her off me and kick sightlessly in her direction. The fat crepe sole of my Clark's school sandal gets her in the mouth. She runs off, howling, her hand dabbing at blood on her face. I'm bleeding as well. A sharp edge on the plastic piping decorating my school bag has caught me on the temple. My elbows and knees are indented and stained with the patterns and juices of the grass, and the collar of my blouse is torn where Pauline grabbed me by the tie. I feel important and scared.

There are consequences to our fight. Pauline has a chip in her front tooth, caused by my wild kick. And Mum, appalled by the state of my clothes when I stagger home, keeps me off school until I am swapped into another class. There is another consequence, of course, less obvious. Pauline Bright and I are connected. We are certainly not friends, but we are on our way to something. And Pauline Bright is trouble.

```
Call sheet: 'That Summer'
June 17th 1975.
Director: Michael Keys
Director of Photography: Anthony Williams, BSC.
First AD: Derek Powell.
6.30 a.m. call.

CAST: Dirk Bogarde [COLIN], Lallie Paluza [JUNE],
Douglas Alton [MAN IN CAR], Vera Wyngate [WOMAN
IN CAR].
LOCATION: Hexthorpe Flats, Doncaster.
```

34. EXT. SCRUBLAND. DAY.
```
COLIN and JUNE fish in the pond. JUNE catches a
fish, gets wet.
```

35. EXT. SCRUBLAND. DAY.
```
JUNE talks to a WOMAN passing by, who is
suspicious. COLIN reassures her.
```

36. EXT. SCRUBLAND. DAY.
```
JUNE kisses COLIN goodbye.
```

VERA ALWAYS HAD a bacon sandwich on location. She knew she shouldn't, but the smell was irresistible, and there was bugger all else to do once you'd been in make-up, and getting up so early – five o'clock to be ready for the car that picked you up from the hotel – gave you an appetite. Anyway, she was resigned to doing character parts at her age, so an extra pound here or there didn't much matter. If anything, it was all to the good. She wished, though, that the costume was a little more forgiving. The view of herself in the mirror of the make-up van was a depressing one, even allowing for the early call and the make-up girl's intention of making her look as dowdy and nondescript as her few lines required. It didn't help that the little girl, Lallie, was sitting in the chair next to her, eyes clear and brilliant, skin vividly freckled and unexhausted. She was a funny-looking kid really; not what you could call pretty, but if youth came in a bottle it'd sell out in five minutes. While a make-up girl methodically powdered her, Lallie kept breaking into a Jimmy Cagney impression. Vera was far from charmed by this. She doubted the child had ever seen Jimmy Cagney; what she was doing was an impression of an impression. It was all too early, anyway, for any kind of performance.

'Do Dirk,' she heard the make-up girl, Julie, urge, silencing the cries of 'you dirty rat'.

'Oh I couldn't possibly,' said the little girl, and then Vera really was amazed, because the child's face captured perfectly the saucer-eyed, self-conscious melancholy of their leading man, along with the light regret of his voice. The make-up girls laughed.

'Michael, dear boy, would it be possible to have a word?' the child continued, and segued into the director, Mike, whose patrician drawl would be easy enough for anyone to take off, although not everyone would note so accurately the barest hint of a stammer in his intonation, the way he headed off certain words before they could be formed into anything troublesome.

'She's like a little parrot, in't she?' said Julie, blotting Vera's mouth with a tissue.

'Ar, Jim lad,' Lallie cawed. It was all too much, that degree of attention. Bound to ruin any child. Vera felt suddenly uneasy about talking to the make-up girl, in case Lallie was gathering material to 'do' her later.

'Is that me finished, darling?' she asked, and heard herself, camply over-theatrical. Once Julie had frowned and re-pencilled an eyebrow, Vera was glad to pluck off the tissues guarding her neck and go outside to the catering van for her bacon sandwich.

She'd had better – the watery bacon made the bread go limp, even through the butter. Which wasn't butter, of course, but sulphurously yellow marge. Still. Nice, with a strong cup of tea, and a ciggie. It was only the second day of location filming, and Vera's first. Close to her last as well, bar her opening of a door to field a question from a policeman later in the week. Oh well, it was a job.

There was no sign of Dirk, sequestered in a modest caravan, or of Mike, possibly sequestered with him, going over that day's scenes. Vera could see the director of photography, Tony, already setting up his first shot by the pond, where she was due to stop and deliver her economically suspicious lines. Tony was a distinguished-looking man in his fifties with a leonine head of white hair; DOPs always seemed to have that same air of civilized self-containment about them, like little boys adept at Meccano, which they all very likely had been. You always knew their nails would be clean, an assumption certainly not to be made about directors.

Vera and Tony had actually been an item on a film (which one – *Summer Sins*? *And You Beside Me*? Some lovey-dovey rubbish) in the mid-fifties; her an overripe Rank starlet and him a slightly younger camera assistant. It was nothing but a nice memory to her: cheap spaghetti in Soho trattorias and polite sex back at her flat in yet-to-be swinging Chelsea. Tony in bed was, like Tony professionally, unintrusive and precise. She had an image of him going down on her, his hair, then ash blond, masking his face, his concentration touchingly absolute.

Of course it was traditional for leading ladies to fall in love with their cinematographers, possibly out of some sort of survival instinct, since the glow of mutual attraction ensured the best close-ups and the most flattering lighting. There was a story about an American star (Myrna Loy? Jean Arthur?) who had had her career ruined when she married, so spurning the DOP on whom she had always relied to give her a dewiness on screen that had deserted her in life. Maybe it was spite, or maybe he just saw her more clearly without the haze of sex and wanted to pass that revelation on to the audience. Either way she was over, playing the kind of roles Vera was now pleased to get, bitter mothers and nosy bystanders. Vera had never worked with DOPs good enough to make a difference to what she'd once had, apart from Tony. And there the timing had been wrong: him on the way up, and her on the way down.

Vera watched as Lallie left make-up and skipped along towards the cluster of lights. She wondered if Tony would still feel a frisson, with an eleven-year-old leading lady. After all, the kid hardly needed to look any younger; angles and keylights were an irrelevance. And in any case, tastes had changed. As far as Vera could see, glamour had become a word filthier than any of the ones now so fashionably bandied about on screen (not in this one though; apparently they were hoping for an 'A' rating, Double 'A' at worst).

There was a harassed-looking woman following the girl, picking her way around the mud in inappropriate high-heeled boots. A chaperone: Vera recognized the style. Among the crew of any film involving kids, you could pick out the least maternal, hardest-faced woman, and that would be the chaperone. Then she saw that high-heels-and-no-knickers was actually making her stumbling way to the catering van, abandoning her charge.

'Lallie! What d'you want?' she shouted. Her voice wasn't the standard nicotine bass Vera was expecting, but jarringly soft and girlish. She had another look. The chaperone's make-up was heavier than any the actors were wearing – it included false eyelashes – and her nails, lacquered metallic brown, looked as though she could use them to open tins. But she was younger beneath all this get-up than Vera's first sight of her had led her to believe.

'Lallie!' the woman called reproachfully. 'I said what d'you want for your breakfast?'

'Not hungry!' shouted Lallie, uninterrupted in her nimble journey across the mud.

'She's never hungry,' the woman confided breathily, almost whiningly, to Vera, rolling her black-fringed eyes. She had a gentle northern accent – Teesside, Vera guessed.

'It is a bit early,' Vera consoled, inhabiting her homely headscarf guise.

'Chocolate biscuits, she'll have,' said the woman who had served Vera her sandwich with a Rothman's (now smoked) parked in her mouth.

'Oh aye, she'd live on them,' breathed the chaperone.

'Kids,' Vera said, since the tone of the scene demanded it. There was a little silence after this. Vera saw Lallie reach the illuminated point where Tony conferred with his crew. She danced around them, inaudible at this distance, but no doubt treating them to another round of her impressions.

'Do you ever get a bit of peace?' she asked the chaperone, who had lit her own cigarette and was devouring it with a cup of the polystyrene tea.

'This is it,' the woman told her, hoisting her fag.

Vera's elbow was cupped by the First AD, a nervous boy with chronically bad breath.

'We're ready for you now,' he muttered, unconscious of his affliction. 'Mike wants to do a run-through.'

'With you in a tick, darling.' Vera downed her tea and held out the cup for the canteen woman. Then she smiled a goodbye at the chaperone, who sighed, exhaling smoke, still watching the ever-moving Lallie.

'Don't know where she gets it from,' she said. 'She wears me out. Her dad tries to look after her a bit at the weekends, but he's been working away.'

Not a chaperone then. Vera, accommodating this adjustment, tried to find some resemblance to the daughter in the mother. There wasn't any, as far as she could see, even allowing for all the make-up. But she'd lay money Lallie could imitate her mum a treat, clever little love.

SATURDAY NIGHT, AFTER a good Saturday. Swimming, chips, comics, Christina, and now Lallie. Tapping down the stairs in a blue-sequinned catsuit, pausing to gurn and exclaim 'Shut that door!' before reverting to herself and scuttling rhythmically to the bottom of the stairs for her I-gotta-be-me finale. A cola-bottle chew, dissolved to a sliver of flavour, sits on my tongue. The next part of the show will be Lallie and Marmaduke.

Mum opens the door to the lounge, bringing in the Saturday steak-and-chips smell with her.

'Darling . . . '

I frown in irritation. Canned laughter accompanies the discovery of Marmaduke, in a frilled apron over his butler's uniform, dusting Lallie's stamp collection with a huge feather duster, stamp by stamp.

'I wondered if you wanted to come to work with me next week after school?'

The formality of the suggestion would strike me as odd if I wasn't intent on Lallie, who has sprung out of nowhere, telling Marmaduke to use a bit of elbow grease on the Penny Black, then grabbing the feather duster and doing a quick Ken Dodd. 'How tickled I am,' she splutters at him.

'Only I thought it would be nice for you,' Mum continues.

'I'm watching this,' I tell her, exasperated.

'Don't you be like that when I'm trying to talk to you, young lady.'

Now I've missed the next joke, and catch only the laughter. But I know better than to spark Mum's irritation. She wouldn't think twice about turning off the telly altogether, and has even

27

taken a few steps towards the set, as though this is already in her mind.

'Sorry,' I say, hoping that this might be enough to get her out of the room again. But she sits next to me and cuddles up, with the delicious smells of the hair salon and the even-more-delicious cooked fat of her tea on top of that.

'It's OK, I know it's your favourite.'

I feel a bit embarrassed. It's not the same, watching Lallie with Mum there, even though it's a particularly good show this week, with plenty of Marmaduke bits. He has to cook Lallie a special meal because she's invited a boy round, called Algernon Smithington-Smythe, who wears a monocle and talks with an extremely posh accent. Marmaduke keeps getting everything wrong and ends up head first in a large meringue. My dad comes in at the end, saying 'Load of rubbish,' which he always says, and pretending that he's going to turn over because he thinks the programme's finished, which is also traditional. Mum then says what she always says, when Lallie's doing a song from *The Sound of Music*, being Julie Andrews.

'Not what you could call a pretty child, is she? Terrible nose.'

'Talented, though,' says Dad, and Mum's 'mmmmn' of uncertain agreement suggests talent is no compensation for a lack of looks. I'm fairly sure that I'm prettier than Lallie. My nose is quite small.

Mum clears off to do the pots, later than usual. She doesn't reappear for the police programme I'm allowed to watch before bed. After that's over, I'm supposed to be sent upstairs, but a film starts without Dad saying anything. Once I realize he's forgotten about me, I don't dare speak or move in case it reminds him that I'm still up, particularly as the plastic stuff the settee's made of squeaks a lot when you shift on it.

The hands on the clock above the gas fire creep steadily towards ten. Still no sign of Mum, still no order to go to bed.

It's a kind of torture, because although I'm very interested in the film, and know that it's far too grown-up for me to be watching, there are a number of things I don't understand. I'm dying to ask Dad to explain the plot for me, but can't risk drawing attention to myself. A man and a lady in a dark, scary old house are looking for someone who's missing – the lady's sister? Why do they know she's in the house?

The house looks a lot like Lallie's mansion, although in Lallie's show you only ever see her room and sometimes the dining room. There's a scary old man who keeps telling the main man and lady to 'leave this place', but they don't pay any attention. As they're looking for the missing sister or whoever she is, the lady opens a door and sees someone in the other room. It's another lady, probably the sister, but she has her back to the main lady, so you can only see her blonde hair and pretty dress. The main lady says 'Judy?' but the sister doesn't say anything so she taps her on the shoulder, and the sister turns round suddenly and it's not her face but a skull, grinning horribly, with a rat running out between her teeth. The lady on the television screams at the same time as me, but not as loud. Mum runs down the stairs and wants to know what the matter is. Dad looks confused and foggy – I realize he has been asleep in his chair and not watching the film at all. My heart is still punching hard from the shock. 'This isn't fit for her to be watching,' says Mum, and packs me off to bed. Even though I get her to leave the landing light on, I don't go to sleep for ages in case I see that empty-eyed skull in my dreams.

It troubles me for days, and I make all sorts of excuses about going to bed. One night I jerk awake and think I see the corpse hovering in the corner near the door, blonde hair billowing around it, then wake up properly with a scream thick and unscreamed in my throat. And this is how Pauline Bright draws me in. I'm playing two-ball with Christina and some other girls at morning playtime, and I see her chasing after a couple of the rough boys in our year, Neil Rigby and Darren Soper. Pauline spends a lot of playtimes on her own, but if she does play with anyone apart from her brother or sister, it's with boys like them. Sometimes she tries to barge in on skipping or a game of two-ball with the girls, but when there's enough of us we gang up and chase her away, telling her she smells. If she's in the mood, she lets the boys snog her and touch her where they shouldn't, but she always demands to touch their willies in return. Other times she just fights them, and she's quite capable of making them run off crying to tell a teacher. Today she's after Neil and Darren, her jaw thrust forward and eyes hideously crossed, legs spastic and arms outstretched; a monster.

'So then she turns round and she's like this, right –' she shouts, 'and she jumps out on you, but you can't gerraway and she pulls you back in – there's like a secret passage and she pulls you in through the cupboard and that's where she keeps you and there's all these other people she's caught and she eats their flesh and that.'

Pauline catches Neil by the back of his jumper. He stretches it to the limit, arms wheeling, but can't escape.

'Some are just skellingtons,' continues Pauline, still shouting. 'That's all that's left of them and she's even eaten your sister you were looking for, but then you escape—'

She lets Neil's jumper go and he runs off round a corner. She staggers after him, pulling a fresh monster face. Christina fumbles the ball on a simple overarm against the wall – not even over-under – and it's my turn. I have to concentrate on the game.

In the dinner queue I manoeuvre a place next to Pauline. It's risky, given her threats to do me since our fight on the playing field, but I can't resist.

'Did you see that film on Saturday night?' I ask her. I'm anxious, both in case she says no and in case she says yes. 'The one in the mansion when the sister's gone missing and the lady jumps out but she's got a skeleton face?'

'That weren't the best bit,' Pauline says, scornful. 'The best bit, right, was right at the end when the bloke gets this knife right through him and you can see it pushing out of his back, like, and he's all bleeding and it even comes out of his eyes.'

I think about this as the queue edges forward.

'What about the skeleton woman?' This is what I really need to know. If I know what happened to the skeleton woman, she might stop erupting into my dreams.

Pauline flicks a look at me. It's quite difficult to see her eyes because she's got a bushy fringe that straggles halfway down her face. Her hair is dark and heavy, and I can smell it from where I'm standing, part of the sour, alarming Pauline smell. She punches me on the arm, not hard, but enough to startle me.

'Give us your dinner ticket,' she says, matter-of-factly. I hand over the blue ticket and am surprised when she holds out a grubby yellow one in exchange. Only then do I want to object, since I've never had free dinners in my life, but we're at the front of the line now, and Pauline has yet to tell me the ending of the film. I pocket the yellow ticket and hand over another blue one to the dinner lady in charge. I can always tell Mum I've lost one, although that isn't like me, as she's bound to remark.

I'm actually pleased when Pauline follows me to sit at my table, although I can't continue our conversation immediately as I have to perform my duties as a table monitor. This involves doling out food to the other children at my table from the various tins that arrive from the kitchens. There aren't enough teachers to go round, so well-behaved tables like ours have to make do with monitors.

Another girl, Cynthia, comes and sits next to Pauline. She's a regular at my table, and she's a disaster. She's coloured – there aren't that many coloured girls at our school – and she wears glasses so thick that her eyes are nearly lost behind them. Her shoulders, caving together for protection, are too narrow to hold up her bobbled grey cardigan, which bows around her arms like a shawl. She maintains a constant, gummy smile to stop being got at, but it never works. Most of the kids round the table call her nig-nog and blackie in a quietly taunting way that frightens me, the way anything frightens me when I know that grown-ups wouldn't like it.

The main taunter is Rodney Wallace. He looks like a rat, with white hair and eyelashes and a perpetually reddened nose. He likes to kick Cynthia under the table, but not in a way that the teachers will notice. From meal to meal, when Cynthia gets up to go, I see the bruises, some purple on the shiny darkness of her legs, some older, yellowing. I don't know what to do. Cynthia just smiles her blind smile and huddles her shoulders closer, trying to ignore Rodney's swinging legs and the sambos and niggers that come her way.

Today, when Rodney approaches, Pauline is in his place.

'I sit there,' he dares to tell her.

'Fuck off, knobber,' spits Pauline, and Rodney retreats, muttering threats which he sensibly keeps below a level Pauline could hear. I'm glad he's gone, although I'm breathing through my mouth so that the Pauline smell doesn't offend me. I slide a few extra chips on to Cynthia's plate. I always give her big portions, to make up for not protecting her.

'Tell me about the film,' I urge Pauline. 'What happens to the skeleton lady?'

Pauline doesn't know to keep her mouth closed when she eats. Through her mouthful of chewed chips I can see the uneven edge on her front tooth, the one caused by my kick.

'It's ace,' she tells me, and a few bits of chip escape back on to the plate. 'The other bloke, the one with the big nose—'

'The professor,' I encourage her.

'He comes in after she's stabbed the posh bloke, the skellington one, and they have a scrap and you think she's going to win

32

because she's right strong and that but then he's got this gun and he starts shooting her and all her bones go everywhere but bits of her keep running towards him and then he manages to get her right here –' Pauline jabs at her chest – 'and she's dead but then for a second she goes like she was before she was a skellington, all like pretty, and he snogs her and then she's a skellington and then she turns to dust and there's just her dress left.'

We leave a little silence as I imagine the scene. It is deeply satisfying.

'Why does he snog her?' I ask, tying up loose ends.

'They were supposed to get married, before she turned into a skellington.'

'Skeleton,' I correct her, 'not skellington. Skelly ton.'

'Skelly ton,' muses Pauline. 'It were an ace film.'

'My mum and dad wanted to watch summat else so they turned over,' I tell her, glossing over the fact that I'd already been sent to bed. I'm not allowed to say 'summat', but it's easier talking like that to Pauline. Pauline stuffs most of a sausage into her mouth.

'I can watch what I like, me,' she says. 'Mucky films, owt. Horror ones are the best though. Some of them get a bit mucky an' all.'

This intrigues me.

'Do you see them doing it?' I ask.

'All't time,' says Pauline airily. She scoops out the few squashed chips left in the serving tin with her hand.

'You're supposed to use the spoon,' I admonish. 'And I'm supposed to do it because I'm monitor.' I demonstrate my power by using a serving fork to spear the last sausage, which I put on Cynthia-the-disaster's plate. She smiles nervily at the sausage instead of me, bobbing her head as though it too might rear up and kick her.

'What you give it to't blackie for?' asks Pauline, reaching across to retrieve the sausage. I bar the way with my arm, which is still holding the fork, but Pauline reaches over me, pushing me in the face.

'If you take it, I'm telling,' I warn her.

'Fuck off, lezzie,' spits Pauline. Lezzie is the worst insult we possess. I shoot my arm up in the air, thrusting so that my bum leaves my seat with the effort, panting to get the attention of Mrs Bream, who teaches the fourth years and is one table across.

'Miss – Miss –'

Mrs Bream gets up and comes over.

'Miss, Pauline Bright stole a sausage, Miss.'

Pauline is chewing furiously. Mrs Bream looks at her.

'I never, Miss,' Pauline protests, bits of sausage meat tumbling from her mouth.

'And she called me a rude name, Miss.'

Sighing, Mrs Bream tells Pauline to come and sit next to her, guiding her softly by the arm as though she's giving her a treat, which she is in a way, because beautiful Mrs Bream, with her perfect, bell-like pageboy and trendy dresses, is one of the most-loved teachers in the school. I feel stung, and even more so when Mrs Bream says, in the gentlest way possible, 'You know, Gemma, it's really best not to tell tales, lovey.'

Pauline's smile is triumphant as she takes her place next to Mrs Bream. And maybe because of this small victory, or because of the bond of the film she's ended for me, I let her play with me when we're released into the playground. Christina objects, but I ignore her, and Pauline and I play the skeleton lady together until the bell rings.

35. EXT. SCRUBLAND. DAY.

A car pulls up at the edge of the track. COLIN
is startled and backs away from JUNE as a middle-
aged WOMAN, dowdy and suspicious, rolls down the
window. Her HUSBAND is at the wheel, picnic rug
and basket visible on the back seat.

> WOMAN
>
> [to JUNE] Everything all right, love?

> JUNE
>
> I'm fine. Aren't I, Dad?

COLIN registers surprise at her invention. The
WOMAN sees it.

> JUNE
>
> Me dad and me had come for a picnic but he
> was telling me off because I forgot to bring
> the sandwiches.

> WOMAN
>
> Can we give you a lift?

> COLIN
>
> You're all right.

The car drives off. JUNE shoots COLIN a look.

Filming in cars was always a pain in the bee-oh-tee-tee you know
what. Given the schedule, Vera couldn't see why they didn't alter
the scene so that she and Douglas Alton, who was playing her
husband, were going for a country walk instead. Douglas agreed

with her, although both of them were far too professional to do more than comment within ten feet of the director as he conferred with Tony about the first set-up of the day. The long shot of the car driving along and stopping would be picked up later with underpaid doubles standing in for her and Douglas, and they were to begin instead with a two shot of her rolling down the window to talk to June, with Douglas in the driver's seat, slightly to the left of her in the frame.

'Could have done it with a back projection down at Elstree and kept our feet dry, love,' Dougie muttered as Tony agonized over lens sizes.

Vera had known Dougie for years. When Mike had talked through the scene with them, she had been unsurprised to hear him suggest that he put the car into gear without actually driving away at the end. Dougie was the laziest actor in England. The decline this film marked into his first non-speaking part perfectly suited his inclination to do as little as possible. She herself had once witnessed him argue that the character he was playing was far too patrician to pour himself a drink, insisting that he should stay in his chair and let a servant do it for him instead. In that case, he had won. Over the car, Mike prevailed. Well, they would see. Dougie's idleness apart, when all the other elements had run smoothly in the scene, Sod's law just begged for the engine to stall, killing the take.

After another half an hour to set up and run through, they were ready to begin. The AD, nervous, nasal Derek, delivered Dirk and Lallie's lines, nervously and nasally. Since the shot was actually from Colin and June's point of view, the two leads didn't appear in it, and rather than get his star actors to stand out of sight and mouth the lines, Mike preferred to keep them in their caravans, out of the cold. Besides which, as he had confided to Vera over an early cigarette at the catering van, it was merry hell trying to arrange the schedule around the strictly limited hours which Lallie, as a minor, was legally allowed to work. Even with her mother as chaperone, and more willing to bend the rules than the usual stage-school harridans, they had to save every minute they could.

To that end, any shot which didn't require Lallie's face was in fact a shot of Lallie's double, a stunted, bewigged twenty-five-year-old called Sue, to whom access was unrestricted in more than merely the professional sense. Vera could see her by the sound equipment, joking with the grip. She wore an adult bomber jacket which made the child's costume beneath seem provocative. Her drab hair was coiled up to accommodate the wig which sat on the hair woman's waiting hand, being brushed out by her assistant. As Vera watched, Sue squeezed the grip's bum. Gripped the grip. She couldn't share this with Dougie, who would have appreciated it, as Derek was shrieking, 'Turn over!', and they were seconds away from a take.

With the car engine supposedly idling, but to be added in the dub, Vera had to roll down the window, suspiciously eye the character of Colin, played by the absent Dirk Bogarde, but fictitiously standing to the right of the camera, then drop her eyes to the height of June, aka Lallie, also missing but represented by a strip of tape on the chest of Derek's jumper, and deliver the line, 'Everything all right, love?' Derek responded with Lallie/June's 'I'm fine. Aren't I, Dad?', and Vera had to catch Dirk/Colin's non-existent little flash of surprise at the child's resourceful pretence that they were father and daughter. Then came her line, 'Can we give you a lift?' and Colin's reply before Dougie drove them away, out of the frame.

It was a couple of takes before the eye lines were sorted out, with the piece of tape meant for Lallie positioned and repositioned on Derek's chest, then she fluffed by changing her line to 'You all right, love?' and was admonished by the script girl (always a girl, although well into her forties), then for three takes, with eye lines and script lines perfect, she was encouraged by Mike to 'take it down', until on the seventh take, when Vera felt that she had taken it down as far as was possible, short of just thinking the scene instead of performing it, a plane flew over.

'Shit!' shouted Mike.

'Go again!' shouted Derek, remorselessly.

During the eighth take, Tony announced a slight camera shake so they cut and went to take nine. Take nine was a print. Nine takes wasn't bad, particularly given the car. Everyone swarmed in for the next set-up and Vera moved off for a fag.

Vera felt pleased with herself. She was, after all, a pro. She watched Sue-the-double, her Lallie wig now in place and jacket off, playfully massage the bicep of the boy who had been helping the boom operator. Shameless.

'Fuck me, darling, did I win medals at Rada so I could work as a cunting chauffeur?' moaned Dougie recreationally, as they wandered off for their celebratory cigarette.

'Couldn't cadge a fag, could I? I've run out.'

With a start, Vera realized Sue-the-double, her wig off, was grinning at her from the other side of the horse-chestnut under which she and Dougie stood to smoke. The ground beneath it already looked like a pub ashtray, after a single day of shooting. Vera handed the girl a cigarette and readjusted her stare. She could see now that it was the real Lallie cavorting with the muscle boy over by the lights, not her adult counterpart. She could see too that it was just innocent horseplay, as Lallie jumped at him and demanded a piggyback. Vera was too vain to wear her glasses, except for a role.

After another forty minutes or so (Dougie had some profession-ally bitter stories to impart about a telly he'd done recently), they moved on to cover the next part of the scene, for which Dirk and Lallie were required. The make-up department had applied their best efforts to dimming Dirk's glamour in order to make him a convincing kiddie fiddler, although in Vera's opinion there was a theatrical abundance to the fake dandruff scattered on the greasy shoulders of his windcheater, and not much could be done to alter the confident, rather camp individuality of his stance. Although their paths hadn't exactly crossed at Rank but had run parallel, in that they had appeared in many of the same films without actually sharing many scenes or even remotely similar billing, their acquaintance had never sparked into friendship, not even at the bantering level she shared with Dougie. Such was the polite remoteness of Dirk's conversation whenever they met that Vera always felt compelled to reintroduce herself, hoping each time to fix herself in his memory. It never worked. Dirk was forever the austere but devastating senior prefect and Vera the ink-stained inhabitant of a remedial stream. Today had been no exception.

Vera watched the kid's mother – what was her name? – detach the child from her game with the forbearing crew member and lead her, skipping at the restraint, to the business end of the set. What it must be like to have all that energy, Vera thought, infinitely accessible. No one had made the offer to replace Vera and Dougie with a couple of strips of gaffer tape. Although to be fair, considered Vera, a kiddie like Lallie probably needed something real to get a bead on, so to speak.

They ran the scene with the four of them. Both Dirk and the girl were word- and note-perfect. Mike raised his eyebrows at Tony and Derek, and adjusted Dirk's position slightly. They went for a take. As far as Vera could tell, that too seemed perfect, although Mike immediately asked for another one.

'Can you come in just half a second sooner on Dirk's line?' he asked Lallie. Lallie nodded vigorously. She did too – her tone unfaltering and not a fraction of a second out either way. After Derek's 'cut', the miraculous, unique point of concentration distintegrated once more into the myriad activities necessary to set up for another shot.

This time the whole scene was to run in close-up on Dirk, so Lallie was taken away for a brief respite that would presumably contribute to her precious tally of tutored set-time. The adult performers had just re-established themselves under the smoker's horse-chestnut, when Dirk stopped in ravenous mid-inhalation.

'Christ,' he remarked.

Vera turned and saw a dark globule of blood had appeared under one of Dirk's distinctively snubbed nostrils. It was already distending into a thickish trickle. It looked like make-up, straight out of Hammer – golden syrup and food colouring.

'Your nose is bleeding,' she informed him gratuitously.

The second nostril began to bleed. After anxious consultations and the leading of Dirk to his caravan with his head tilted back at a forty-five-degree angle, Lallie was re-summoned for what Mike intended as some pick-up shots. Vera didn't mind. Her own time was paid for, after all. But when Mike told Lallie what he wanted from her, the kid asked him, politely enough, if it wouldn't make sense for her to run the whole scene again, shooting it on her.

'Wouldn't you rather wait until Dirk can do it with you, darling?' Mike asked solicitously. Well, as solicitously as he could, given that Lallie's suggestion would be the best use of everyone's time.

Lallie shrugged.

'I'm not bothered,' she told him. 'He—' she gestured to Derek – 'can give me the mark so the sight-lines aren't off.'

So that's what she did. She played the whole scene to a piece of tape on Derek's forehead (he was slightly shorter than Dirk). Mike ordered two takes, but Vera, watching out of shot, could tell that he'd be happy to print the first, if he had any sense.

                          WOMAN
          [to JUNE] Everything all right, love?

                          JUNE
          I'm fine. Aren't I, Dad?

     COLIN registers surprise at her invention. The
     woman sees it.

<pre>
                    JUNE
Me dad and me had come for a picnic but he
was telling me off because I forgot to bring
the sandwiches.

                    WOMAN
Can we give you a lift?

                    COLIN
You're all right.
</pre>

The car drives off. JUNE shoots COLIN a look.

The look that Lallie gave Derek's forehead was complicit, seductive and yet terribly, painfully innocent. A flick of the eyes that lasted less than a second. She gets it, thought Vera. She gets the whole thing. Afterwards, she wondered if it really could have been as good as she thought. It was like the momentary triumph of seeing a goal scored at a football match, without the benefit of the action replay. She hoped the editor would see it too, but there were no guarantees. Maybe Mike would decide the look was too knowing, that it was too dangerous to give the story that weight, although the script hinted at it, that the child was that powerful, but ultimately, of course, tragically, only as powerful as a child can be.

Heading back to the caravans, Vera patted Lallie on the shoulder.

'Good work there,' she congratulated her. 'Quite splendid.'

Lallie rolled her eyes and contorted her mouth into a quick Barbra Streisand. 'Gee, ya really think so?' she spat in loud, third-hand Brooklynese. Vera walked on ahead. She could admire the talent without admiring the owner. It was almost a given in this business. Just because the kid was a genius, it didn't mean Vera had to like her.

THERE WAS NO phone at the Brights' house on Adelaide Road. In cases of particular, often criminal emergency, they used a call box at the end of the street. Letters were neither sent nor received. So there was no warning for Pauline whenever her mother reappeared after one of her mysterious periods of work. Joanne was usually exhausted, and slept for the first couple of days. But once she had revived, she changed the atmosphere of the house as no one else could. Her initial tiredness apart, she had none of the family lassitude, rather a large and angry energy that she dispensed on whoever caught her attention. Until her interest waned, this was very likely to be Pauline.

'Look at the state of her, Mam,' complained Joanne, sitting at the table with a fag and a handleless mug of something when Pauline came in from school. Joanne was one of the few people to call Nan anything other than Nan. 'Come and give your mam a kiss then.'

Pauline trotted over and clamped Joanne in a strangling hug. She couldn't get on her lap because it was occupied by Cheryl, Pauline's little sister. Cheryl looked confused but happy. She babbled all the time anyway, as though she couldn't stop herself talking, but her racket today indicated her pleasure at the reunion with their mother.

Pauline hadn't seen Joanne for six months at least. It had been so long that she had begun to forget about the previous visit, but as soon as she spoke it was as though it had been days ago.

'She looks like a fucking gyppo,' Joanne complained to Nan. 'Can't you do summat about her hair?'

Nan sighed. 'I've got enough on my plate without being a bloody hairdresser.'

'What d'you think you look like, eh?' Joanne shook Pauline lightly. Pauline said nothing. 'D'you like looking like a fucking gyppo?' Pauline still said nothing. Joanne delivered a stabbing tickle under her arms, meant for affection. 'When I go to't shop I'll get some shampoo. Eh? Dirty little bastard you are. You're that bloody ugly.'

Nan grumbled around the kitchen. The gas supply for the cooker had been disconnected long ago, and a Baby Belling ring with a frayed flex was balanced on top of it. Nan opened the oven, which was full of old newspapers.

'You haven't seen my tablets, have you, our Pauline?'

'No, Nan,' said Pauline dutifully. Nan took tranquillizers for her teeth. She got Pauline to renew the prescription for her down at the chemist whenever she ran out. Pauline took the tablets herself sometimes, since Nan never counted them. They made you feel better, although they gave you a headache the next day, and if you took more than one, which she had only tried the once, your legs didn't work properly.

'I'll find them for you,' Pauline offered, and escaped the kitchen.

'Never lifts a bloody finger when you're not around,' she heard Nan say.

'Thinks I don't know what the little bugger's like,' Joanne retorted fondly.

Pauline found the tablets down by Nan's rank special chair, which had a perfect imprint of the back of Nan's head and Nan's bum worn into it. Gary was in the room watching cartoons with Pauline's little brother, Craig, as well as Uncle Dave, Uncle Alan, Uncle Dave's current girlfriend, Sharon, Sharon's baby, Christopher, and Sharon's brother, Keith. Craig tried to start a fight for the pill bottle when she picked it up off the floor, just because she wanted it, but he let go after Pauline kicked him in the face.

Pauline was furtively relieved to find that Joanne had disappeared when she returned to the kitchen, sneaking a couple of
tablets into her jumper pocket for herself before she handed them
to Nan. Joanne had run out of Coke for her rum and gone for
fresh supplies. That was just one of the many remarkable things
about her: she always went to the shops herself, instead of sending the kids out like the rest of the family did. When Joanne got
back, she'd bought a lot more than the Coke: cans of beer for the
uncles and Keith, dandelion and burdock and Tizer for the kids,
bags of crisps, a Swiss roll, fags, milk, a bottle of lime shampoo
and another plastic bottle which she flourished at Pauline.

'Get us a towel, gyppo!' she shouted excitedly. Pauline found
one on the floor in Uncle Dave's room, frayed and stiff with
stains. If she ever needed to dry herself she used the candlewick
spread that was the only covering on her own bed, shared with
Cheryl. But since the taps in the bathroom basin had stopped
delivering water, there hadn't been much need for this.

Back in the kitchen, Joanne made her sit on a chair and draped
the towel round her shoulders, wrinkling her nose at the smell.

'I'm off to the launderette tomorrow,' she told Nan. It was the
only time anything got washed, when Joanne came home. She
held up the bottle she'd got from the shops.

'Stay still,' she commanded. Pauline tried, but when Joanne
opened the bottle and poured the stuff on to her hair, the smell
made her eyes water and her throat burn. Joanne told her not to
be such a baby, and used the comb to spread the liquid through
her hair. It made the skin on her scalp burn and then sting like
the worst nettle patch in the world, but she had to wait half an
hour until Joanne bent her over the kitchen sink and rubbed
shampoo into her hair, careless of whether it went into her eyes.
Pauline finally couldn't help crying at the varieties of pain she
was suffering, which Joanne found hilarious.

'Great big bloody baby,' she laughed, and poured another mug full of scalding water over Pauline's head. Pauline pushed her tongue against her teeth to stop herself shouting out, knowing that Joanne's amusement could quickly turn to impatience, which led to other sorts of pain. Finally, Joanne stopped rinsing, and attacked Pauline's head with the towel, scrubbing her hair dry. The friction was agony on her sensitized scalp, but by now all the different pains had blended into one prevailing hurt, so universal that it almost didn't matter.

'How d'you think I get looking the way I do, eh?' asked Joanne, as Pauline snivelled in misery.

Joanne's hair was deep orange, with a white streak at the front. Her skin glowed against it, very pale. Pauline found her mam almost unbearably beautiful. Her eyes were huge, and so dark that they looked as black as her eyelashes, spiked with mascara. Joanne had got rid of her own eyebrows and pencilled brown arcs high on her forehead. The lipstick on her thin mouth was pearly pale, as though she'd been kept in a freezer. She looked very different without her make-up, Pauline knew, lost and unemphatic. But she rarely took it off, preferring to apply each day's brows and eyes and lips over the smudged version from the previous day.

'You're growing up,' Joanne warned her, retrieving a long-handled pink comb from her handbag. 'It's time you started thinking about looking proper and that. You can't always wait for me to look after you.'

There was a strip of dusty orange hairs woven along the bottom of the comb's teeth, a few of which had broken off. Pauline braced herself not to flinch as Joanne began to comb her snarled mat of wet hair, but in contrast to her previous assault, she was surprisingly gentle. This was what it was like with her mam. You never knew when there was going to be a good time, or a bad. Now, suddenly, it was good. Pauline sat on the floor with her head poking up between Joanne's round knees, letting her comb her hair free of its knots as Joanne sang along to the radio she had brought home with her. Her singing was heartfelt and tuneful, and she knew the words to all the latest songs. She even gave Pauline a packet of smoky bacon crisps, which she crunched quietly so as not to disturb the singing or the mood, while Joanne combed and combed, long after the last knot had disappeared and the raging of Pauline's scalp had muted into an almost pleasurable throbbing. The bulb in the kitchen shone down on them, sparing them from the night, just her and her mam, for what seemed like hours.

'See,' Joanne said when she'd finished. 'That's more like it.'

THE LAST PART of school before the summer holidays is awful. Because of Mum having me moved to a different class I don't know anyone properly, and no one can be bothered to make friends with me so soon before we break up. At least at playtime I can find my old friends and play my old games, but Pauline Bright hovers at the edges of skipping and two-ball, tempting me into a bout of skeletons. Her hair is now a horrible greenish-white that reminds me of fresh snot, with a stripe of black at the roots. The teachers were shocked when she turned up like this and tried to send her home, but she claimed that her mum had mixed the bleach bottle up with the shampoo, that it had all been an accident. She came back the next day with her hair in a ratty snot-and-black ponytail (rubber band, which I'm not allowed; I'm only allowed proper bobbles, because uncovered elastic breaks your hair) and told them that her mam had said there was nothing she could do until it had all grown out.

Whenever Pauline opens her mouth, the ragged angle of her front tooth gnaws into my conscience. Some days I succumb, and play skeletons. It's the sort of game I gave up playing when I was at least eight, and I feel slightly ashamed of myself, as well as wary of Christina's contempt. Fortunately she does violin and choir two dinnertimes a week. And the game with Pauline doesn't make us friends, however much we play it.

My mind is on other things. Mum takes me into work, as she'd suggested during her interruption of my perfect Saturday night. She pretends it's because my fringe needs cutting, but usually she whips the scissors out at home and gives me a deft, brutal trim. This time though, she gets one of the juniors (spotty Trish) to wash my hair at the basin like a customer, and puts rollers in after the trim, and sits me under one of the driers which makes me feel, not entirely enjoyably, like an astronaut. By the time she combs out my hair, saying how much better I look, even using a bit of spray, everyone else has left. And then Ian the accountant turns up; Mr Haskell. He's sweating in the heat even though his shirt has short sleeves. I have never, in fact, seen so much sweat on a person's face. Something to do with his fatness, I conclude.

'Hot enough for you?' he asks us both, accepting my mum's wordless greeting of a lilac salon towel and drying off his face with it. He hands the towel back to her, also without speaking, then beams at me.

'Who's this dollybird?' he asks. 'A famous model?' I blush happily, and oblige when Mum wonders if I'm going to give Mr Haskell a kiss. I blush again when I remember the jam rags. But he seems unconcerned.

We return to the Copper Kettle, where Ian once more orders my dream pancake combination. 'Your usual, madam,' he says. I'm perfecting a method of eating it, where I swirl each disc of banana in a pool of butterscotch, before using it as a template to cut out a corresponding disc of pancake with the blade of my knife, skewering the resulting forkful and eating it. The concentration demanded by this process obliterates the surrounding adult conversation, although I noticed when I sat down that Mum was unequipped with a biro this time, and that while Ian has a pile of papers with him, they remain on the seat beside him. I'm chasing the last drops of sauce with the final absorbent morsel of pancake when Mum asks me a question.

'So, Gems, what do you think about us having a holiday?'

I swallow the last of the pancake, nodding. We always have a holiday, usually abroad. I've been to Spain more times than anyone in my former class (I don't know anyone well enough in my current one to ask them about holidays). I'd most like to go to Butlin's, like Christina; she's told me there are lots of competitions there which I'm hopeful of winning, talent contests that I think might lead to meeting Lallie and being in her show. But I know better than to say so, because I know that going to Spain is better, and that being better is what Mum's best at. We always have new clothes for our holidays. Only Dad wears shirts from his non-holiday life, but even he puts on hats and aftershave.

'Just you and me,' Mum elaborates.

'Is Dad busy?' I ask, eyeing my plate and wondering if Ian will mind if I lick it clean. I know Mum would, but if he thought it was OK, she might let it pass.

'That's right.'

Experimentally, I dab at the edge of the plate with my finger and transfer the film of syrup to my mouth.

'Where are we going?' I ask.

Mum's arms are crossed on the table in front of her, each hand nursing the bare, fleshy top of the opposite arm. She sits very straight, as she always does.

'Ian's very kindly invited us to stay with him,' she tells me.

'Oh.'

It seems fine to me. I presume that Ian has a house in Spain, or is inviting us to stay in a hotel with him. It isn't until the next day, when Mum nervously expands on the holiday arrangements, that I realize we're having a holiday ten minutes up the road.

'The good thing is, you'll still be able to go to school,' says Mum, busying herself with her mascara brush. I'm sitting on the bed, watching her through her dressing-table mirror. She puts on the amazed expression she uses for mascara application. 'You can get the bus.'

I don't consider it much of a holiday if I still have to go to school.

'Has Ian got a swimming pool?' I ask hopefully.

'Don't be so spoilt,' snaps Mum, viciously rodding the mascara wand in and out of its pot, and we leave it at that. Dad gives me a five-pound note when we go, all packed up, and tells me that I can come home any time. It's only then that I realize that something quite important is happening. I feel sorry for Dad, not coming with us, and I prolong our farewell hug to let him know. As usual he detaches himself first, as though he's late and has to get a move on.

Ian's house is in a posh part of town, Old Cantley. Cantley proper isn't particularly posh, but Old Cantley is. It's a detached house, Mum points out. I'm not sure what this means, but I know it's desirable, as is the fact that it's a dormer bungalow. This means it has stairs, although I always thought the whole point of a bungalow was that it didn't. It's quite a bit bigger than our house, and brand new. It has a particular smell, of Ian's soap or aftershave, and the mints he sucks. Despite the sweating and the fatness, he always seems extremely clean, and his house looks very clean as well, which is bound to appeal to Mum.

'Your room, modom,' Ian says, when he takes us to the upstairs part. The single bed is pushed up against a large window with a deep sill, which is a bit like the bed arrangement in Lallie's room in her TV show. I love it, and tell him so. He nips my nose between his finger and thumb with his soft, fat fingers, just for a second.

'I like a woman who's easily pleased,' he grins, and Mum shoos a backhand his way, without really hitting him.

'Cheeky bugger,' she says, approvingly. Then they leave me to settle in while Ian takes Mum to show her her room. I breathe in the new smell that surrounds me. I like it, but it seems to collect in my stomach and turn hard, like a stone. Only when I leave the house, when I go to school on the bus and breathe in everything familiar, does the hardness dissolve. Then I remember about being in a different class, and it comes back.

FRANK DENNY, OF Frank Denny Management, never felt entirely comfortable out of range of a phone. Journeys by train were a torment to him. At least in the car you could take regular stops and make calls along the way (he kept a bag of change from the bank in the glove compartment for just this purpose). Not that he was a fan of motoring per se. He was a nervous driver – he always had too much on his mind to concentrate entirely safely – but he bit the bullet and decided to make the run up to Doncaster in the Rover. He needed to sort out the Lallie situation in person. Good as he was on the phone, and few were better, some problems were best resolved face to face.

'When will you be back?' Laurence asked him, faffing about with sandwiches for the journey, although Frank had told him he'd be stopping at motorway services, likely more than once.

'Expect me when you see me, Lol,' he'd told him. It might be an overnight, if he really needed to lay it on with a trowel and take the mother for dinner. Although he definitely needed to be back and rested by tomorrow lunchtime because he was booked to take out another client who needed as much time and attention as he was about to dedicate to Lallie. Being a good agent, as he always said, was like having a big family where every child was your favourite.

The traffic wasn't too heavy up the M1, and past Watford Frank relaxed enough to concentrate on the situation as it stood. LWT were cutting up rough about another series, although the contract still had two years to run. Light Ents wanted to axe the show in favour of a couple of specials; 'showcase' was the word they had used. Frank's unusually hairy ears (he kept them

trimmed) filtered euphemism with one hundred per cent effi-
ciency; he knew the score. Lallie wasn't getting the audiences
they had imagined – Bruce and *The Generation Game* were just
too strong. But it needn't be the end of the world, as he and the
Head of Light Ents had agreed. Frank was committed to emol-
lience because he was in the process of finessing a tasty contract
for another of his clients, a club comedian who was ripe for a TV
breakthrough. LWT was dangling a cast-iron game-show format
for him tantalizingly out of reach; the crucial distance was Lallie's
mum's compliance in the conversion of Lallie's contract from a
series into two of these so-called showcases a year. As a bonus,
they were willing to release the kid for film work and fit the timing of the shows around it.

Frank knew that LWT was a bit nervous about the current
film. Disney was one thing, the dirty-mac-artsy-fartsy brigade
was another. Still, he was very hopeful about a contract with
one of the American studios, if not Disney itself. It wasn't for
nothing that he'd said to the mother, Katrina, when they'd been
approached about the film, it could well be a springboard to
greater things. And the director, whatshisname, couldn't have
been more enthusiastic when Lallie had read for him. (Now there
was a man who could do with a hit.) Of course, hearing him
on the phone raving about Lallie after the audition had come as
no surprise to Frank. As he'd attested himself in more than one
interview, the first time he'd seen Lallie, singing in a Tyne Tees
TV rehearsal room, the hairs had stood up on the back of his
neck (also kept trimmed). You just knew. A star was a star, aged
eight or eighty-five.

But the American business, although highly promising after the
letter that had landed on his desk yesterday, was also tricky. How
old had Hayley Mills been when Disney got her for *Pollyanna*?
Twelve? And she was pure blonde Anglo-Saxon peaches and
cream. Lallie's dad had some Mediterranean blood in him from

somewhere – hence the name – and puberty was bound to be around the corner. Not that Frank claimed to be an expert on these matters, far from it, thank God, but the costume department on the show had already moaned about how much she was growing during the last series. Maybe Katrina could fill him in more precisely about Lallie's development, if that was the word he was looking for. The things he had to worry about. A grown man.

Making good time, Frank stopped at the Leicester services to stretch his legs and ring the office. He sorted Veronica out with the calls she could safely make, and made three himself, one of them quite tricky. He got to the set towards two, Lol's sandwiches untouched on the passenger seat beside him. There was no excitement for Frank in visiting a set; he considered them the most boring places in the world. But, jaded by his unremitting professional routine of rich restaurant lunches, he had an unadmitted weakness for the blandness of catered food. He'd been looking forward to lunch all morning.

It didn't disappoint. He sat on the bottom deck of the decommissioned double-decker being used as the location canteen and tucked into mince with instant mash and textureless cubes of mixed veg as Katrina smoked over him and drank tea. Lallie had been taken off for some fittings, so he didn't have to beat around the bush.

'A showcase,' Katrina echoed, when he broached the LWT proposal. Her tone was neutral. So far, she was just looking for elucidation.

'Think Morecambe and Wise, Stanley Baxter type of thing.'

'You mean a Christmas show?'

'Christmas, Easter, the big bank holidays – the idea is, Lallie's a treat for the audience, not something served up to them every week.'

Katrina caught back the smoke she had begun to exhale, re-inhaled and blew it through her nostrils instead, a feat Frank knew to mean that she smelled a rat.

'So she wouldn't be on every week?'

'No. Which, let's face it, is going to be a relief all round, the way they scheduled the last season, poor kiddie.'

'She was a bit knackered by the end,' conceded Katrina.

'Economies of scale,' said Frank. Katrina seemed to like the phrase.

'For the same money though,' she clarified.

'Money in the bank,' he reassured her. 'Plus –' he leaned forward, pushing aside his cleaned plate, and dropped his voice – 'thinking of the future, this is the perfect way for Lallie to make the transition into being an adult entertainer.'

'She's not twelve until next April, Frank.'

'They're not children long these days.'

Katrina stubbed her butt end into her cup, where it hissed against the dregs of her tea.

'That's true.'

Frank could see that the bulk of his work was done. He pulled his bowl of square jam sponge and glossy custard towards him.

'How's the filming going, anyway?'

Katrina shrugged. 'Can't tell. She's enjoying it – you know what she's like.'

'Loves the work.'

'That's what she says to me. All the time. "I love it, Mam." Always has done – well, you know.'

'Born to it.'

'That's what I've always said – it'd be cruel to stop her. But the minute she tells me she's not enjoying it . . . '

Katrina expanded her fingers into stars, denoting an explosion of finality. Frank nodded.

'I mean, it's not my idea of a good time, hanging round all day, bored as arseholes if you'll excuse the language. But I'm not doing it for me, am I?'

Katrina had made good money in the clubs, singing, before

Lallie's career had taken off. Frank had experienced many times the volubility of Katrina's regret about this sacrifice. He wanted to conserve his stamina for the drive back.

'I was talking,' he diverted her, 'to America. About the film. You know, the studio.'

Katrina's eyes stopped their sightless journey over the view from the bus window and jumped to him.

'They're very interested in our girl. One of their people wants to come and see her for himself.'

'A producer?'

'An executive. You know, since they're already putting money into this – I wouldn't be surprised if they had something else lined up for her.'

Delivering this news was like plugging Katrina into a socket.

'They want to visit the set?'

'I'll clear it with Mike. It shouldn't be a problem.'

Katrina sighed. 'Shame they don't want us to go to America.'

Frank quelled a frisson of irritation. *What do I have to do for you people? What would be enough for you?*

'Well, fingers crossed, eh?'

Judging the moment, he pulled out the revised LWT contracts from his briefcase and slid them over to Katrina. Then he took his Parker ballpoint from his breast pocket and primed it for her with his thumb.

'Just there – unless you want to hang on to them and have a read. I've marked the changes.'

Scarcely glancing at the amended paragraphs, she hoisted the pen.

'Did they mention what the project is?'

'They like to play their cards close to their chest,' he told her, with unfounded authority.

'Who's playing cards?'

Shit. It was Lallie, bouncing up the aisle.

'There's our girl,' said Frank, offering himself for a kiss. Lallie gave him a professional peck on the cheek and said hello. Then, alerted by her mother's animation, she asked what they were talking about.

'They want you for a film in America, hen!' crowed Katrina. Lallie yelped in excitement and bundled into her for a mutual clinch of celebration. Katrina squealed back at her, the two of them jiggling exultantly.

'Steady on,' said Frank. 'They're interested in seeing you, that's all at this stage.'

But it was too late. He could see that the cat was out of the bag before it was even conclusively in. Why did she always have to whip the kid up? He and Lol didn't treat the boys like that. They had even become accustomed to spelling out 'walk' in a sentence unless they were about to take them out, otherwise the frenzied excitement and subsequent whimpering disappointment were unbearable. Of course the boys were highly strung, like all Jack Russells, but then so was Lallie. Like he always said, she might be a kid but first and foremost she was an entertainer.

She hopped on to his knee, flourishing his Parker and tucking it back in his breast pocket.

'Here, kid, have a cigar on me.' It was – who was it? Bob Hope? How the hell did an eleven-year-old kid from Gateshead even know who Bob Hope was? Frank stretched to retrieve the contracts, dislodging Lallie from his lap. She was more of a weight on him than she had been, definitely, although she still looked skinny as a snake. Still, best for him to sort out this trip ASAP, considering. And at least he could count on the big cheese from the studio running to a chauffeur.

To Pauline, a cataclysmic outburst of rage from Joanne was as inevitable as her eventual departure from Adelaide Road. In fact, it was difficult not to regard one as contingent on the other. Pauline didn't consider slapped legs and pulled hair and name-calling as part of this tally; the nature of her mam's real anger actually rendered these casual tokens of attention puzzlingly desirable. Because when Joanne decided that Pauline was a miserable little cunt, unfit to be her daughter, she punished her by refusing to speak or even look at her. She wouldn't have her in the same room, or say her name. Then, it was as though Joanne had killed her, and Pauline was left to float around the house like a ghost, a ghost that lacked even the small consolation of being scary.

It hadn't happened yet. Pauline was adept at reading her mother's moods and smelling her breath, and stayed out of the way if either seemed volatile. Craig and Cheryl were too little to have learned these lessons, but although a few bruises came their way as a consequence, Pauline knew that the larger reaches of Joanne's anger were reserved for her.

'Where've you been?'

'School.'

'School. Read this then.'

Joanne flourished a newspaper at her. Pauline took it. The *Express*. Someone must have been to visit her mum and left it.

'Which bit d'you want me to read?'

'I don't care. Any.'

Pauline never got a chance to read out loud at school. It was always the others, even if she bothered to put her hand up. She

57

started to read out a bit about a man who'd killed his wife with a tyre iron but Joanne lost interest after she realized that Pauline wasn't going to make any mistakes.

'What's the time?' she asked, chopping off Pauline's flow of words like scissors.

'Don't know.'

There were no clocks in the house, and Joanne didn't wear a watch. But Pauline could hear the *Nationwide* music from the telly.

'I think it's about six,' she offered.

'I've got to get ready,' said Joanne, without making a move. She looked ready from the neck up, but her body was still in a bra and jeans. She lit a fag and slumped to smoke it so that her soft white torso stacked on top of itself and over her waistband. A row of lush purple bruises the shape of fingertips stood out on the flesh of her back.

'You looking at?'

'Nothing.'

Pauline drifted away, belatedly sensing danger. She'd been less alert to it than usual because she wasn't feeling well. Her head was thick and her legs felt woolly, as though she'd taken too many of Nan's pills. She'd felt sick all day as well, too sick to eat her school dinner. She staggered upstairs to her bed, which was empty of Cheryl. The candlewick bedspread had been washed, and there was a sheet. Joanne had been to the launderette. Pauline crawled beneath the covers, breathing the launderette smell and loving Joanne. When she woke hours later in the dark it was with a lurch of dread. Cheryl was in the bed with her, rolled next to her on the slack mattress, but Pauline was shivering with cold, despite the combined heat of her sister's body and the summer air. She was about to be sick.

Their room was closest to the bathroom, and Pauline ran, but before she could reach the toilet a hideous gush of sour liquid erupted through her mouth, splashing up from the patchy lino and over her clothes. The awful taste in her mouth, a few shuddering breaths, then the next wave assailed her, interrupted convulsively by the next, and the next. It was everywhere. She was crying now as well as shivering, and she'd shat herself at the same time as being sick. She tried to be quiet. Not because she was worried about waking anyone else in the house – she could hear voices downstairs and there was never an hour when someone wasn't awake and about their business – but because she didn't want to draw anyone to the scene of her shame. There were no towels to clean up the mess, and the empty toilet roll, furred with dust, mocked her from where it had rolled to the foot of the washbasin. She'd have to get the bedspread.

Still sniffling with shock and self-pity, Pauline waddled shittily back to the bedroom, where Cheryl slept on, the bedspread kicked off her. Returning to the bathroom, she retched on the landing outside, but there was nothing left to come up. She wrestled with the cover, turning the one bath tap that worked feebly on it before giving up and stuffing as much of the bedspread as she could down the toilet to get it properly wet. After a few plunges she cast it, heavy with water, on to the mess on the floor and stamped up and down its length, swabbing hopelessly at the vomit.

It wasn't that Nan or the others minded stink and shit and mess, it was what they lived in, although even they probably drew the line at this. But Joanne would mind, she was different from the others, and Pauline knew she would blame her. Especially since she'd been looking for something to blame her for. It made it worse that she'd been to the launderette, that Pauline was covering the newly pristine bedspread with puke.

'What's all this in aid of?'

In her panic, Pauline's first thought was that Joanne was wearing a swimsuit. She'd never seen her in a swimsuit.

'I was sick.'

As soon as she spoke she couldn't stop herself crying, as though the tears came from the same place as the puke.

'Don't be cross wi' me, Mam, I'm sorry. I was sick, I couldn't help it, I'm sorry, Mam . . .' On and on she wailed, unable to stop, as though she was Craig's age and not ten.

'State of you. You messed yourself and all?'

Pauline continued to cry, abject, as her mother left the room. After a few seconds her tears stuttered, uncertain of the outcome. Was she being left? This would be better than she dared to hope. She reapplied herself to shoving the bedspread back and forth with her toes, sweating with nausea and effort. Joanne reappeared, wearing her plastic leather coat open over the swimsuit, which Pauline now saw was some kind of underwear which pushed up her tits and crammed in her waist, and had bits dangling off for stockings, although Joanne's white legs were bare. She was carrying a bucket full of water.

'Take your clothes off then. Get in the bath.'

She wasn't angry, as far as Pauline could tell. She had the face on she wore when she had a job in hand. Pauline gestured to the stuff in the bath, an assortment which included broken-down shoes, unstapled porno mags and an ancient, flexless bar heater.

'Well, shift it then.'

Pauline complied as quickly as she could, not wanting to shatter this fragile interlude of grace. Joanne even helped her, finding the plug in the process. She put it in the plughole, commanded Pauline to get in, and poured in the bucket of cold water. Although she was still shivering, Pauline was grateful, after all the recent weirdness her body had visited on itself, for the normality of the water shocking her skin. Joanne went off to fetch another bucketful, as Pauline tried to wash off the sick and shit. It took four buckets altogether. Joanne chucked the last one over her as she stood in the bath, like a shower, she said. Then she brought a dry towel from somewhere and let her wrap herself in it. Throughout this, Pauline tasted the sick in her mouth and was terrified that she might vomit again. She knew how easy it would be to overtax the miracle of Joanne's patience. But nothing happened.

Joanne followed her back to her room, told her to get back in bed with Cheryl. As Pauline climbed in she looked around.

'Where's the flipping blanket?' she said.

She doesn't know, Pauline realized. She didn't recognize it, heaped in a corner of the bathroom floor, covered with sick and mess. And the dread came back to her, as sour as the taste of vomit.

'I haven't seen it,' she lied.

'I washed it,' Joanne told her indignantly. 'Put it back on the bed today.'

'Sometimes our Craig takes stuff,' said Pauline, faking more sleepiness than she felt. 'It's dead warm, any road.'

As soon as Joanne had gone and she was reassured by a few minutes of silence, Pauline was up again and back to the bathroom. She dragged the unrecognizable, stinking bedspread back and stuffed it under her bed. Anything was better than letting Joanne see what had happened. She'd be first out of the house in the morning, however ill she felt.

By the time the sun was up Pauline no longer felt particularly ill. What she did feel was starving, and she had to nick a bottle of milk from the nicely decorated house five doors down to stop the ache in her gut. After this, she distributed her soiled clothes among a few local dustbins. She'd realized on waking that she had to retain her school pinafore dress because there was nothing to replace it. But it was more badly stained than the water from the kitchen tap and a frantic rub could remedy, and she could smell herself even in the weakness of the early sunshine.

Pauline walked on to school, although it was at least an hour before lessons would be starting. To wash the bedspread, she needed money for the launderette. Scavenging about their house before she left had only unearthed a few coppers and two five-pence pieces. The one thing all Brights took care of when they had it was money. It wouldn't be a problem to shake some down from the littler kids in the playground, she knew. But then, cost aside, she had no idea what happened once you were in a launderette. Pauline didn't like new environments, where it was likely she'd be disapproved of, if permitted to enter at all. She knew better than to go into a launderette unarmed with any redeeming knowledge of its procedures. Ignorance would make her stink twice as badly as she already did.

Still groggy, she slumped against one of the school gateposts and dozed in the sunshine. When she woke the gates were open, and other kids were milling through, some accompanied by parents. Pauline could see in their faces how bad she looked and smelled. She glowered back at them, defying anyone to comment. Among the arrivals was that Gemma girl, not with her mum, although Pauline had seen her mum with her at school before, always pulling and plucking at Gemma as though she was making her out of plasticine. Seeing Gemma's round blue eyes open rounder at the sight of her, Pauline shouted 'Fuck off!' before another thought struck. She hopped into the playground after Gemma before she could get herself into a group with her friends.

'Hey.'

Pauline shoved her on the shoulder, making Gemma's perfectly divided high bunches waggle like spaniel's tails as she turned to address the blow.

'Leave me alone, you,' Gemma warned.

'I'm not,' said Pauline. 'I need to ask you summat.'

Gemma stopped, wrinkling her small nose.

'Yuck. Have you been sick?'

'Six times,' exaggerated Pauline. 'There were nowt to come up in the end.'

'I got a bug one time we went to Spain,' Gemma said, 'and I was sick fourteen times in two days.' She looked at Pauline's pinafore. 'You'll get done for not wearing a blouse. It's the rules.'

'I ant got owt else.'

'Anything.'

'You what?'

'You should say anything else.'

'Do you know about launderettes?'

It turned out that Gemma did, and seemed flattered to be asked. She went quite often with her mum, she said, although now that they were in Ian's house he had a washing machine so her mum didn't need to go any more. Pauline recognized this as a boast, although its content was too obscure to impress her.

'You'll need lots of five-pence pieces. And powder,' Gemma told her. 'You can buy it there, but they charge a fortune for it.'

Pauline mused on this. 'You'd better come with me.'

'When?'

'After school.'

'I can't. I've got ballet.'

'Dinnertime then.'

'We're not allowed.'

'They'll only think you've gone home. We'll be back for the register, it's not like twagging.'

Pauline could see the impossibility of this in Gemma's face.

'You know the skellinton lady, I saw her in another film the other night,' she lied. 'She showed her tits and everything.'

'She never.'

'I'll tell you about it later,' she enticed, 'if you come with me.'

'We'll get done.'

'We won't. If we do, I'll say I made you. Please. Go on. Please. Then I'll tell you about her.'

Gemma exhaled. 'You really smell, you know.'

Pauline hadn't mentioned anything to Gemma about the soiled bedspread, now waiting in a plastic bag among the lower branches of a leggy lilac bush in the Brights' garden. So it took some persuading to get her back there before they set out again for the launderette. Gemma was very anxious, however much Pauline reassured her, that they'd miss the two o'clock register. Pauline was more anxious about being caught by Joanne retrieving the bedspread. This was unlikely, since Joanne rarely stirred before mid-afternoon. But she was very relieved once they were out of the garden and walking to the launderette a safe few streets away. Many five-pence pieces jingled in the pocket of the PE shorts she was now wearing, along with an overlarge PE T-shirt similarly culled from lost property after an appalled Mrs Bream had intervened at morning assembly. Pauline had waged a campaign of terror during playtime, mindful of the fortune that Gemma had told her washing powder would cost. Throughout this, Gemma had ignored her and played two-ball with that Christina and her other snot-bag friends.

'Why can't your mum wash it?' Gemma asked her as she watched Pauline lug the stinking bag with both hands and the help of a leg to boot it along.

'She's working,' said Pauline. Gemma accepted this.

'My mum works,' she told her.

Coming on top of the warmth of the day, the heat of the launderette was nearly overwhelming. Pauline liked it, but Gemma, who had turned pinker during the walk, fanned her hands in front of her face in distress.

'Let's hurry up,' she pleaded.

At their arrival, a woman with a fag in her mouth and a single fat curler at the front of her hair peeped out from a doorway at the back, but only stayed long enough to exhale her smoke before disappearing, uninterested. Gemma held out her clean, fleshy palm.

'Give us some money and I'll get the powder for you.'

Pauline crammed a mound of five-pences, tinny-smelling from her pocket, into Gemma's hand, and watched her march with officious confidence to a metal box on the wall.

'Put the cover in there,' she commanded, nodding at a row of queasy-green washing machines with porthole doors, as she slotted coins into the box. By the time Pauline had crammed the bedspread into the machine nearest the door, Gemma was by her side carrying a thin plastic cup full of gritty soap powder. Nudging Pauline aside, she slammed the washing-machine door closed with her hip and tipped the powder into a little compartment that pulled out on a box at the top of the machine. The sequence of movements, and the forced seriousness with which she performed them, looked borrowed from someone else. Gemma sighed heavily and pushed her bunches back, flick flick, as though their weight was oppressing her shoulders, which they barely brushed.

'You need twenty-five p more. That's five five-pences.'

'I know,' said Pauline, but handed Gemma the coins obligingly enough. Gemma pulled out a metal arm concealed in the machine's middle which accepted a row of neatly placed coins, them rammed it viciously into its housing and pulled it back, empty. The machine gurgled into life. Pauline regretted allowing Gemma to perform this final, satisfying operation, but it was too late now. Next time she'd know.

'There,' said Gemma. There was a row of orange plastic chairs for them to sit on. They sat and watched the soapy waves breaking against the porthole.

'Go on then,' Gemma prompted. 'You can tell me now. About the film with the skeleton lady in.'

Pauline slumped in her chair, chewing a bit of her fringe. She felt dreamy and warm.

'Can't be bothered.'

'You said—'

'I told you, I don't feel like it, right?'

Gemma peeled her back away from her chair, rigid with outrage.

'You said you'd tell me. You promised.'

'I didn't say when, did I? And I didn't promise, any road.'

'You're a liar.'

'No I'm not, you are.'

Gemma stood. 'You are a liar and if you don't tell me, I'm telling. I'm telling Mrs Bream you left the school without permission.'

Indignation had pinked her face a shade deeper. Pausing to
hoist her white socks over the plump crowns of her knees, she
made for the door.

'You can't,' Pauline called after her. 'You'll get done and all.'

Panicked by this observation, Gemma stopped.

'If you tell, I'll tell,' Pauline promised.

'They'll think you made me. I'll tell them.'

'An' I'll tell them you showed me what to do.'

Pauline could see tears filling Gemma's eyes like the water rising in the washing machine. She turned and ran off, away down
the street. Pauline didn't care particularly, she was too tired. She
hoisted her legs on to the row of chairs and curled up, falling
asleep to the churning rhythm of the water.

IAN DOESN'T LIKE Mum smoking in the house so she has to go out into the garden with her mug of tea in the morning, before she leaves for work. He and I sit at the table in the dining room eating our breakfast, while she stands in an open slice of the sliding French door, smoking out into the garden and talking back to us. This is new to me in all sorts of ways. Mum and Dad and I have never talked in the mornings, and Dad's a smoker as well so I'm used to waking up over my toast while they smoke over me, silently. This new, sociable way of breakfasting is quite nice, although both Mum and I have less time than we used to because of the bus journey. We walk to the bus stop together then take separate buses into our different bits of town, while Ian drives the opposite way to his office in Bawtry. Mum and I chat as much as always, although I never ask her the two questions which weight my stomach: when are we going back to Dad, and what happened to Ian's wife.

Of the two, the Dad question is the more urgent and frightening, while the one about Ian's wife is pure curiosity and so becoming unbearable. Her photo is everywhere in his house. Tanned, she squints into the sun on foreign holidays, inclines her head towards Ian as they stand holding hands more palely on the front lawn, and, wearing something sequinned, raises a glass of wine at a party. She looks the same in all of them, round-faced and fat and placid. She looks very like Ian. In fact, the reason that I know not to ask any more about her is that when we first moved in I asked him, looking at one of the photographs, if the lady was his sister.

'Now, Gemma.'

It was as though a door had flown open which Mum hurried to shut before anything blew in from outside. But it was too late. Ian's mild, bulbous brown eyes had already welled with tears.

'That's my good lady,' he said, with a sigh. Mum started talking about spotty Trish getting engaged, and that was that. Now I know better than to ask. Ian's wife died. I wonder if she died in the house, and that spooks me at night, although I realize she's unlikely to have died in my bedroom. One night I have a dream where she turns into a fat version of the skeleton lady with a rat running through her skull teeth. It's then, stumbling from my room, crying and terrified, that I discover that Mum doesn't sleep in the other spare room, but with Ian in his bed. It's a surprise like a small, cheap firework, amazing for less than a second. I'm not stupid. And I'm pretty sure I know the answer to my question about Dad, which is why I don't ask it.

It's nearly time for school to end, and there's talk of Mum and Ian and me going on another holiday, a proper one this time. Although with the hot weather, staying at his house has felt like being in another country, with everything in it tasting and smelling entirely different.

'What do you fancy, señorita,' says Ian one teatime, holding out a fan of holiday catalogues like a giant pack of cards ready for a trick. 'Minorca, Majorca, Marbella?'

Mum giggles and chooses one.

'When are we going?'

'Not for a couple of weeks,' says Mum. 'Why do you care?'

I've already told them. It's the single most exciting piece of news I've personally ever received in my life, and they've already forgotten about it.

'Lallie,' I say. 'You know.'

'Lallie.' She rolls her eyes at Ian. 'Oh, don't worry, we know better than that. You and your Lallie.'

Her words spark a warning against my feelings. This is why

I don't talk much about Lallie to her, particularly when Ian's around; she'll just make fun of me. But I had to tell them this, what Mr Scott announced at assembly after his account of the parable of the talents, which was gripping enough in its own way. In case we can't be relied on to convey the astonishing information accurately, we've also been entrusted with a letter to take home, giving the dates when Lallie and the rest of the film people will be using the school, and when we can sign up for the film people to see us in case they want us to be in the film. I've read it so many times I know it off by heart.

'July the third they're having the auditions.' Auditions. It's a word familiar to me only from *Ballet Shoes*, and here I am sending it out of my mouth as casually as my own name. 'So we'll need to be here.'

'I know.'

'Then July the fourteenth to fifteenth they'll be in the school, from eight a.m. to ten p.m.'

'I'll put it on the calendar,' Ian promises. He takes these things more seriously than Mum does, or seems to.

'Bit late for kids, ten o'clock,' Mum observes.

When she says things like that, I'm worried she's not going to let me go to the audition at all, and I ask her about it so much that she snaps at me to stop mithering. Which means all evening I have to resist the urge to talk about it, not because I think she needs to be reminded any more, but simply because I want to. I long to talk about Lallie, about the audition and the film and how my life might be transformed for ever at the beginning of July. Instead I have to sit through *Sale of the Century* and a boring war film while Mum smokes outside during the adverts, and Ian eats chocolate Brazils from a noisy bag perched on the arm of his chair. The sucking sounds he makes are slightly disgusting, and although he offers me the bag, I decline. I don't like Brazil nuts, anyway, they remind me of toes. I retreat into my meandering private fantasy where Lallie and I become great friends and live in her house with Marmaduke the butler. The starting point for this dream is now fixed as our meeting at the school. At the audition.

On Saturday, when Christina and I get back to her house from swimming, her mum is stretched out on the settee in the living room watching the wrestling with Elaine, who's eating crisps. Christina's mum rears her head from the settee and fires a question at Christina in Glaswegian.

'Mum's saying she's going to ask your mum about coming to Butlin's with us.'

This is surprising, as well as exciting. But I can't see Mum and Ian wanting to go to Butlin's.

'I think we're going to Spain.'

Christina's mum starts talking to me. She always calls me hen. I work out that the invitation is for me alone. This is much better, and makes the offer more likely to be accepted by my mum. Both Christina and I are very excited by the prospect of going on holiday together, and her dad, when he comes in at teatime, tells us off for excessive giggling. As ever, the attempt at stopping spurs us to new and more hysterical heights.

When we see each other at school on Monday, Christina again describes the pleasures to come: the bunkbeds we'll share in the chalet, taking turns to sleep on the top one, the expanse of the pool and the unbelievable fun of its wave machine, the hilarity of the redcoats, particularly a boy one called Denny, who looks a bit like David Essex. Unexpectedly, Mum proves enthusiastic about me going, and by the unseen machinery of adult life communicates this to Christina's mum. It's all arranged. My excitement about this and about meeting Lallie finally dissolves the anxiety I've had about our failure to return to Dad, and for the first time since our holiday to Old Cantley I lose the stone in my stomach. Although Pauline Bright still lurks around me at playtimes, since the launderette I've ignored her, and even skeletons can't tempt me.

A fortnight before school breaks up, I get in one afternoon to find my bed covered with new clothes, neatly arranged into outfits like the ones for the cut-out Bunty on the back page of my comic: two sets of shorts and T-shirts, with matching socks below, a blue spotted bikini and matching hat, a sundress and sandals. To the right of the sundress, just where my hand would be, is a clear plastic handbag with a bright orange handle. Through a zipped compartment on its side stares a little doll with matching orange hair. From the door, Mum peeps in to see my reaction.

'To look nice for your holiday,' she says, as I cuddle up to her in a bliss of gratitude. 'You should thank Ian – he bought them for you.'

Ian's still out at work, so I hang on to her.

'Lucky girl,' says Mum.

'I know. I can't believe it, Mum. School, then the auditions, then Butlin's.'

Although I know Mum likes it when I'm grateful for gifts, my delight is real. But as I coil into her, I'm met with tension. I pull back, already dreading something. Mum's eyes slide.

'I thought you knew, Gems . . .'

And she tells me. The Butlin's holiday clashes with the audition at the school, since the only week Christina's dad can get off work is the week before we officially break up. Going on the holiday will mean missing the whole thing. I'm submerged in sudden despair, as complete as the sea closing over my head.

'Why didn't you say?' I can hardly speak for tears.

'I thought you knew.'

That's all she'll say to me, although of course in the obscurity of the arrangements, no one has explicitly mentioned dates to me, or acknowledged the importance of the days I've ringed on Ian's kitchen calendar in purple felt-tip. I howl, I sob. I don't accuse or rage, although I know somewhere that Mum has seized on Christina's mum's offer as a way of punishing me for my love of Lallie. Her attempts to calm me down evaporate when I start clawing the new clothes to the floor in a blind desire to hurl myself on to the bed. I feel the sting as the flat of her hand catches my calves.

'Un-grate-ful – little – beggar!'

She punctuates each syllable with a slap, and I scream in outrage. It doesn't hurt, but the world is reduced to my snot and my tears and my difficulty in breathing through the sobs in a way it hasn't been for years. I press my fists into my eye sockets and give myself over to the stars exploding behind my eyes.

'What's all this in aid of?'

Ian stands at the door in his short-sleeved shirt, setting down his briefcase with a look of mild amazement. Mum and I both stop. There's something shameful about him walking in on us, and much as I'm hating Mum, I don't want Ian to see her rage.

'She's got herself in a state,' says Mum, as though she's suddenly on my side, the side of me not getting into a state. 'About going away.'

'Be– be– cause – because of Lal– Lallie,' I heave. 'I won't be able to—' And at the thought of what I won't be able to do, I'm submerged by another wave of despair.

Above this, I don't know what takes place between Ian and Mum. At some point they leave me, and eventually my crying abates to vacant shuddering breaths. A smell of lamb chops travels upstairs. Then Ian comes in, holding out a flannel he's soaked with cold water.

'Here.'

He sits down on the bed next to me, which doesn't leave me much room. Folding the flannel in half to form a rectangle, he places it over my eyes. The flabby coolness of it is soothing, as is the dark it leaves me in. Ian's minty smell gets in the way of the lamb chops, like sauce. He doesn't try to say anything, but he doesn't leave. Occasionally a tearful gasp overcomes me, as sudden and inescapable as a burp. The first time this happens, Ian lays his big heavy hand on my stomach, as a comfort. For some reason I can't help thinking again about his wife, his good lady, and wondering why she died.

'Teatime!' It's Mum from downstairs, louder and more ferocious than normal, which is what she's trying to be.

'Come on then.'

Ian lurches and shifts from the bed, pressing his hand down on my middle before he takes it away. There's a gap between my skirt and blouse and he has to peel the part of his hand that has made contact with my skin painlessly away.

'Sweaty.'

He means himself, not me. Then, trying to dry the sweat off, he briskly rubs his palm up and down the front of my knickers. It's easy to do this because in writhing about while crying I've worked my skirt into a bulbous band that sits above my waist.

'Sexy.'

He says it the way he calls me a dollybird. He's commenting on my knickers, which are pale green with a faded purple fairy printed on the front, dipping her wand in a pond spangled with lilac stars. They're my favourites. In the second that Ian's hand moves up and down the fabric, my privates feel charged and wrong. Ian taps my thigh and twitches my skirt.

'Come on then, or your mum'll have our guts for garters.'

He takes the flannel from me and leaves it in the bathroom, over the basin. Then we go downstairs together, towards the table with its waiting symmetrical plates of lamb and mashed potato and carrots, his and mine with Mum's safely in the middle. It's not the right sort of food at all for such a hot day. But I eat it anyway, because I should be grateful to Mum for making it, and for the new clothes, and for everything she does for me every day of my life.

FROM THE MOMENT she arrived in the UK, Quentin realized she wasn't going to be who anyone was expecting. Coming out of the arrivals gate at Heathrow, she quickly spotted the hapless guy with glasses and an overlarge chauffeur's hat who was holding a sign that read 'Quentin Montpellier'. The lettering was increasingly squished at the Montpellier end. When she approached him and introduced herself, he did a weak double-take.

'Wasn't expecting a lady,' he said, and then dropped the sign to free up a hand. 'Welcome to England.'

As the chauffeur dipped to pick up her luggage, Quentin caught him taking a peek down her top, which was low-cut. She wasn't wearing a bra. Poor little guy, she thought, as she tended to on these occasions. It would have been hard to begrudge him on any score since Britain already seemed like such a cheerless place, even though the sun when they got out of the airport turned out to be shining as brightly as it had when she left California. Despite what everyone had warned her about the rain and the fog, it continued to shine throughout the long journey, which mainly took in the freeway. It had to be said, though, that the surprising weather didn't help in any way.

'Not the scenic route,' said the driver, who had introduced himself as Len. 'Hot enough for you?'

Quentin had, in fact, asked him if he could switch on the air-conditioning, which made him hoot with laughter. No air-conditioning in the car, he told her, and suggested she open the window instead.

'Get a bit of a breeze going.'

Quentin had been to Europe before, and once to London. She

realized she had to adjust. The head fuck was everyone superfi-
cially talking the same language, albeit with the accent, which
she'd never found as cute as everyone claimed. But it was still
Europe.

She'd taken her last pill on the flight with a couple of double
vodkas, and the residual buzz from this kept her dozing for the
first hour or so through Len's unextensive conversation. As the
medication began to wear off, England and the freeway and Len
looked even worse. The sunshine was like a strip light, exposing
every flaw – and there were plenty to expose. The place looked
like Poland. Not that she'd ever been to Poland. *Oh shit*. Quentin
tried to guide her mind away from the decision she'd taken in
the airport bathroom to ditch her holiday stash of Quaaludes and
Valium. She needed a clear head. But there was clear and there
was painfully clear, and she was erring on the side of pain right
here already.

'How much longer till we get there?' she asked Len. He considered, allowing for traffic, and said it would be another hour
and a half at least, maybe two. From the way he said it, Quentin
knew that the first estimate was a lie, designed to console. She
took out a script from her hand luggage and managed to concentrate for nearly thirty pages, making notes in the margin.
After that it got so predictable she lost interest and resorted to
the bad thing, wondering if she could get hold of anything once
she was on set. Vague nouns weren't a good sign. Thing, anything, stuff. Drugs. Crews always had drugs on them. Or maybe
it would be different in Europe, more cultivated. Like what?
Sipping absinthe from exquisitely engraved hip flasks perhaps,
while exchanging *bon mots*. She'd sign up for that.

OK, stop, Quentin told herself. *Consider your position. Your
brand-new, box-fresh position. Vice-president, production. Not as
good as it sounds, but it sounds pretty damn good. You can do this.*
She was pleased with herself for the pep talk. There was no point

in being nervous, since she was the scary one. No one here knew her. To the people she was about to meet, she was the job. The job her father had actually made actual calls about actually to get for her.

'My father's family is from Scotland,' she announced, leaning towards the back of Len's head. 'On my grandfather's side. He was called Quentin Macphee Gordon.'

'You lot always know where your families come from,' said Len. 'Yanks, I mean.'

And then, some seconds after this had closed the conversation down, he unexpectedly revived it.

'Sounds French, Montwhatsit.'

'My mom's family is French Canadian, originally,' Quentin explained, despite her resentment at proving his point. 'I took Mom's name when my parents divorced.'

Len had no answer to this. After nearly an hour more of their sporadic couplets, he announced that they would soon be there. Quentin gratefully hunched closer to the window. She had imagined, since they were travelling north, that the countryside would be rather like that in which her grandmother had been born. But there was still freeway, mainly, and a notable flatness. She'd been expecting moors. Didn't moors go up and down like Heathcliff's moods, hills and dales, mountains and valleys, et cetera, et cetera?

'Are these the moors?' she asked Len, just in case.

'Nah, have to go further north for that, love,' he told her, and she could tell her ignorance slotted right into his prejudices. *Yanks.*

The schedule she'd been sent ordered her to go straight out to the location. Quentin suggested that once Len had dropped her off, he could take the luggage on to her hotel in case she was late checking in. But she could see he was looking worried. Challenged, he explained that she'd been booked into a hotel in Manchester, a city apparently another couple of hours' drive away across something – mountains? – called the Pennines. Quentin could imagine the way some PA back in the production office in LA had checked out a map and figured that the apparent distance to Manchester would be nothing in this bonsai country. But of course, being so tiny, two hours was a big distance, and apparently the freeway didn't go everywhere.

If Len had been an American driver, he'd have got on to finding somewhere else for her to stay during his downtime when she was visiting the set. But the lost look of his eyes behind his fishbowl lenses told Quentin that any further prodding would produce a more despairing version of his already contagious anxiety. She forced herself to quell the instinct to worry about Len. Incredibly, it wasn't her job.

'I'll be fine,' she told him. 'Just wait here, or whatever.'

The location looked even more like Poland. It was a school, and although it was a modern building, it seemed entirely without modern amenities. The many large windows, presumably intended to give the place a sense of space and light, were cramped with childish artworks and dulled with dirt, and looked out on to a brutally circumscribed area of concrete. Quentin felt a surge of dread. Confinement, limitation, despair. *Bullshit*, she tried to convince herself. *This is chemical. My body thinks it's four in the morning. Everyone's low point. This building is the architectural equivalent of four in the morning. For all I know, the whole frickin' country might be. I'm just passing through.*

'B– bleak little place, isn't it? We were pleased. Mike Keys.'

The man poked his hand forward for her to shake it. Weaselly little guy. The director.

'I must say I was expecting someone much older and not nearly so attractive,' he told her, automatically checking out the non-cleavage. Incredible, really, that a movie director would be insensitive to sight lines, but every guy in the universe thought he had secret X-ray vision when it came to staring at tits.

77

'Of course, the art director's had a bit of a go,' Weasel-teeth continued, as oblivious to Quentin's lack of response as he apparently was to her power. *Power, goddamn you.* 'It's actually all rather sweet inside.'

Of course. They were making a movie. They *wanted* the school to look like this.

'Interesting,' said Quentin briskly. 'This wasn't the original location, right? You changed it.'

'G– gosh, yes we did.' *Good.* She could see his surprise that she was up to speed. Did he really think she'd flown thousands of miles to provide him with frankly disappointing T & A? 'That was early days. The other place was a bit gothic – bit too obvious. I just felt it'd be more interesting to use somewhere modern and, you know, try to subvert it, make it sinister. We did send you photos.'

'Yeah, I saw them. It looks great. Suitably creepy and depressing.'

'But modern!'

Quentin registered Mike's little anxiety about the modern thing. Probably his age. He was what, in his mid-thirties? So maybe worried that he was losing touch with the youth market. *Nobody at the studio has any hopes for this movie as regards the youth market, honey.* Or maybe, she realized, as Mike continued to yabber away fanatically about the world of the movie as he led her into the school, it's an artistic thing. *Europe, Quentin. This is an art movie. Guy's a fucking artist.*

Inside, the hopeful array of kids' pictures and projects, the world so trustingly and inaccurately represented in primary colours and cardboard and tissue paper, was enough to choke her up. Benign, not in the tumour sense, but like Santa. All love and optimism and related shit. Each painted coat peg was surmounted by a label with a child's name (Judith, Darren, Rodney, Pauline) printed in clear black teacher's script. As though this was the way life went, a place for everyone, and so clearly and democratically marked. Even the teacher's writing on the name cards, striving for impersonal authority but betraying the compromised asymmetry of a human touch, raked at Quentin's vitals. That falling short, the contamination of the real. Poor little kids. She couldn't remember a time when sights like the wavering tail of the 'y' in Rodney didn't give her a pain in the guts.

'Let's make a movie!'

She heard herself produce this exclamation as they reached a huddle of lights and cables in the corridor that was being set up for a shot. Her loud American voice aroused curiosity, which was presumably what she'd intended: to announce her arrival. Was this what the job was going to do to her? But she encountered a few friendly smiles among the response to her dumb-ass effusion, so maybe it was OK. Oh, God, she was tired. *Check out the crew.* That skinny guy adjusting a lamp had the promising look of a speed freak about him.

'Bit of a nightmare with the lighting,' Mike said, following her gaze but not her intention. He gestured to the lack of space. 'But we can't say you didn't warn us.'

Quentin smiled professionally. Her predecessor, Danny Larson, had lobbied to build sets for the main interiors, including the school, but Mike and the English producer, Hugh, had insisted on shooting everything on location, with all the problems of cramping that entailed. As long as it looked OK and didn't hold up the schedule, it wasn't Quentin's job to care. Danny had a thing about set-building because he'd majored in architecture – this was Quentin's theory anyway – and he just loved fooling around with the models the designers sent him and arguing about dimensions and building methods to console himself for the loss of what he had concluded, age forty-two, would have been the nobler career choice. *Asshole.* She really, really wished she hadn't fucked him. Even with thousands of miles between them, it made Quentin feel bad to think about it, befouling the nest of her new job. Everyone would be saying she got the job because she'd fucked Danny, or, to get the hierarchy straight, Danny had fucked her. When actually, she owed the gig to her dad. *Calling Dr Freud* . . .

'So . . . ' Snapping herself to attention, Quentin could see that Mike was itching to get back to work, to tweak some lights and confer with that silvery-haired cinematographer of his and then shout 'Action', presuming that was the word they used over here.

'Is Hugh busy?' she prompted. Mike looked shifty. There was absolutely no way he'd know about her and Danny Larson, right?

'He is, I'm afraid – meant to say – got a batch of rushes up from the processors which are looking a bit wonky.'

'Wonky.'

Quentin could see he thought she was challenging him, when she was just unfamiliar with the word.

'Nothing serious. Just a slight colour problem – he's sorting it out now.'

'So maybe there's someone who could take me to him . . . '

Mike hesitated. Right there, Quentin had had enough. With the journey and the lack of sleep, and maybe the craving for chemical alteration, she felt as though she'd already slipped into watching what they called rushes and she knew as dailies; repetitive, discontinuous interludes which needed an editor's hand to splice them into the illusion of action with consequences that lead to another action. And so on, building to a climax. Instead of which she had the view of the shrunken English freeway, Len's gnomic expressions of anti-American prejudice, the school, all spooling off into pointlessness like the black frames that ended a reel of film. Nothing. *Nada*.

'Anything I can do, Mike?'

Gratefully, Quentin felt the arrival of organizing energy. It emanated from a small, wiry woman around her own age with bright eyes and too much make-up.

'Oh, Katrina . . . '

She couldn't readily place the woman in the crew, but Mike didn't like her, that was for sure. Quentin offered her hand, just to yank his chain.

'Quentin Montpellier.'

'Ooh, American—'

'That's right!'

'From the studio,' Mike muttered grudgingly. Katrina's eyes widened. *See, asshole*, Quentin mentally addressed Mike. *She can see it. Power.*

'And you are . . . '

'Katrina. Lallie's mummy.'

Ah. Lallie's ambitious mommy. So Mike was pissed with her for muscling in, and who could blame him?

'She'd love to meet you, hasn't stopped talking about it – she's mad about America, terrible—'

'Well, I'd love to meet her too,' Quentin reassured her, professionally. 'Maybe Katrina could take me to see Hugh, Mike?' she suggested. 'I wouldn't want to hold things up.'

And so she was borne off by Katrina, who enlisted Len to transport them to the hotel where Hugh was staying. This was presentable enough by Polish standards. Despite everyone in the cast and crew who wasn't local being billeted there, they still had rooms for Quentin and Len, and Len was even galvanized by this happy outcome into dealing with the luggage without being asked. Katrina, calling the receptionist by name (no one wore name badges, Quentin noted, although they did have odd militaristic burgundy uniforms), eased their passage. She had talked a lot in the car, and Quentin was struggling to understand her, not just because of the accent, but also because Katrina seemed to assume a lot of prior knowledge on Quentin's part, particularly of Lallie.

'. . . course, we've been keeping our heads down with Mike,

but he's got a lot on his plate, hasn't he? I wouldn't like it, everyone "Mike Mike Mike" all the time, poor man doesn't get a minute, but Hugh's lovely – Uncle Hugh, Lallie calls him, which is funny because she's got a real Uncle Hugh back home – a friend of Graham's nan's actually, I mean, not a proper uncle as such, but she calls him Uncle Hugh, and he's nothing like this Hugh, but she says to me, "I've got two Uncle Hughs now, mam" . . .'

Katrina had unselfconsciously followed Quentin into her cramped room. It was really dusty, although since most of the people she'd seen since she arrived also appeared dusty, she was beginning to think this was a British thing. The receptionist had mentioned a shower, but Quentin, remembering her previous European trip, held no illusions about its prospects. This didn't prevent her using it as her excuse to hustle Katrina out without causing offence.

'Twelve hours on the plane . . . need to freshen up . . .'

Katrina obligingly made for the door. 'Just give me a knock when you're ready. Two two five. Then I'll run you along to Hugh.'

'That's OK, Katrina – I'm sure I can find him myself.'

Quentin caught the fall of the woman's face as she pulled the door after her. Thwarted ambition? Being the mother of a kid actor was all about that. Get close to the rep from the studio. Or was she hoping to buddy up with Quentin so that she could bitch some more about Mike? The garrison mentality of location shoots guaranteed relationships were as overcharged as they were overdiscussed. Or maybe, Quentin realized, the woman was just plain lonely. She was a mom. She spent her day hanging around a place where everyone else was incredibly busy and focused. That was it; the poor bitch probably just needed a friend. With that thought she felt guilty. And the guilt led to the other thoughts about what she might procure to bring about a more insulated state of mind. She took herself to the shower.

The unit uncertainly grouted to the tiling above the bath waited a couple of seconds before drooling lukewarm water from its rectangular head, tickling unsatisfactory pathways over parts of Quentin's skin. Even so, when she got out, she had to admit she felt better.

Without swabbing herself with the thin hotel towel, Quentin lay on the bed. She goose-pimpled and cooled, bobbing in and out of consciousness the way, as a kid, she used to tread along the shallow end of their pool with her head almost submerged, alternating between the heat and chatter above the water and the soundless, cool isolation of the world beneath. At some point she must have drifted under completely because suddenly she jolted back into the room. A man was staring at her. She yelled. Instinctive pervert-response.

'Good God – I'm so sorry.'

He erased himself with the closing door, and it wasn't until she met him down in the lobby, twenty minutes later, that Quentin was entirely convinced that he didn't belong to her dream.

'Well, it's one way to break the ice,' said Hugh.

Urbane. Quentin had never before met a man to whom this word truly applied. Although appropriately and convincingly apologetic about their encounter (Katrina had told him where to find her, he'd knocked and, getting no answer, tried the door), he was also utterly unembarrassed. Not even a token peek down her cleavage, either, although let's face it the sight of her from soup to nuts should have been recent enough.

'Maybe some sort of producer's prerogative? *Droit de seigneur*? Could try to convince you it was some quaint custom we have . . .'

Already, Quentin could tell that Hugh was the real deal. If she could have popped, snorted or smoked him, he could hardly have permeated her so instantly and so blissfully. *He's the man. He's in charge. He can handle it all.* He led her through the dingy hotel corridors like an astringent washcloth cutting through years of accumulated grime; she felt cleansed in his wake. Everything about him looked extraordinarily alert, even his skin. Although it was poreless and fresh, perfect, in fact, the perfection it emanated was the accomplishment of maturity rather than any residue of childishness. Still, it made him look wholesome, despite the urbanity, incorrupt. He was of that indeterminate middle age that turned women invisible but made men look as though they were wearing a good suit. Which, in fact, he was. She didn't want to fuck him, exactly. She sort of wanted to swim in him.

'Sorry about the hike – but the lift's due to be condemned,' he told her as they took a flight of stairs at a light run, weightless in his case. 'Except of course no one will bother to do it until there's actually a disaster of some kind.' He dipped back towards her, making some gesture. 'So glad.'

Probably gay, she realized with pang. Although it was harder to tell with English guys. Already she was worrying about how she'd feel when they parted. She'd come down, she knew. She wanted to live in Hughland. For ever. She was even in love with his watch, an assertive Rolex which suggested that time would be kept, really kept, accurately and reliably. *He's chosen that. That's the kind of man he is. Jesus, Quentin, get a grip.*

They were on their way to watch dailies, as per the schedule, because this was her job. One of the larger rooms – the hotel didn't run to a suite, as Hugh explained – had been cleared of its bed to make a viewing room. There was a projector on a chest of drawers and a decent-sized screen at the far end of the room, slightly askew on its tripod. The curtains were drawn. Another man, youngish, with a corpse pallor suggestive of the hours he spent in these shaded rooms, was threading film into the projector as they arrived. Hugh introduced him as Bri. He nodded, paying no attention to Quentin. She totally knew the type. Nothing personal, because a guy like him just didn't do personal.

'Do . . . .'

Having tweaked the screen straight, Hugh waved to one of the armchairs placed in front of it, economically adapting the end of his gesture into an indication for Bri that he should start up the film. They both sat. The dry-leaf skittering of the reel feeding through the sprockets began, calming to an automatic whirr as the countdown flashed up on the screen, the numbers huge in the middle of their target-shaped cipher. 4, 3, 2, 1. There was no sound, of course. Hugh jabbed a cigarette into his mouth and lit up, first proffering Quentin the packet, which she declined. His chair was at a slight angle to hers, so that the definite edge of his profile teased her line of vision to the left. He inhaled as though the smoke was essential to the continuation of breathing.

'Sorted out some of the earlier stuff for you to see . . .'

The screen flashed an apocalyptic white, then it began. A clapperboard, mutely snapping. This dipped from view, revealing muddled activity which dissipated into a suddenly empty frame. Now there was just an expanse of parched dun grass, surmounted by a flat grey stripe of sky. The shot held, second upon second, waiting in thick light like the view through a dirty window. A smudge appeared on the line of the horizon.

'*Lawrence of Arabia*,' remarked Quentin.

'I think we're calling it an *hommage*,' Hugh told her.

The smudge grew, and resolved itself into the figure of a child. The kid. Lallie. Our heroine. She came erratically closer, running, then walking. Her distress was immediately readable, as was the fact that she was a child unwilling to accommodate her distress.

'Titles here. Plenty of room.' Hugh gestured to the space to the right of the approaching figure.

'What about the fight with the mother?'

Hugh shot her an appreciative grin. *See, Hugh, I'm on the ball, Hugh.*

'Pre-title. Haven't got it yet, of course. Means we can just jump straight in.'

The little girl had almost reached the camera. Her hair snaked unkempt around her face, her clothes were slightly too small for her. Not, it was clear, a kid to whom anyone paid much care or attention. She palmed furious tears from her face, then swerved off to the left and disappeared behind the silhouette of Hugh's profile. A second, then the girl's face poked back into view, confronting the camera. Now she was grinning, although her cheeks were still streaked with tears. Lallie's lips clearly formed the shape of 'OK?', before she was nuked by the flash of light at the end of the shot.

'That was OK,' said Quentin. There it was; a whole new world, right there. She watched two more takes, one marred by a lurch of the camera as it pursued Lallie across the barren grass.

'It looks good,' she told Hugh. It was the truth. And she felt good. It was fine, she could do this job. The movie was going to be more than fine, maybe. Her name on the credits. She basked in the moment as Bri threaded the next reel of film and Hugh leaned to stub out his thoroughly smoked cigarette in a crowded ashtray.

'It's going to be great,' she told him.

Hugh arched into his seat and palmed back his lively brown hair. 'I do hope so.'

'But I guess every film's a masterpiece in the dailies,' she added, because it was something her dad used to tell her, along with 'There are no rights or wrongs in this business, baby, only opinions', and 'Never put an actress in silk after thirty'. She didn't believe it or anything. At this moment, noting the pristine band of shirt cuff which divided the flesh of Hugh's hand from the pressed linen of his jacket, at this exact moment, she felt as though she'd flushed that paternal brand of cynicism away at LA airport, along with the Ludes and Valium. Yay for her.

IT HAD HAPPENED, finally, and like stifling heat breaking into a storm, the catastrophe brought a kind of relief. Pauline walked back into the house one afternoon while it was still her mam's morning. She could see Joanne had just got up: although she was dressed as much as she ever got dressed in the day, her breath smelled, and her hair was matted with stale hairspray. This was a usual sight, as was the avidity with which Joanne sucked down the smoke from her fag. At least three mugs of tea and at least three fags to go with them – that was the minimum Joanne required to transform into something human. Shooting a look at her, Pauline deduced she was on her opener, and so to be avoided.

'You got summat to say to me?'

Pauline swerved for the living-room door.

'I said, you got summat to say to me, gyppo?'

'No.'

Pauline edged around Joanne's chair, palming a biscuit from the packet in front of Joanne. She dropped it as Joanne's hand shot out from behind and grabbed her by the hair.

'No?'

'No, Mam.'

Pauline bent her knees and twisted back to lessen the strain on her scalp as Joanne wound the hank of hair tighter round her fingers.

'Fucking let go!' Pauline protested.

Joanne laughed. It wasn't real laughter. 'Happy Birthday, Mam,' she whined, in loveless mimicry. Shit.

'I forgot . . .' Pauline panted. 'Please, Mam . . .'

But instead of letting go, Joanne pulled all the harder. In a tearing burst of pain, the hair came away in her hand. Pauline screamed and lashed out. This gave Joanne an excuse to punch, her fist still clenched round the sundered clump of piebald hair.

'Fucking stop it, will yer – please, Mam, I forgot – fucking – I forgot, Mam—'

Joanne only had the chance to land one blow with full contact before Pauline, agile with experience, squirmed under the table and rolled herself into a ball. Joanne had to be content with aiming a few ineffectual kicks before giving up. Seconds later, when Pauline finally dared open her eyes and uncurl a little, she saw Joanne's pale legs, crossed implacably in front of the chair as she lit her second fag. A few inches away lay the remains of the pink wafer biscuit, pulverized during their scuffle. And she knew, blankly and intolerably, that there would be no more blows, because Joanne had passed into the state where Pauline was dead to her.

She had forgotten her mam's birthday. It wasn't surprising. No one reliably remembered hers, and for the last two or three years Joanne had been away working at this time of year. But that was the way it went. Joanne would hold this resentment a long time if Pauline couldn't think of a way to redeem herself. Which she would, because she had to. Because nothing was worse than this.

Pauline hadn't been to school for a while now. She disliked the laxness of the pre-holiday weeks, the playing of bingo and the sop of watching of 'special films' because everyone was waiting for the term to end. She had learned to ignore the alien chatter of the other kids about caravans and the seaside and going on planes, because the summer holidays were just an annual hole in her time, filled with aimlessness, sunny if she was lucky. This year, though, the chatter was even more animated, because it was fixed on the school being used in that film and the possibility of everyone becoming film stars. This was the real reason Pauline was staying away. When the notice had gone up for everyone to put their names on for the film people to see, she had joined the queue like everyone else. Mrs Bream had smiled and written her name, but Pauline had seen the look aimed from the back of the hall by Mrs Maclaren, thrown like a ball that Mrs Bream had refused to catch. Pauline knew what it meant. *Gyppo. Pisspants. Pov.* And to punish herself for that stupid lapse into expectation, she had stayed away and stayed away, until she could be sure it would all be over and there would be no chance of her hoping something special might happen to her.

Twagging school, at least she'd made herself some money. Shaking down kids in the playground was only a minor source of Pauline's income. If Nan told her to piss off when she asked for money for the chip shop, or she'd decided to invest in a really desirable toy for herself, or once, exceptionally, for Cheryl (because she'd accidentally made her need to have stitches at the hospital when they were messing about on a wall with glass embedded in the top), Pauline went down to Wentworth Road.

It was an older girl, Dawn, who'd introduced her to it. Wentworth Road was the last rung in the ladder of streets surmounted by Adelaide Road. There had been two further roads, bombed during the war, fringed by a common that was now largely subsumed by a ring road built in the sixties. Wentworth Road itself had suffered an amputation in the bombing, and its abrupt truncation, skirted by the malnourished grassland of the bomb sites and the lethal boundary of roaring traffic, rendered it a real estate no-man's-land. At the top of the road a depressed-looking newsagent limped on from year to year and at its bottom, a dead end, a similarly lacklustre trade in street prostitution managed to survive. The real pros operated nearer the top of the ladder; it was here, where they could literally go no further or no lower, that punters picked up junkies and kids.

Pauline couldn't remember the face of the first man she'd

wanked off, because she hadn't looked. She had been frightened, not of being hurt, but of doing something wrong, the way she had been frightened when she walked into that launderette the first time. But Dawn had explained it all really well, although not that his spunk would go everywhere, like wee. After that surprise, she didn't have to think about it much any more. Sometimes they wanted to put their hands in her knickers and rub there, and once a man had asked her to put his willy in her mouth, but she had said no, and he hadn't insisted. It never took long, and she got pounds and 50p pieces. The men were usually, although not always, in cars, but she didn't get in with them because she had listened well to the warnings at school about getting into cars with strange men. They might drive off with you and do all sorts. So instead Pauline took the men into one of the backs, the alleys that punctuated the ladder, which were either deserted or occupied by people engaged in similar activities. A lot of dogs crapped in the backs, so you had to be careful where you trod.

She didn't go down Wentworth Road much as a rule, but the boredom arising from her truancy and the impossibility of staying in the house to be erased by Joanne had led her to make nearly five pounds that week. It didn't look like five pounds, because it was mostly coins, but Pauline had counted it assiduously and knew how much was there. Enough to buy Joanne something really special for her birthday. Enough to bring herself back to life.

When this idea came to her, Pauline was in the woods, vainly searching for blackberries, which were still pale green and inedible, phantoms of their future selves. Legs scratched from the brambles, she walked back into town, over Hexthorpe Flats, heading for the Arndale Centre. Her mam loved jewellery. She already wore a fair amount, real gold, as she always told Pauline during the good times, when she allowed Pauline to hang round her and take stock of it on her body. Small gold sleepers in her small white ears, whose inner whorls were sympathetically gilded with wax. A ring on her little finger made out of a real sovereign, and then on the next finger along a signet ring with her initials on it. On the other hand, a fat gold ring with three small stones embedded in the front: diamonds, her mam said. The ring was slightly too small and made the skin above it bulge uncomfortably, but Joanne never took it off, even to have a bath. Around her neck, two gold chains: one thin and slippery, one thicker and less alluring, the thick one with a pendant also engraved with her initials; on her left wrist, a charm bracelet. This was Pauline's favourite. It was the crowning part of her ritual to tell the charms devoutly, like the beads of a rosary: a pair of dice, an old-fashioned car, a heart with a red stone at its centre and, best of all, a domed birdcage with a tiny canary and a door that actually opened. She thought she might buy her mam a new charm for the bracelet. Even the idea warmed the chill inside her.

Preoccupied by her plans for redemption, it wasn't until a man shouted that Pauline realized she had walked into some unusual site of activity on the Flats, which, as their name suggested, usually had nothing, not even trees, to interrupt them. There were a lot of people milling around parked vans, and big lights on stands which made it look like a confusingly different and cooler time of day. Her first thought was that she had strayed on to a fairground being set up, even though it was the wrong time of year for fairs.

'Oy!'

A skinny bloke in an anorak grabbed her T-shirt at the shoulder. Pauline smelled his breath before she broke into a run. No point hanging around to be blamed for something. Skimpy breaks of trees fringed the Flats, like the receding hair on a bald man. They never thickened into something more substantial, since you could always see the pale land behind them, but they were the only form of cover in sight and she bolted for them instinctively. Once she realized that the anorak man wasn't going to follow her,

Pauline began to enjoy the sensation of skittering through the sparse trees, heading for town with her plan. And just as she was leaving the last straggling line of birches, she glimpsed another girl, not running, but labouring under the weight of a man who had her pinned against one of the narrow tree trunks. It took Pauline's legs a second to stop, and in that second she processed the various pieces of information her eyes had taken in in flight: the man wasn't hurting the girl, as she'd immediately thought, but submitting to the piston movement of her small hand on his cock. Both of their heads were bowed to the effort, joined in the endeavour, although the man's eyes were closed, and the girl's wide open. The girl was a smear of dark hair and an orange T-shirt, the man was a massy length of green-and-white-striped shirt and jeans. The two of them vanished as Pauline resumed her run, so fast now that her breath began to tear the edge of her lungs. Pauline understood what she had seen, or thought she did, and there was no reason to linger.

The Arndale, opened five years before, was busy with civilized consumption. Pauline took a minute to wash the worst of the woods from her hands and face in the fountain that was the shopping centre's focal point, its waters splashing against the legs of a monumental abstract Adam and Eve whose pinheads, streaked with verdigris, which Pauline assumed to be bird shit, reached almost to Boots on the second floor. There were coins flashing in the shallow green pool, silver as well as coppers, but Pauline ignored them and headed for the doors of H. Samuel. She had enough money, from the look of the window displays.

The lady who worked there was briskly unsuspicious. When Pauline told her what she was looking for, she laid out all the gold charms they had on the counter, taking them from velvet resting places under glass. Pauline recognized some of the charms Joanne already had, the heart and the birdcage. But there were others: a gold teddy bear whose legs swung when you flicked him, a teapot with a minute hinged lid, and a shining guitar. Pauline considered. She was drawn to the teddy bear, but concluded that her mam would prefer the guitar, given her love of music and her current dislike of all things related to Pauline. It cost four pounds eighty and the woman, without being asked, put the charm in a special box and wrapped it in H. Samuel paper tied with thin ribbon. Then she dropped the parcel into an H. Samuel bag, safe from Pauline's fingerprints.

'Fuck you been up to?'

Nan was shuffling around in the kitchen when Pauline got back, performing her version of tidying up, which meant sorting piles into larger piles, freeing up the decreasing space at ground level while creating skyscrapers of clutter.

'Is Mam in?'

'No. Mind that—' Nan reached across Pauline to stave off the collapse of a cairn of tins. Pauline left her and went up to Joanne's room. It was always Joanne's room, even when she was away, and as such had more of a decor than any other room in the house. It was papered, Joanne had done it herself, in flock wallpaper stamped with a huge quasi-paisley pattern in chocolate, purple and crimson. There was one magazine-sized blank patch on the wall, high up above the wardrobe, where the paper had run out and it hadn't been worth buying another roll. You might not notice it straight away, but once you did it was the first thing you looked at each time you entered.

The bed was made. This was unusual. The shiny mauve nylon cover had a see-through frill around it, as though it was trying to be a negligee. It had dulled from a mix-up in the wash. Devoutly, Pauline took her gift from its bag and placed the H. Samuel box on the pillow, superstitiously centring it not just on the pillow, but even within the middle stitched diamond of the bedspread covering the pillow's summit. The formality of the offering looked pleasingly special, although it now occurred to Pauline that she should have bought a card, a birthday card. That's what people did. She made another journey to the newsagent on Wentworth Road, and from their time-bleached selection chose the most expensive, adorned with a vintage car and a fishing rod, and returned to place it below the box.

Then she waited, settling herself cautiously beside the present and card. Only after she had slept, waking to synthetic heat radiating from the bedspread on to her sticky skin, did Pauline realize that it was all too late. Once again, Joanne had gone to Leeds, and she had been doomed to limbo.

THERE'S A ROW about the photographs of Ian's good lady. I work it out, eventually, although at first I think it's a row about me and my 'behaviour', as Mum calls it. I wake a few days after the upset over the trip to Butlin's and the filming to the familiar sound of Mum's anger jabbing against the more surprising rhythms of Ian's response. I haven't seen or heard him angry before, and he doesn't sound angry now, not compared to Mum, who's an expert. His tone (I can't hear words at this point) is completely unlike my dad's short bursts of defence. He sounds like an actor doing a big scene in *Coronation Street*.

'If you really feel like that—'

'Well, I bloody do!'

'– then I may as well walk out of this door, turn right into Cantley Lane and stand in front of the next bus—'

'Don't be so bloody stupid!'

'Well, that's how I feel. There'd be nothing left for me, Suzanne, nothing at all . . . life was empty for me, you know that . . .'

I go into the bathroom and run the tap while I have a wee. I don't want to hear any of it. I wash my face and brush my teeth at agonizing quarter speed, water running all the while, and by the time I venture down for breakfast, Mum's smoking silently into the garden while Ian crunches toast, sad-eyed. We all ignore each other while we go through the morning routine, Mum's leftover anger used up in the roughness with which she scrapes my hair into its bunches.

On the way to the bus stop she suddenly speaks.

'You know Ian's wife died of cancer.'

Cancer, I know, is as bad as swearing, its outcomes and diagnoses only ever mouthed in front of children. No wonder we aren't allowed to speak of Ian's good lady.

'It was very sad. She was only forty-nine. I used to do her hair. Big lady.'

That's all Mum seems to have to say, until we reach the end of our bus journey and are due to go our separate ways. She kisses me goodbye and flicks at my fringe in irritation.

'You, er, we've decided that you can stay, for the wotsit. Filming thing. I'll have a word with Christina's mum. They shouldn't be out of pocket, so . . . it's very good of Ian – generous – I hope you're grateful.'

I am. I say so, although my feeling is beyond words. This surge of ecstasy, the mystery of the argument between Ian and my mum, and the possible involvement of his good lady have somehow all come together into the change of heart I hadn't thought possible. Wonderful Ian: I know my gratitude should be laid at his door, because I can still feel all Mum's resistance to my devotion to Lallie, however carefully I protect her from its full force. And yet mysteriously she isn't cross with me, or him, but rather his wife. Even in my relief and pleasure, I feel bad about her. It's almost as though satisfying my dearest wish was what killed her.

I sit under this puzzling feeling all through our morning assembly, the last of the year, while Mr Scott gives out prizes and talks about holidays. When he mentions Lallie and the film, a lightning stab of glee shoots through me, followed, with a two-Mississippi delay, by a thunderclap of guilt. And then, an answer offers itself, in the form of Mr Scott's sermon of the day. This, like most of his sermons, takes a recent incident to illuminate its message.

Mr Scott's chest hair pokes through the buttons of his sports shirt, sparking gold in the sunlight to match the hair on his arms. The same light bounces from his aviator frames as he trenches back and forth at the front of the hall, and occasionally catches the face of his manly watch, itself once the subject of one of his lectures. I can't now remember which moral quality it revealed, but I know that it is waterproof to a depth of several hundred metres and is the same kind worn by airline pilots.

'Lallie Paluza,' he says, making it count. My heart beats faster. What is he going to say about her? Surely nothing bad? What if he condemns her in some way and I'm forced to disagree, even to dislike him? I love Mr Scott.

'A clever girl. A very clever girl, with lots of talents. Acting, singing, dancing . . . '

Actually, even I have to concede that Lallie's dancing isn't up to much. I'm up to Blue Riband in tap and modern and Grade Three in ballet and all round I'm better.

'Now it looks as though she's going to be a film star – like some of you.'

There's a murmur of half-laughter, to show our appreciation.

'But something you might not know about Miss Paluza—' Mr Scott reaches the end of his walk and pauses before taking the return journey. I doubt very much that he's going to tell me something I don't already know. He reaches for the vaulting horse near the door where he's stacked a pile of papers to do with the assembly and takes down a newspaper cutting. Nudging the nosepiece of his specs, he reads:

'Ten-year-old entertainer Lallie Paluza gave a lift to children at Great Ormond Street Hospital in London during a recent visit. Leukaemia sufferer Abigail Vaughan, eight, pictured, is shown enjoying one of Lallie's impressions during a party where the child star presented the hospital with a cheque for two hundred and fifty pounds raised for the hospital during her pantomime season.'

He turns the cutting to face us so that we can see the grainy picture of Lallie in close-up with a moon-faced little girl, both cocking their thumbs to the camera. This is old news: Lallie stopped doing panto – it was *Aladdin* this year – months ago, obviously. But I haven't seen the article before – it must have come from another paper, not the *Mirror*, which is what we get, or used to get before we went to Ian's. And they've got her age wrong.

'Leukaemia is a kind of cancer of the blood, it's very serious,' Mr Scott tells us. 'Cancer' reaches out of the sentence and grabs me. 'But there's no doubt that getting a visit from someone famous must have given this young lady a lift, however poorly she was feeling, the way your granny or grandad or your auntie Betty get a lift when you pay them a visit. And you might be saying, "Ooh, I don't want to go to Auntie Betty's, her house smells funny and she always gives me sloppy kisses and she's never got any chocolate biscuits," but the point is, Auntie Betty loves seeing you – I don't know why, looking at the lot of you, but she does, and that's what's important . . . '

I drift away. Auntie Betty makes regular appearances in Mr Scott's assemblies, and enjoyable as I find her, today I'm more excited by the message. Lallie does good things. Lallie isn't selfish. Perhaps there's someone I could visit in order to be like her and set things right with Ian's good lady? My nana, Mum's mum, lives in St Helens, and Grandma and Grandad, my dad's parents, always spend this part of the summer at their caravan in Filey. It's encouraging then, when Mr Scott says that doing good things doesn't have to mean visiting our relatives. It could mean helping our mum do the washing-up or our dad to wash the car or being nice to our little brother or sister. It could mean being friendly to someone we don't particularly like, or noticing when someone in the street needs help, perhaps a little old lady needing help to cross a road, although that only seems to happen in the *Beano* . . .

After school I see her. Pauline Bright. I'm on my way to get an ice lolly from the newsagent nearest the school. When I catch sight of her, scuffing up grass at the edge of the Town Fields, I realize she hasn't been at school for ages. I wonder if her absence has something to do with our trip to the launderette, which didn't end well. It seems extremely clear what I have to do, given that I have twenty pence and lollies are ten. Although when I approach, proffering her the second Strawberry Mivvi, she does nothing to reach for it, just glares at me.

'It's for you,' I say. 'You eat it.'

As soon as I say that, I know it's a mistake. Probably even Pauline has eaten an ice lolly before.

'I don't want it,' she says, and walks off. I have to go after her. What am I going to do with two ice lollies? One will melt while I eat the first. I point this out. She tells me to eff-word off. Only then does it occur to me that she's actually annoyed with me.

'Are you being mardy about the launderette?' I ask, panting after her. I've started my lolly and am having to lick it to stop it dripping down towards my elbow. ''Cos that was your fault. You said you were going to tell me about the other skeleton lady film.'

'Shut up, Fatty.'

'It's true!'

I wasn't going to run after her, but it seems unbearable that she might win. 'Fatty' is wounding as well. No one has ever called me Fatty before, although that doesn't mean it might not be true.

'Do you want to come to my house?' I shout after her. She stops, amazed.

'Yer what?'

I can scarcely believe the invitation myself. I'm desperate. At least I know that no one is home. I usually have tap on a Tuesday, but we've broken up after our exams. I can easily get rid of her before Mum gets back to cook tea, I tell myself, as we get on the bus (I have to fork out the extra two pence for Pauline). I watch the melted syrup from the lolly bleed a path through the grime on her hand. Maybe I could offer her a bath? Various scenes from Enid Blyton books involving gypsies come to mind. Tassie, in the *Castle of Adventure*. They gave her clothes, as well as a bath, and she turned out to be quite pretty, although they couldn't get her to wear shoes; she'd preferred to wear them hung round her neck by the laces. Pauline's shoes are surprisingly new and shiny, with stacked heels and gaps at the back where they're too big for her. They delay her walk strangely as the extra bits catch up with her feet. This slows us down on the journey from the bus stop, and makes me nervous, as though Ian and Mum are going to get home and see us by the time we reach the house.

'Hurry up!'

Pauline gapes.

'It's a dormer bungalow,' I explain, pulling the chain holding the key from under my school dress.

Inside, it's just as we left it that morning: mugs and plates in the sink, Mum's lipstick-ringed cigarette butt splayed into a saucer on the worktop nearest the French window, Ian's minty smell thick on the furniture. Now what? Now that I've brought Pauline here, what am I actually expecting us to do? I take her up to my room, largely bare of my toys, which were left at my real home. We hang about there, Pauline flicking her two-tone hair out of her eyes. She seems nervous, although unusually open to whatever I suggest. I don't quite dare the bath.

'You can see the rest of the house if you like.'

I give her the tour, using pride borrowed from Mum to point out the fixtures and fittings. The bathroom has a dimmer switch, which I demonstrate.

'Is that your mum and dad?'

Pauline dawdles by a framed photograph in the hall by the bathroom, showing Ian's good lady. She's bent in, uniquely, to Ian, who is more commonly the invisible person behind the camera. They are at some kind of do, a posh one, Ian's wife in a sparkly evening dress and Ian with a dickie bow.

'No. He's not my dad. That's his wife. She's not alive any more.'

Pauline ponders the photo.

'I haven't got a dad.'

She says this casually, as though staking common ground. *Either*, is what she means.

'I've got a dad,' I object. 'We're sort of here on holiday . . . '
And as I hear myself say it, its last trace of reality evaporates into
the nonsense it is. Will I actually ever see Dad again? As I flail,
Pauline squints at Ian's wife. Iris.

'Was she killed?'

I must look blank.

'In an accident or owt?' Pauline grins. 'Or did he kill her?'

She staggers a few zombie steps towards me, evoking our playground game. Now here is a thing. Our best thing.

'He says she got poorly, you know. With cancer. But . . . '

I pull a face, stagger a few steps myself.

'What if he buried her under't house?'

We both hurtle downstairs giggling, spooking each other,
chasing, becoming Iris the skellington lady and Ian the murderer
finally hounded into his own grave. Every photo around the
house feeds the game, the noise and excitement growing to fill
the awful space I've opened up around Dad.

'Oh my God!'

I seize a picture from the living-room dresser, in which Iris sits
astride a sad Spanish holiday donkey, holding a knife in a tooled
leather sheath in the slack two-handed pose used by anglers for
their catch. The very same knife, as I point out to Pauline, hangs
on the wall above the photo. Tassels of blood-red cord dangle
from its hilt, the raised patterning of the scabbard picked out in
green and brighter red.

'Oh my God, maybe that's what he did it with and he's like kept it!'

Pauline is already balanced on the arm of a dining chair, flail-
ing for a tassel. To both of our surprise, as she tugs, the knife
slithers from its sheath, making her lurch off balance. Falling, she
catches her chin on the dresser's edge, landing in the gap between
that and the chair, still holding the knife above her. I would have
howled, but Pauline just swears and stands up. I think of her in
scraps, the way she piles into bigger kids without caring.

The blade is long and slightly curved, melodramatically bright. Pauline tests the tip against her finger.

'Don't!' I warn.

To Pauline's disgust and my relief, it leaves only an indentation. She points it at me, being Murderer Ian, threatening.

'Don't!'

The face she pulls is hideous, cartoonishly enraged and zombified. I scream. She chases me. Nothing bad happens. Even when she catches me and I trip and she kneels on my shoulders and hisses, 'You're dead!' and I feel the blunt blade on my chest, I scream out of the hysterical assurance that no real harm can come to me, along with the terror that it might.

'You're nesh, you!' she crows, sitting back, running the length of the knife uselessly against her palm. I wriggle out from under her.

'You shouldn't play with knives. It's dangerous.'

I'm thinking of Ian's good lady, running around the room with her head chopped off, like a chicken. And then, horribly, I hear the complicated give of the front door latch. Ian or Mum, I didn't know which would be worse. Immediately careless of safety, I snatch the knife off Pauline.

'I'll get done!'

She's better at danger than me. As I push the knife beneath the skirt at the bottom of the settee, she's already making for the French doors out into the garden. It isn't until she's climbing over the fence, showing her knickers (which seemed to be men's Y-fronts), that I realize there's been no further noise since the latch had gone. Cautiously, I round the corner to the hall. No one is there. What if it was a burglar, who has gone upstairs? I creep back into the living room and retrieve the murder weapon. Then I sit, holding the knife pointed at the stairs for a lifelong minute or two. Nothing. Gradually, my pulse calms. There's nobody in the house except me. Not Ian, not Mum, not a burglar, and not Pauline.

About an hour later, as Mum serves savoury pancakes, me

facing Ian, and above him the knife on the wall (I replaced it earlier, teetering on the dining-room chair), it strikes me how lucky it was that Pauline had known immediately she needed to get out of the house, that me getting done would have been caused more by her presence than us being discovered mucking about with knives.

After tea, as I uncomplainingly dry the pots for Mum, she remarks on how quiet I am and begins to ask questions about school.

'Someone tried to get into the house,' I blurt.

She stops scrubbing the basket of the chip frier.

'What do you mean?'

'I heard the door go, I thought it was you back or Ian. It was someone trying to get in.'

'Don't be daft.' But she's worried, I can tell. She moves off, hands dripping, to talk to Ian, who is watching the news round the corner of the open-plan.

'She says someone was trying to get into the house when she was back from school.'

After a slight delay, Ian appears with Mum.

'What's this about someone trying to get in?'

'I heard the door go.' This is, after all, the truth. I absolutely did. I must have done.

'You mean you thought you heard someone using a key to get in?'

This hasn't occurred to me, that the phantom would have had to have a key. I don't like the way things are going. Why have I started this?

'I don't know.'

Ian hitches his trousers, angrily excited by the possibility, or by the possibility that I'm lying; I can't tell which.

'Were they rattling the door?'

'A little bit,' I concede. Now I think about it, there could have been rattling.

Ian marches off, Mum following, to have a look at the door, to see if there are signs of forcing the lock. What if there are? The prospect makes me queasy. They move outside, murmuring. The image of Ian's headless wife comes to me again, her large body in one of the flowered dresses she wears in the photos lurching around the living room behind me, blood spurting from the neck. She gathers behind me, ready to pounce. I wheel from the sink and race into the garden, where Ian is crouched by a flowerbed.

'See?'

Satisfied, he prods at the earth next to some trampled flowers. Mum has her arms folded. She isn't eager to believe my story.

'And here.' He's triumphant this time. Mum leans in to look. There is the clear indent of Pauline's shoe in the soil near the fence.

'Must have gone over the fence.'

'What are you going to do?'

'I'll have a word with next door. Might be worth letting the police know.'

Unexpectedly, Mum takes my hand and squeezes it, pulls me close for a sideways hug. She's sorry for not believing me, I can tell, as well as annoyed in that way she has whenever she's worried about me.

'You can come to the salon after school and we'll travel back together. I'm not having you on your own in the house. It's only another week until you break up. Nothing to worry about, anyway.'

Anyway. After I've gone to bed I can hear them talking, still galvanized by the event I've provided for them. And the next morning, I notice that many of the photos of Ian's good lady have been removed, but whether by Ian or by Mum, or why, I have no idea and don't dare to ask. As with the Lallie audition and the cancellation of the holiday, I feel obscurely and guiltily involved. It isn't something I want to pursue. And I definitely don't want it to pursue me.

QUENTIN DIDN'T REALLY like kids. Like all the stuff in the school, they gave her the Fear. All that trust and shining hope and shit. They were like puppies locking on to you with the big soft eyes and eager little tails at the very moment you tied the sack over their heads and slung them in the river. The thought of having a child of her own to fuck up made her want to down anything mood-altering she could get her hands on, even those Vicks inhalers they were into in high school, snorting the menthol stuff on the tiny sponge you could prise out from the plastic case. There was a thought . . . could you get those in the UK?

She hadn't been near a store. She was in the location–hotel–location bubble. Which was fine, surprisingly, but she'd been insulated by having Hugh around, which was something to get her out of bed in the morning even if she hadn't been stark awake by three from jet lag. But today, he was back in London. No one would expect the producer to be around the whole time, and God knows he had things to do, but it didn't mean she wasn't going to miss him, as she'd told him lightly as they'd said goodnight a few hours before. He'd kissed her forehead. Who ever did that? He was like an uncle in a forties movie, and so, definitely queer. Didn't stop her craving him though. Already nearly eight hours since her last hit and who knew when she'd score again? Actually, he'd said he'd be back the following night, when they were doing some of the search scenes. She could almost definitely make it till then.

Quentin heaved herself to the bathroom. She'd started taking baths, since she had been told that there wasn't anything wrong with the shower. That is, it wasn't malfunctioning, it was just existentially inadequate. She was supposed to be meeting Lallie and her mother for breakfast. This had been Katrina's suggestion, although something of that nature had definitely been on Quentin's to-do list, since Clancy back in the office wanted her to put out feelers about the *Little Princess* movie. There was only the hotel to eat at, or the catering bus, so they were plumping for the hotel. Quentin wasn't sure if she was relieved or irked that Katrina would be chaperoning. Truth was she'd been avoiding the kid as much as possible. It was impossible to avoid the mom; she'd made herself indispensable in fetching cups of coffee, for one thing, as though she was Quentin's own personal runner. And Quentin had had to borrow a tampon from her, which always created a bond. Particularly as the woman had then donated the whole goddamn box. But the kid, well.

The hotel dining room was usually full of crew and actors, all grey from lack of sleep and tanking down large plates of fried food. Like that would help (well, maybe it did; they all seemed to live on the stuff. Or maybe that was the reason they were grey?). But that day everyone was already out on set, shooting some of the police scenes, by the time Quentin came down at nine. Only one of the older actresses was left tucked away in a corner, smoking and reading the newspaper. And there were Katrina and Lallie, right on the middle table, Katrina wearing enough make-up for a drag act and Lallie unusually pale and silent. Her greeting was polite enough, but Quentin had seen her bouncing around the set and knew she always had energy to burn.

'Bit tired,' said Katrina, rolling her eyes.

It was as if she had taken a key and wound Lallie up. She produced an impression. Garbo. 'I vant to be alone.' Beneath it, Quentin could see there had been words. Maybe Lallie hadn't wanted to come. After all, it was work for her too, shaking that little money-maker. Poor kid.

'Shall we order breakfast?'

Lallie had a poached egg, Katrina stipulating on her behalf

that it should be kept apart from its accompanying toast. Which should be unbuttered. Quentin approved of the juvenile finickiness. From what she'd seen, this was a country generally in need of a little more active discernment. She herself had been negotiating for yogurt for a couple of days, and that morning it cashed out in the shape of a narrow pot, gingerly proffered on a saucer, with a vaguely alarming logo: 'Ski'. What the hell did skiing have to do with yogurt? She delved, cautiously, as Katrina smoked over her fried stuff and Lallie methodically opened the three foil pats of butter that had come with her order.

'So you do like butter,' Quentin observed.

'Yeah, but I don't like—'

'She doesn't like melted butter,' interrupted Katrina. 'She likes butter on toast when it's gone cold. Don't know where she gets it from!'

Katrina, Quentin had noticed, was always eager to promote her daughter as some sort of freak, whose eccentricity was unique but whose talents were firmly connected to her. She watched Lallie mush the rectangle of cold butter on to the toast.

'It's nicer,' she said, firmly.

'So.' Quentin gathered herself, smiled. Time to shake her own money-maker. She wondered what Hugh was up to. Breakfast at Claridge's perhaps, or rough sex with some boy he'd picked up; did he give or take? It was hard to work out in one so confidently dominant and yet alertly receptive. Well balanced, that's what she loved. Complete even. Maybe that was it. Maybe he didn't need anyone. Maybe he did it with himself in the mirror, or only with boys who looked like him, like a certain movie star her dad had told her about. While looking at himself in the mirror. And where was the harm, as she'd thought at the time? The movie star was so beautiful, why wouldn't he want to drown in his very own swimming-pool-blue eyes? Of course with Hugh, it wasn't narcissism exactly. There just didn't seem that much of a gap between him and the world, a gap that cashed out as any kind of need. *Ah, that need, that fucking need, Quentin.* To work.

'Have you ever read *A Little Princess*?' she addressed Lallie, smiling her smile.

'*A Little Princess*, *A Little Princess*, ooh, I'm not sure we've read that one, have we, luvvie?'

Lallie chewed her toast.

'No.'

'She's not much of a reader,' confided Katrina. 'Too much to do.'

'Well, I'll make sure you get a copy.'

And then she pitched it, aware that as long as there was a ticket to Hollywood on the table, she could have said it was about a kid giving blow jobs for peanut-butter sandwiches and the mommy would sign her daughter up. It was tempting, but Quentin stuck to the truth. Weirdly, *A Little Princess* was a book she remembered well from her own childhood. Particularly the ending, when the dad came back. Or was that the one about the trains? It didn't matter: in a movie the dad would end up coming back for the girl, since that was obviously what everyone would be rooting for.

If she did say so herself, Quentin did a good job. She knew, because Lallie switched her attention from cutting exact triangles from the white of her egg to listening to her. The story began to live in her face. She loved the ending too, Quentin's version. Katrina was also excited, if only for her own reasons. They were all still talking about it and asking questions when Lallie's tutor came to find her. The tutor was a hesitant woman in her forties, too fat for her fussy purple blouse. Quentin knew as soon as she saw her she had a drink problem. Holding it together, maybe not yet starting until after lunch, but in another ten years she'd be a wreck. No wonder. *Nice career, hon.*

'Off we go! Fractions today.'

Lallie took her time drinking a glass of milk, enforcing her status as the tutor hovered, unconfident of taking a seat. Quentin didn't suggest she did, and it clearly didn't occur to Katrina, who operated only out of commitment to the cause of Lallie. Finally, Lallie got up.

'I'll get you a copy of the book,' Quentin told her.

'Ooh, we'd love that, wouldn't we, hen?' said Katrina. 'I'll have to read it and all.' At last, she included the tutor. 'She's talking about our Lallie being in a film, in America. *The Little Princess*. You know, from a book.'

The tutor smiled indefinitely, revealing mottled teeth. 'Lovely.' She scooped Lallie along. 'Isn't it set in England, though?'

'Well, they'll set it where they like, won't they? Doesn't have to be in England.'

For a moment, Quentin was apprehensive that Lallie and the tutor would go and leave her to Katrina's mercies, but after a moment to stub her cigarette with all the vehemence of grinding it into the tutor's eye, Katrina headed off with them. Maybe she sat in on the lessons? As soon as they'd gone, although she had been desperate for them to go – hey, she could do Garbo herself – Quentin felt the drop, another of those time spools. Maybe another cup of coffee. The coffee here was weird, with a gross kind of skin that clung to your lip, like algae bloom on a stagnant pond. When she glanced around, she was surprised to see the room was empty except for the older woman in the corner, and that all the other tables had been cleared.

'I think there's someone in the kitchen, would you like me to knock?'

The actress waved her baton of folded newspaper at the door behind her shoulder. Quentin could see she was nearly done on the crossword.

'Oh, that's OK—'

But the actress – she should know her name, probably – was already leaning over and calling through an opened gap: 'Excuse me, service?'

Over Quentin's 'No, really, it's not a problem', the woman said she fancied another cup of tea herself. Then, tilting the cup, observed that perhaps it had been coffee? She was no Hugh, but the thespian self-confidence was better than nothing. When the waiter came, smelling of cigarettes, Quentin ordered the drinks and invited the actress to join her.

'Vera Wyngate.'

Quentin introduced herself. She recognized Vera now from what she had learned to call the rushes. She looked really different with her own hair. Seeing her as herself, Quentin thought she might be familiar from another movie, but it would be kind of rude to ask. If you have to ask, it doesn't count. Although she had that instant actress intimacy which made her seem almost American, and so potentially impossible to offend. It was nice to be with her, drinking the weird coffee. Vera seemed about as lonely as she was.

'Back home this time next week, touch wood,' she told Quentin.

This was London, apparently. Not married 'any more, thank God', no kids. Although she knew Quentin was the producer, Vera was the first person she'd met on the movie, including Lallie, who wasn't trying any sort of angle on her. Even Hugh. *Hugh Hugh Hugh.*

'Have you worked with anyone before? The director? Hugh?'

See, it felt nice just to say that, to be in a world where other people potentially knew him. This was Vera's first time working with asshole Mike apparently, 'But I've known darling Hugh since he was a baby, practically. His father was a producer too, you know. Sidney Calder. Terrible man.'

The way Vera said this, Quentin could see she'd fucked Hugh's dad. He'd fucked her. Danny-wise, probably. *Live and learn, or just keep on living.*

'With the ladies?' she empathized.

'Oh, awful, darling. Not that he had much to offer, apart from a part – I mean in a film, because that part –' Vera gestured and grimaced – 'not much to write home about, let me tell you. Hugh definitely gets his looks from his mother, I don't know about anything else, I hasten to add – Hilary Longton, do you know her? She was a lovely actress. Of course Sidney made her give it all up when they got married and had the boys. Hugh adored her, I think. Well, everyone did. Such a shame. She used to turn a blind eye, although Sidney would have just carried on in front of her if she hadn't, I think. Of course the boys were at boarding school.'

Poor little Hugh. It was like they were related. Movie brats. She hadn't known that. Although she imagined it was all a little different here, kind of simultaneously downscale and yet classier than her Hollywood biog.

'But Hughie's an absolute sweetie.'

The way Vera spoke, Quentin could see she didn't get it. Him. No matter. Vera shepherded her cigarette ash into one corner of the plastic ashtray, confidentially rearranged her shoulders.

'But now – what do you think about the girl?'

For a sick heartbeat Quentin thought she was talking about a girl in connection with Hugh, a fiancée, as he'd probably call her, some pissy bitch with a creamy complexion and crystal vowels. But of course, she realized, once she'd interpreted Vera's offstage flick of the eyes, she meant Lallie.

'She's quite a package.'

Vera nodded. 'Isn't she just.'

Okay, so there was real dislike there. What was that about? Jealousy?

'Poor little thing,' said Vera, unsympathetically. 'Of course it all comes from the mother.'

'That's traditional, I guess.'

'God, yes. Don't put your daughter on the stage . . . of course there's a kind of genius there.'

Quentin never responded well to the G-word. She'd grown up in a town of geniuses, and the über-geniuses were always distinguished by how many people around them they could destroy, the über-über-geniuses by how spectacularly they could destroy themselves into the bargain. Lallie would have to rack herself up a few habits and burn through a few waster husbands before you could start approaching that word. And she didn't even need a bra yet.

'And she loves the limelight, no doubt about it. Mind you, don't we all? Not you, darling. I'm sure the backroom stuff is much more well adjusted.'

Yeah, right. Quentin thought of all the kids she went to high school with, the fuck-ups with geniuses for parents. Herself probably included. True, the spawn of actors were more straightforwardly damaged: addictions, suicidal tendencies, nymphomania. The producers' and writers' and directors' and designers' kids took a more smorgasbord approach to neurosis, in her experience. There was a kind of hopeless simplicity, in the actors' kids, in knowing you'd never be as beautiful or successful as your mom or dad, whereas such as she, well, they all had to work that stuff out, be their own personal Hamlet . . . anyway, that wasn't Lallie's potential problem. And Lallie's potential problems weren't her problem either. She was here to pretend to be a producer and functioning human and recruit Lallie for the other movie, maybe. She was kind of getting that Vera wasn't unduly preoccupied with Lallie's welfare herself.

'Are there problems?' she asked. 'On set . . .'

'Not that I can see.' Vera's regret was obvious. 'Works like clockwork, poor mite. Absolute trouper, Mike's probably told you.'

Quentin was yet to have much of a conversation with Mike. He was too twitchy, and come to think of it, Hugh had intervened between them without her really noticing. Silent diplomacy.

She liked that. But it wouldn't have mattered if Mike had sat her down and told her that Lallie threw tantrums and turned up four hours late every day and demanded he personally wipe her ass. She could see from the rushes – *everyone always loves the dailies: thanks, Dad* – that Lallie was something else. It didn't matter, the Mom and the W.C. Fields impressions and the tacky TV show (which she hadn't seen, but from what the agent and the Mom had said about it she could tell it was tack all the way). Because what Lallie had, money couldn't buy, although God knows it was going to give it the old college try. And she, Quentin Genevieve Montpellier, was heading up the line. Just step into this sack, kid, there's a heap of dollar bills at the bottom, and excuse me while I find something to tie it up with.

It was really only because of Gemma that Pauline went back to school before it broke up. Admitting this, especially to herself, would have infuriated her. As far as she was concerned, she went back because there was nothing better to do now Joanne was out of the house. At least at school she existed, if only to get done and spend hours standing outside Mr Scott's office waiting to get done by him. And it was just as bad as she'd feared about the film and the auditions; it was all anyone talked about, even the teachers. Everyone was excited because the film people had been in at the weekend already and left stuff that showed the way they'd decorated the school to look different, and they all surrounded Mr Fletcher the caretaker in the playground at playtime to ask him everything about it, Gemma included.

Because of her talking to Mr Fletcher, Pauline didn't realize until dinnertime that Gemma was avoiding her. In the queue, she talked to one of her snot-bag friends as though Pauline's voice didn't make noise. It was only when she pushed her on the shoulder that Gemma did this crap pretending to notice her face. They weren't allowed to be on the same table at dinner itself, but Pauline could see Gemma from where she was sitting, serving up mince from the tin. Pauline finished her own meat and veg and square of flan ages before Gemma, then bided her time mouthing her tepid glass of water, metallic from the jug, with grey bits of mince sunk at the bottom. The moment Gemma pushed back her chair, Pauline was making for the door to meet her.

'Do you want to play skellingtons or owt?'

Gemma said she didn't, that she was going to play two-ball with Christina, who was already installed by the Juniors' wall. So

Pauline followed her, watching, which was tolerated, although no one invited her to have a go. And when the bell shrilled for afternoon lessons, she got in the line behind Gemma and pushed the box into her hand.

'What are you doing?'

'It's a present for yer.'

Gemma opened the box containing Joanne's charm.

'It's a guitar. You put it on a bracelet, like. It's gold. I got it for me mam's birthday.'

Gemma dangled it. 'Gold? Really?'

'Cross me heart.' She could see that Gemma liked it.

'Why hasn't your mum got it if it's her present?'

'She already had one the same so she said it was all right if I wanted to give it to someone else.'

Gemma put the guitar back in the box, careful to centre it in its little red satin bed before she slid it in the pocket of her dress. Pauline felt so happy she sat in her class until four o'clock without bothering any of her neighbours, just thinking about Gemma's house and the life she lived there. She got done for not listening to the teacher, but not the way she got done for pinching or kicking or taking pencils. Ever since she had been to Gemma's house, she had run this daydream to herself, like a groove in a record. When Gemma had gone to the toilet, before they had played the murder game, Pauline had taken the opportunity to have a really good look around her bedroom. It was like the telly. Everything matched. She had opened a drawer and there were Gemma's knickers and vests and socks laid out, clean and separate from each other. She didn't recognize the socks at first, because they were balled in pairs. When she got home that night after she'd scarpered over the fence, she found as many socks as possible – she and Cheryl did what they could from a common pool – and tried to arrange them in these satisfying spheres. It wasn't the same. Pauline realized that she needed Gemma's kind of white socks, and she didn't own any white socks; the best pair she had was some pale green pop socks left by Joanne. She'd been wearing those ever since Joanne had gone, although one of them was now full of runs.

'I'm not allowed pop socks until I start secondary,' said Gemma critically, focusing on the ladder. But Pauline was listening. She nicked a blue pair from a shoe shop in town which kept a rack of them by the door and presented the packet to Gemma on her way into school the next day. The day after that, it was a Kit Kat, and on Thursday, a purse that had made its way to the house, brand new and shiny red, with a big-toothed zip all the way round. When Gemma undid the zip, curious to examine the inside, it disclosed a row of long metal loops, one of them holding a key. This disappointed them both.

'It belonged to my mam,' said Pauline. 'She said you could have it 'cos she's got a new one but she must have forgotten to take out the key, like.'

Gemma seemed satisfied by this.

'Do you want the key back?'

'Yeah.'

Pauline took it, although she knew it didn't open any door round at hers. Her lie made her half believe the key really did belong to Joanne, so it was nice to have. Gemma didn't play with her for long, though, at playtime, and at dinnertime play she couldn't find her at all. Now they were in different classes there wasn't any queuing to do together either, except at dinner. She got kept in after the last bell for swearing, and as Mrs Maclaren started her weary telling off, Pauline could hear the noise of everyone else spreading through the playground and disappearing through the gates.

'I've got to go, Miss.'

'You're not going anywhere, Pauline, until you've realized what and what isn't acceptable behaviour in my class.'

'I know, Miss, I'm sorry, Miss, but I've got to go and look after me little brother, Miss.'

'Well, he'll have to wait, won't he?'

Pauline was sure she could hear Gemma laughing in the mix of voices below the window. Mrs Maclaren had quickly finished telling her off and was tidying up the classroom, picking up dropped pencils, repositioning chairs casually upended on desks that might topple on to Mr Fletcher when he came to clean the floor. As she turned with a duster and began swiping her maths lesson into the chalky fog on the board, Pauline made a run for it. She was so quick down the stairs she didn't know if Mrs Maclaren was coming after her, but once she was out of the gate she allowed herself a glance round and sure enough she was, gasping fury and shouting for other people to stop her, as though she'd stolen something.

'Come on!'

Pauline grabbed Gemma's school dress and pulled her past the gate. Gemma ran, docile. She wasn't as fast as Pauline, and tried to ask what was happening. Pauline tugged her for a good way across the playing field, until she could see that Mrs Maclaren wasn't going to continue the chase. The teacher was waving her arms a few feet beyond the gate, the stupid bitch.

'Can I come to your house?' she asked Gemma.

'You what?'

'I can't go home 'cos me mam's poorly and she says I'm not allowed to stay hanging round town.'

Gemma cast a look back at stringy Mrs Maclaren, who was retreating into the school.

'Why were you running? What did you do?'

'She started chasing me – I didn't do owt. I reckon she's turned, you know, like what your dad's girlfriend did at your house.'

Pauline rolled her eyeballs and lurched, knock-kneed and zombified. Gemma almost giggled, swerved away so she couldn't get her.

'So can I come then?'

'I'm not allowed,' said Gemma. 'I've got to meet me mum at her salon.'

'I'll come with you then.'

Gemma looked horrified. 'You can't. I'll get done.'

'I meant I'll come into town with you, spaz.'

She could see Gemma couldn't think of an excuse. It was a free country, anyway.

'He's not me dad,' Gemma said, as they headed for the subway where the perv lurked. 'When you said my dad's girlfriend. He isn't my dad.'

They didn't say much else to each other, but Pauline was content with the two of them together, side by side, as long as it lasted. She didn't know what Gemma had meant by a salon, so it was a surprise when they stopped outside a hairdresser's and Gemma said it was her mum's work. A customer was coming out as they stood by the front, which was brown glass with cartoony pictures stuck against the window of women with hairdos. Before the door shut again, Pauline inhaled an acrid tang. The customer looked nothing like the vast-eyed women in the pictures, although her hair did, exactly.

'You'd better go, I'll get done.'

Gemma hustled her out of sight of the window, towards the men's clothes shop next door.

'I'll get done!'

She left her there and went inside the salon, releasing another waft of cooked hair. Pauline edged round and peeped, to see Gemma marching through the reception and past the waiting women there, towards the back, which was divided from the front by a wrought-iron screen that allowed incoherent glimpses of basins and driers and bits of Gemma with bits of her mum, reflected in bits of mirror. Pauline sank down and sat on the pavement, her back against the window of the men's outfitters.

Dreamily, she scratched at her knickers, where she itched. She decided to wait, so she could talk to Gemma when she got out. It was another warm day.

Pauline absorbed herself for a while smearing pictures into the glass of the men's shop window. The lower section where she was sitting was painted black from the inside. As she finessed a knob and balls, the owner hammered on the glass and told her to clear off. So, for a while, she made slow circuits of the precinct. A pub, a haberdasher's, some kind of office business you couldn't see into, a bakery. She realized she was hungry. Staring at the uniform rows of long doughnuts piped with cream and a single scab of garish jam, she saw herself reflected. Her own hair was monstrous. Pauline had thought at home of taking the scissors to it, but it belonged to Joanne, the transformation of the peroxide, and as long as it stayed her body possessed something of her mother, even if her true ugliness advanced every day with the dark regrowth. One of these days, she saw, catching herself in the bakery window, her real hair would be longer than the white bits. By that time Joanne might be back.

She nicked a doughnut. It was a simple matter of waiting until the woman at the counter was talking to a customer, then leaning in from the open door and plucking one from the display. Pauline didn't run off, because experience taught her that the running was often what alerted them that you'd nicked something. Licking a channel through the cream, it occurred to her that she could offer the doughnut to Gemma, who loved sweet stuff. Then she remembered that she'd already given her the purse thing that day, and allowed herself to eat it, taking her time.

Lolled against a wall, she was still scavenging sugar from her chin and fingers when Gemma finally left the salon with her mum. It took a second for Pauline to recognize the mum because her hair was a different colour from when she'd last seen her at school. Today it was a dense brown. She had Gemma by the hand and was giving her a talking to of some kind, tugging Gemma back towards her now and again as though she was trying to escape, which she wasn't. Gemma's face held the rebuke. She'd got a comic in the hand her mum wasn't hanging on to.

'What are you looking at?'

Pauline was amazed. Gemma's mum was staring straight at her, savage.

'I've seen you hanging about – what do you want, eh?'

Ordinarily, Pauline would have told her to fuck off. As it was, she and Gemma stared at each other, locked in bewilderment.

'I – I go to school with her.'

'She does, Mum.'

Gemma dropped her comic and had to pick it up. Her mum had a look entirely familiar to Pauline from Joanne – it meant free-roaming rage that had just found an outlet.

'What's your name, eh?'

'Pauline.'

'Pauline what?'

'Pauline Bright,' offered Gemma, cravenly.

'What, from that lot down Clay Lane?'

She didn't need a response. Gemma's mum pulled Gemma's arm like she was cracking a whip.

'I don't want you hanging round her!'

'I'm not, Mum, honest!'

'And you, leave her alone from now on or I'll get the police on to you!'

'I wasn't doing owt!'

The habitual phrase leaped from Pauline with a new meaning. Injustice seared a blade of tears in her throat.

'I know you've been fighting – I sent a letter to the school! So stay away! I'm warning you. Scruffy little beggar.'

The woman's face was ugly beneath her make-up, rearing towards her. Pauline spat. Then she ran.

'I wasn't doing owt, you fucking bitch!'

She stopped running when she couldn't breathe easily any more. She didn't want to go home, so she took a long loop back to the bus station and watched the buses arrive and depart, the people getting on and off, until the short night darkened. She hadn't even done owt either, except try to be nice. She fucking hated Gemma's mum, the fucking bitch.

Call sheet: 'That Summer'
July 3rd 1975.
Director: Michael Keys
Director of Photography: Anthony Williams, BSC.
First AD: Derek Powell.
2.00 p.m. call.

CAST: John Reed [PC MERCHANT], Anne Fortune
[MARY], TBC [LITTLE BROTHER], Vera Wyngate [WOMAN
IN CAR].
LOCATION: Moxton Rd, Carr Hill, Doncaster.
Scenes 80, 83.

80. EXT. RESIDENTIAL ST. DAY.
PC MERCHANT arrives to break the news to JUNE's
mother and father.

83. EXT/INT. RESIDENTIAL ST. DAY.
WOMAN IN CAR sees PC MERCHANT leave JUNE's house.

Today was Vera's swanswong. When she'd been sent the script,
she'd had pages more, including a court scene, but it had all
been cut. Since she got paid the same fee, she really didn't mind,
although actually it was always nice to work – not just to have a
job, but to turn up and have a natter and get to know the lie of
the land. Of course that was clear the moment you set foot on set;
whether it was a happy crew, whether there was a star or another
cast member creating intrigue and unhappiness with the director (usually, in her experience, and God knows she'd done this
herself in her time, because they felt they were being ignored),

122

whether there were two stars jostling for supremacy or creating some magic because they were either at it or so desperate to be that the thwarted energy crackled its way into the can. All these things and a million others were apparent in a couple of hours, but none made a blind bit of difference to how good a film was. A happy set was absolutely no guarantee of a good film. One of the most enjoyable experiences of Vera's career had been on a heated biopic of Edward Elgar called *Hidden Rhapsody*, which had turned out a tortured stinker despite incontinent daily giggles. Of course the script had never been in its favour – come to think of it, most of the giggles had been triggered by the lines they had to say.

She couldn't really tell whether this one was any good, script-wise. It was sparse, as seemed the fashion these days, and the story was a little grim for Vera's taste. Personally, she liked a love story. But the atmosphere on set, beyond the industrious concentration you took for granted as men and women dedicated themselves to sorting out the myriad problems they specialized in (floor cables, a squeaking door, a shiny chin), was uncharacteristically hard to discern. Make-up were always the first port of call for cast intrigue, but that afternoon, Vera could get very little out of them as they drabbed her down. It wasn't that they weren't forthcoming. There just seemed, disappointingly, little to tell.

'Mr Bogarde's a lovely man. Very professional,' the girl observed, sponging pancake onto Vera's jawline with an even roll of the wrist.

'Hiya!'

The friendliness in the voice was toffee-apple sweet and just as brittle. The mother, of course, smart as paint as usual, ciggie on.

'Hello, darling.'

One had to be friendly. One was, in the end, friendly. And surely if there was gossip, this woman, having the least to do, might be the source of it.

'Ooh, mind if I take the weight off?'

Yvonne? Julie, was it? No, that was the make-up girl – perched on the vacant chair between Vera and the actor playing PC Plod.

'You all right, Katrina?'

Katrina. Katrina pulled a face into the mirror, and for the first time Vera caught a glimpse of the daughter behind the slap. Maybe that's why she wore so much make-up, to cement the mobility in her features that would have made her part of a joke.

'All go, as per. Costume tests. Don't know why they can't do them at the hotel, but there you are. His Nibs wants to have a look.'

This explained why Katrina and the girl were on the set when they weren't on the call sheet. Of course the business of filming was just the tip of a vast iceberg of other business concerning filming. Don't think everyone's looking at *you*, as her own mother used to say.

'That's a nice colour.' The girl in charge of Vera nodded at Katrina's nails, which were lacquered cinnamon brown. Katrina splayed her fingers critically.

'I'm not sure, me. Did it in a rush.'

'Ooh, reminds me, you've not got any on, have you, love?'

Vera waved her naked hands at the mirror. She knew better. Woman In Car wasn't the manicure type, poor old drudge. The girl caught her left hand, scanned her nails just to be sure.

'Haven't you got nice hands,' she said. Vera did, as a matter of fact, but it was, after all, the most meaningless of compliments, even to a woman her age. Although wasn't it dear Viv Leigh who had been told early in her career that her hands were too big, and so had slogged to find ways of gesturing on stage to disguise the fact? They must have been like absolute shovels for anyone to notice, really. Vera suspected malice on the part of the producer who had made this observation, wresting back power from all that beauty. She knew the type. Darling Hugh's dad had been a prime example – it might even have been him who had given Viv the complex.

'Do you know, darling Viv Leigh was told—'

But Katrina had started at the same time as her, leaning in with the promise of scandal. Vera aborted her own anecdote.

'Anyway, girls, big news.'

She cast a melodramatic look at PC Plod, on the other side of her. He had his eyes shut.

'We've had a chat with the American producer.'

The second girl funnelled her mouth. Lallie's face reappeared beneath Katrina's mask of make-up, pantomiming excitement.

'They want her to go over. Do this film.'

'What film?' asked Vera's girl.

'It's from a book. *The Littlest Princess*. Lead part. I can't believe it, me.'

Katrina and both girls jiggled in unified excitement. Vera smiled.

'I mean, they'll do screen tests and that. Fly us over. I've never been to America.'

'You won't want to come back!'

'Lallie won't. She's mad about anything American, her. She's heard about this ice cream, what is it – thirty flavours or something.'

But Katrina was in too good a mood to pursue the line of disparagement.

'What about her TV show?'

'Oh well, now you're asking. It's early days, isn't it? The agent'll sort it out.'

Vera could see that any American mess of pottage would buy Lallie's English career as far as the mother was concerned. And who was to say she was wrong about that? She herself, fresh from her first film (*Small Talk*), had once had that prospect spread before her. It had lasted all of a week, and had coincided with her being squired around town by a rather dishy Yank producer who was raising finance for a Roman epic. What was glorious was that she would have gone to bed with him anyway – only American men and Scandinavians had those chests – so when he started talking about plane tickets and test scenes and how good she'd look in a toga, it was pure gravy. It had all evaporated, of course. Within weeks, he'd flown back to the States and forgotten her. But the excitement of thinking, age twenty, that all of that was going to be hers had been like nothing else.

'She'll go down a bomb,' said Vera. 'Americans eat up talent. Is it the woman you've been talking to? Quentin?'

The girls sniggered. 'Quentin.'

Vera's girl stopped dabbing.

'She doesn't wear a bra!'

'It's all the rage, isn't it?' said Vera. 'Maybe she's a women's libber.'

'I couldn't go without a bra, me,' said Katrina, who was small-breasted. 'Wouldn't feel right.'

She cast another look. The sleeping policeman continued comatose. Everyone had forgotten there was a man in the room.

'Talking of . . . ' Katrina addressed Vera's make-up girl. 'Do you think our Lallie needs a bit of help?' She skimmed her chest.

'Is she developing?'

Katrina nodded as though she'd just asked for sympathy.

'Just starting.'

'Bless her.'

'It doesn't notice,' said the second girl. 'What do wardrobe say?'

'They put her in something quite tight, you know, a T-shirt, and you can really see.'

'Bless her.'

'Oh God, talking of, I'd best get back.'

Katrina looked for somewhere to put out her cigarette. The make-up girl reached over Vera and gave her an ashtray.

'It's just –' Katrina dragoned smoke through her nostrils as she mashed the butt – 'I thought, best to get it sorted out now before the Yanks have a proper look at her, you know?'

She mimicked squashing her own breasts down, giggling.

'She needs to be eleven.'

The girls laughed. Katrina unfolded herself from the chair, picked up her handbag. With a reorganizing glance back at the mirror, correcting a smudge of eyeliner, she was gone.

'Bless her. How old is she then?' asked Vera's girl.

'Forty-two,' said Vera.

The other girl, Julie, tapped excess powder from her brush, with a cautionary look down at the inert policeman. 'I think she's thirteen, or coming up to it,' she mouthed.

Vera wasn't surprised. She herself was three, or was it four years younger than when she'd started out. They'd shaved off a year at the Charm School, as was standard, and along the way she'd dropped a few more. No doubt, once she was in sight of sixty, she might hover in the late fifties for a bit. Age range early forties to early fifties, as her agent would doggedly maintain.

Released from make-up and costume, Vera settled herself with a cup of tea and a ciggie. Her scene wasn't scheduled until the end of the day. It was supposed to come after the scene where PC Merchant – he had revived suspiciously quickly once Katrina had gone – delivered the news to the girl's mother. But despite appearing as a single scene on the call sheet, he actually delivered the news in close-up, medium and long shots, with his car pulling up, with the mother opening the door, with the little brother noticing the car from inside the house and calling out 'Mum', so there were many permutations of lights to set and cables to lay.

It was a lovely day, and she had a chair and a paper, although she'd nearly finished the crossword. Happily, she knew Anne Fortune, the actress playing the mother. Like her, Anne had descended from more glamorous roles, although in truth she'd never been in Vera's league, looks-wise, so as the years piled on she'd always got more work, particularly as she was legitimately northern and hadn't erased her accent. Since it was Anne's first day on set, she looked to Vera for names and faces, the basic drill.

'Who's that?'

It was the American girl, Quentin, arriving with Hugh. Anne hooted at the name, although she was careful not to let Quentin see once she knew she was from the studio. Vera and Anne watched the two of them make their way through the crew, Hugh holding the girl's elbow and dipping to breathe names as she deployed those marvellous teeth. She really did wear the most extraordinary clothes. The younger generation had their own way, and Vera lived close enough to the King's Road to see most of it, but surely if you were a professional woman who expected to command respect you needed to take that into account? Quentin's glossy hair slithered over bare brown shoulders, while her bra-less nipples, nuzzling the thin stuff of her blouse, stirred a wake of wistful male glances as she and Hugh advanced. Delicious, of course. Vera liked her, actually. Quentin spoke to her as though she mattered. And she emanated such a lot of anxious energy; it was hard not to respond and soothe, even knowing that Quentin retained the power of life and death, professionally speaking.

'Hey, Vera!' That lovely smile, as though you'd just given her a present. Hugh was right behind with his own charming smile, not trying quite as hard. Seeing him, Vera realised that she owed him the work. Of course she did: those evenings after a day on set having drinks at his parents' Chalfont St Peter spread, with Hugh and his brother paraded to do turns for them, wearing side partings and pyjamas straight from Wardrobe. She'd always been nicer than necessary to Hugh, as a way of expiating her fear that Hilary might know about her lapse with Sidney.

'Vera. You look terrible! In the best possible way . . . '

He squeezed her fondly as they kissed. 'Vera's seen me in my pyjamas.'

Quentin's smile was willing but uncertain.

'Darling, Hugh. You were adorable,' said Vera, squeezing him back.

Vera caught Quentin's visible relief as she got it. Oh dear.

'He used to sing Noël Coward songs for us,' she added for reassurance.

'Let's draw a veil, shall we?'

They moved on. Vera wondered, seeing the two of them together. Quentin's eagerness to understand their interchange was of a piece with her not wearing a bra, parading her vulnerability. She'd never seen that before in an American; openness, yes, tiresomely so sometimes, but not this invitation to wound. Would Hugh be nice to her? He was no Sidney, she knew, but she had heard rumours when his first marriage broke down in his twenties. And come to think of it, there hadn't been a second marriage, despite a long engagement to someone Vera couldn't now recall, someone double-barrelled and horsey. Well, looking at them, they made a handsome couple, although Hugh's Savile Row style was certainly at odds with whatever it was Quentin was calling hers. And she was probably closer to twenty years younger than him than ten, but that was par for the course.

'Hiya!'

Before they could reach Mike, Katrina detained them both. Vera wondered if they knew Lallie's true age. Possibly no one did, with the exception of the mother. Maybe she was consulting them about the bra, although Quentin was obviously the last person to ask for advice about that. Quentin patted the woman's arm, reassuring. Hugh laughed. As they attempted to break away, Lallie appeared. Hopping with energy, as usual, trying to enter the circle of adult conversation, demanding attention and attention and attention. Vera, unfathomably stirred, found herself wanting to shout over, 'No one's looking at *you*,' and in that moment, Lallie glanced up and caught her eye. Because of course Vera was looking at her. The girl twitched a shy smile of acknowledgement, looked away. The tentative quality of her reaction disarmed Vera. Eleven or twelve, what did it matter? She was a tot.

'Ravishing, darling.' Hugh held Lallie at arm's length, appraising her costume. It was school uniform, broken down to show the kind of home Lallie's character came from. Lallie gave him a twirl, followed by a few moments of Bruce Forsyth. Vera could see how delighted she was by his approval. She and Quentin might have to fight it out for him, the good-looking swine.

Hugh chucked the girl's chin as he spoke to Katrina. Lallie's upturned face was radiant with trust. As long as Hugh's hand dawdled, on her shoulder now, she shone. But all the while, her eyes played ping-pong between Katrina and Hugh. No tricks missed.

'I'm not sure we're going to let you take her away,' Vera heard. Hugh was addressing Quentin for Lallie's benefit, and more pointedly, her mother's. 'We want to keep her here. We've got big plans.'

Quentin's smile tightened and held. In front of Vera, the grip started up a conversation with Tony about a dolly track and she couldn't hear any more. She was left with the tantalizing feeling of having witnessed a piece of gossip in the making.

'I presume those two are at it?' asked Anne baldly, once Hugh and Quentin had been driven away in that comfy car of his. 'Oh, I think so, don't you?' she said. That, at least, was certain. But what about Lallie? Was what Vera had seen the thin end of a Lallie-shaped wedge destined to come between the two of them? Quentin had suddenly looked less charming after Hugh's crack about hanging on to her. Perhaps Quentin was a tougher nut than she appeared. Maybe, like the clothes, she simply had a new way, and producers didn't have to be Hughs and Sidneys any more. And she could certainly talk to people, not in Hugh's RADA-royal manner, but arm-touchingly, warmly. Well, they would find out, wouldn't they, if anything went wrong and touch came to shove?

The filming day wore on with no sign of Vera's scene being called. The little boy delivered to be Lallie's character's little brother proved undirectable, and Mike got the shot only through the monkeys-typing-Shakespeare approach of endless takes. In the end, they dropped the dialogue and hoped the child could simply manage to open the door, which he achieved without mishap around take fifty-eight. Anne of course was faultless, but a bulb blew on a light, and Tony and his gang took an age consulting over how best to replace it and then discovering the bulb they needed was back at the unit base.

Waiting for the runner to return on his motorbike, they decided to set up for Vera's scene, but the arrival of the bulb set them back on their original course. Vera could see how it would go. Barring a miracle, her scene was going to drop off the end of the day. One more night at the hotel, at least, and God knows when or if they'd bother to pick up the missing scene. Well, it had happened before and it would happen again. No one was looking at *her*.

I WAKE UP the morning of the audition with a balloon of joyous dread bobbing in my stomach. It's impossible to eat breakfast, although Mum nags, and I know if I don't make the attempt she might decide I'm ill and use it as an excuse to stop me going. She seems to want to do that quite badly, so I'm on best behaviour. Ian doesn't help by making lots of comments about me being a film star and being ready for my close-up. In the end Mum tells him to give over, which is a relief. He's taken aback by her command, which she barely bothers to coat with another tone. It's the kind of thing she says to Dad all the time, but she's never done it before with Ian. It makes me see the permanence of this arrangement between them. The balloon tugs inside me, heavy.

Although we'll be at school, we don't have to wear uniform, and we approach disaster when I appear wearing my dungarees as a tribute to Lallie. Mum says I need to put on a dress instead. I very strongly want to wear the dungarees; they are what I've been wearing every time I've been to the audition before drifting off to sleep, and Lallie has got talking to me about them ('Nice dungarees', 'Thanks'), and we've become friends and live together in her TV house with Marmaduke the butler. Mum, though, insists on a dress. Will it be the same? Will it even be possible to enjoy meeting Lallie wearing a dress? I appeal to Ian, who sides with Mum even though I know he'd prefer to support me. In the end it comes down to an ultimatum: do I want to go to the audition?

We arrive ten minutes before the official start, me in a dress, and the hall is already packed. Christina isn't there – they left for Butlin's at the weekend – so I sit near Michelle and Maria from my class. The mums and dads hover for the spare ten minutes, during which Mum gets out a brush and refinishes my hair. Then they're all told to go away by a woman who was there when we signed up, an oldish woman with lots of interesting rings on her fingers and clothes of a kind I've never come across; they don't match, but she's smart. She has a posh voice, which helps to quell us, and doesn't seem the type to be got around.

'Thank you so much for coming today,' she says. 'As you know, it won't be possible to use each and every one of you, although I think I'm right in saying that there will be a scene in the playground where anyone who wants to can appear . . . ?' She dips her head towards a man, neither young nor old, just grown-up age, who is clearly important. He nods tightly.

'So let's get started! I'm Julia, by the way, the casting director – you'll be meeting me first. And this is Michael, the director, Mike, who some of you will be meeting later. He's a very busy man! Oh, and Pam, my assistant – she'll be seeing some of you as well.'

Pam is one of the other people, mixed in with the teachers, there to shepherd us. She's younger and has a friendly look I like, although Julia clearly doesn't think much of her.

A group of fourth-years is led away by Pam. As it becomes clear that this is all that is going to happen, everyone goes quieter and starts to get bored. I've brought my ballet bag with me, at Mum's suggestion, just in case I need to slip my shoes on (I've brought tap as well) and show them what I can do, and Michelle and Maria and I occupy ourselves for a time with its contents, them trying on my shoes and me showing them a few tap steps sitting down with my knees up in the air.

The fourth-years come back, full of pioneering self-importance, and another ten are sent in. Everyone crowds round the returned group, eager for news, but we're marshalled back in line with a few tantalizing scraps. These are soon amplified into concrete rumours: apparently one boy, Andrew Meeton, had to swear. Maria asserts, disappointingly, that the swear word was 'bugger'. But it reaches me from the other side of the row that what he actually had to do was pull his trousers down and show them his arse. I am suitably shocked, but confident that, being a girl, nothing of that sort will be required of me. Admittedly, the tap shoes are looking doubtful. I eat the two chocolate digestives Mum has tucked into the bag for a snack. The chocolate is melted from the heat, so I lick my fingers and the spaces between my fingers clean, like a cat having a wash.

The next lot out claim they are being given speaking parts. Well, two of them. I start to feel worried: what if all the good parts have been given out by the time they get to third-years? What if all the parts have gone? I count the obstacles in front of me, up to forty-two. Four more groups. By now Michelle and Maria and I have stopped talking and are slumped against the wall. This is not how I expected it to be.

And then I see her. Standing at the door, near the vaulting horse where Mr Scott parks his papers on assembly days. There is a strange second of delay between recognizing her and knowing who she is, then the impossible reality flows into that gap, flooding me with magic. Lallie. As familiar as my mum. There. Not on the telly. In my life, human. Smaller than I think of her, although of course she is literally tiny on the telly screen, but small, smaller than I am. She is with her mum, who I recognize from magazine photos, but she's actually talking to Julia, who now seems less stern. I am so bound up in my thirsty intake of the scene that the thought of telling Michelle or Maria doesn't even form: I am all looking.

Lallie is wearing a peaked cap over her springy hair, and oh God, matching orange dungarees. Her clothes, as I knew they would be, are perfect. She doesn't do anything, just talks – she seems to be chewing gum – with her hands tucked into the bib of her dungarees and one plimsolled foot balanced on top of the standing foot in a way I immediately note and decide to copy. But how can she be so small? Just as a stirring of recognition snakes through the hall like a run of dominoes coming down, she moves on. Julia gives her a kiss – a kiss! – although it is not the kind of kiss I am accustomed to receiving, it's a kiss between equals, her mum puts her hand on her shoulder, and they disappear through the door. The recognition has now become shouts of 'That's her!' and 'Lallie!' and I see her buck as her name is called and turn back to respond, although her mum is still herding her out. She gives an uncertain smile and a wave, just like any girl our age would, with friendliness in it and apology, a botched gesture that she seems to want to take back as she goes. She's gone. For a few seconds I watch the doorway, the way I watch the picture on the turned-off TV even after it's shrunk to nothing.

'That wa'n't her!' Michelle says scornfully. I argue roundly, along with Maria and the others, but she won't be convinced, perhaps because she was one of the last to notice her. And all the time I feel elation and sadness, striped together like toothpaste; elation at the sheer glamour of Lallie appearing in my life, and sadness that her separate existence is now an experienced fact, confirming my failure to be her. We are not even alike, despite the freckles and the tap. She is small in a way I will never be, she is dark, she is her. I am forever me. It doesn't stop me craving the orange dungarees.

Nearly an hour later, we are called in. The balloon in my stomach has now risen to my throat, making me feel sick. I know that if they ask me to sing, it will come out as croaking. My pulse beats in my ears. Pam holds us in a corridor outside the classroom where the important people are and tries to chat to us, but I have to keep swallowing to stop myself from vomiting. She says they won't be long and rolls her eyes. She says there's nothing to be nervous about, and that if we aren't chosen it doesn't mean anything bad, it's just a matter of them looking for children who fit into an idea they have for the script. It's the script, really, she says, and having the right sort of look. The possibility of not being chosen leaks bile into my mouth. I ask if there's time for me to get a drink from the water fountain at the end of the corridor, and she says, 'Of course.'

I'm bowed over the warmish nub of water when someone claps my back, making me wet my chin. Before I turn I already know who it is; no one else barges and pokes like this.

'Give over!' I rub my cheek as though the water has hurt it. 'What are you doing here?'

'Come for't film, haven't I?'

She looks, for Pauline, as though she's made an effort. Two hair grips hold her black-and-white hair back at the forehead, which is noticeably cleaner than the rest of her face below, and she's wearing a dress. She's standing too close to me, like she does, and I automatically start breathing through my mouth.

'You can't come with me,' I say, indicating Michelle and Maria and the nice lady. 'You have to go and wait in the hall.'

As so often when I talk to her, I'm not sure if Pauline is ignoring me or hasn't heard in the first place. She just comes with me when I head back to my group.

'I saw Lallie Paluza,' I can't resist telling her, although it means nothing to her. She puts something in my hand: a Flake, the chocolate almost liquid in its wrapper.

'I don't want it,' I say, and try to hand it back.

'I got it for you.'

'I don't want it!'

But there's nothing I can do because she won't take it, and now the door to the classroom has opened and disastrously the nice lady is telling us to go in. I try to explain about the Flake and Pauline, but they both end up in the room with me, Michelle and Maria. We face a table full of grown-ups; there is the woman, Julia, and the important man, Michael. Also another man who smiles nicely and winks, who is called Hugh. I can see they have a list in front of them and recognize, with relief, the mechanisms that will save me and eject Pauline.

'What's that you've got in your hand?' asks Hugh.

'It's a Flake,' I tell them, to mystifying amusement. 'She gave it me, I don't want it, it's all melted!'

'Why don't you put it in the bin,' Julia suggests coolly, her amusement less genuine than the two men's. I'm grateful for this, as well as scared. She's scanning the list for Pauline's name.

'She's not on the list, Miss,' I say.

'Oh, well,' says Michael. 'What's your name?' and Julia takes up her pen and writes at the bottom, where there's a blank bit.

'Bright, as it sounds?'

If I could kill Pauline, I would. The Flake wrapper has leaked chocolate on to my palm and I lick it away so I don't get chocolate on my dress, but this amuses Hugh even more, I can see, as though he thinks I can't resist eating even at this crucial moment.

They ask us questions, about how old we are and what we're doing for the summer holidays.

'I'm going to Spain with my mum and dad,' I tell them, shame at turning Ian into my dad piled on to the shame of what's actually happened between my mum and dad. When it's her turn, Pauline claims that she's going to Spain too, with her parents, and I want to shout that she's a liar, but I'm a liar too. After this, Michael asks Pauline to come closer to the table, and asks her a lot more questions, about school, and her brothers and sisters, and although Pauline tells some more whoppers robbed from me, about liking reading and making up stories (although she stops short of claiming she too wants to be a teacher when she grows up), the more questions he asks, the more she begins to talk to Michael properly, looking at him instead of off to one side of him like she usually does, and all the time he's staring at her, flanked by the two other grown-ups, who also look and look. I prepare a few of my own answers so I'll be ready for similar questions, but there's no need. They thank us all and the door opens and the nice lady scoops us out into the corridor again. That's it.

Michelle and Maria are giggly and relieved. I turn to Pauline and push her so hard she bangs back against the wall.

'You're a liar, you!'

'Oy, steady . . . ' The nice lady gets hold of my shoulder.

'She told lies.'

'I never!'

'It doesn't matter, chick,' the lady admonishes. 'It's not like an exam. They just want to get a look at you really, sort of get an idea of what you're like. It's not the end of the world, is it?'

But I'm bawling. The door opens, and I think I'm going to get in trouble for making a noise, but Julia wants to say something to Pam and registers my distress only remotely.

'Oh dear.'

She nods the lady away and says something to her. When we get back to the hall, Pam says me and Michelle and Maria can wait outside for our mums and dads to collect us. She asks Pauline to wait with her. Pauline looks worried, as though she might be in trouble. I can't bear to tell her the opposite, that they want her and don't want me, but when I see Mum in the playground, that's what I sob, incomprehensibly – they want her, they don't want me. Eventually, she makes sense of it.

'They must have made a mistake.'

When I assure her that they haven't, that they really do want Pauline, Mum goes in search of an authoritative adult to confirm this, and is passed up to the nice lady. I can see them talking together, the benign head shake that fends Mum off, all too quickly. She has to content herself with an impotent, audible 'Ridiculous!' as she stalks back to me.

'She can't tell us much – supposed to be in charge, you'd think they'd get someone who knows what they're talking about . . . '

She aims this mainly at Michelle's mum, who smiles warily and continues to leave. Briskly, Mum takes one of my bunches and makes it do the splits to tighten the bobble on my scalp. 'They haven't made any final decisions, apparently, but you're right, they're seeing Pauline now. Is that chocolate?' She rubs at a stain on my dress, adjusts my second bobble.

In the car, my snorts convulsively subside. 'Knew she'd get het up,' says Mum to Ian, who suggests pancakes at the Copper Kettle, and refuses to believe me when I say I'm not hungry. He insists on ordering my favourites, and I joylessly post sweet, claggy forkfuls into my mouth so Mum can't get irritated about my lack of gratitude for the treat.

'Even if they use her, it won't be anything big,' she reassures me. I've reached the point of not wanting to talk about it any more, in the hope it might go away.

'Course it won't,' says Ian. 'You have to be trained, like, to take a star part. Go to stage school – that's where they'll look for the speaking parts. Down in London.'

'It's a funny way to go on, getting kiddies' hopes up.' Mum raises her voice, hoping for an audience, and manages to catch the manageress's eye as she stands by the till. Ian goes to the toilet, and once he's left us Mum seems to lose interest in her indignation. Her sipping of her coffee becomes inward and complicated. I exploit this slackening of attention to stop eating, and cut the rest of my pancake into cunning shreds that can be dispersed over my syrupy plate and abandoned. I remember that I've seen Lallie, and haven't even bothered to tell Mum, but I can't quite bear her lack of interest. Then I wonder if Pauline has seen Lallie now, met her even, and the possibility revives the crucifying injustice of it all. I know that even if she has, Pauline won't care. That's almost the worst of it.

'Mum?'

Elbows on the table, she lowers her coffee cup slightly. I don't know what I'm going to say.

'Can I, can I see Dad?'

The cup comes all the way down to the table, like I've pushed a switch. I think she's going to be very angry.

'What d'you want to see him about?'

'I don't know. I just want to see him.'

Mum's head writhes elaborately, as though I've put a cord round her neck.

'Because . . . well, I hope you're not expecting much.'

'I'm not,' I reassure her. I haven't got a clue what she means.

'He doesn't pay a penny for you, you know. Ian's taken it all on.' Dumbly, I wait for her to stop. She's definitely very angry, but at the moment, it doesn't seem to be at me. She takes a punctuating sip of coffee, rattles the cup back into the saucer, slopping. This helps her find what to say next. 'Not many men would, a woman with a child. Everything he's got. You should thank your lucky stars, Gemma.'

Tears stab the back of my throat but it feels crucial now not to shed them. Ian is coming back from the toilet. He drops hugely on to the banquette next to me, making me seesaw up.

'Oh dear, oh dear,' he says. 'Man walks into a bar, there's a horse having a drink, he says to him, "Why the long face?"'

Mum tuts. She doesn't like jokes, even Ian's jokes. Ian squeezes my thigh with his vast chocolate-Brazil-eating hand. It hurts, like a pinch. 'You're a star, you'll see. Isn't she, Mum?'

'I don't know where they're looking, if they want Pauline Bright. Everyone knows, that family . . . '

Dad has been erased from the conversation, as he always is around Ian. I can see that this is the way it will always be now, unless I do something. I remember, sickly, how easily I myself erased Dad when I was telling them about our holiday in the audition. Maybe when I replaced him with Ian, that was the moment God decided that I didn't deserve to star in a film with Lallie. Ian gives me one more heavy pat on the leg, jabs a tickle at my stomach, then takes up the flimsy bill for the pancakes and hoists himself out of the seat to pay.

'What do you say?' prompts Mum.

'Thank you, Ian.'

He does a bow, as is his way. 'My pleasure, sweet ladies.'

I force a smile.

'That's better,' Mum says.

FRANK DENNY GOT the phone call from America bang in the middle of his lunchtime sandwich. It was only twenty minutes he took at his desk, on the rare days when he wasn't lunching a client, and Veronica knew the sanctity of that time, which included a fifteen-minute forty winks with *The Stage* draped over his face. Calls from the Yanks were the sole permitted interruption to this ritual, since the time difference made them oblivious to the inconvenience. However dazed he might feel, Frank was expert at vamping until his brain caught up, which it did like a psychic act narrowing the possibilities by firing general questions until the audience member unconsciously revealed all, sometimes helped by his mark in the form of Veronica posting scribbled notes on his desk and miming additional details. But today it was easy, since there was only one female Quentin on his mental Rolodex.

'How's it all going up there? Pleased with my lovely little girl, I hope,' Frank beamed into the phone, whose ancient mouthpiece hummed with years of his own breath. He realized, with a practised repression of annoyance, that although Quentin was a Yank, she was actually in the country. Veronica wasn't to know.

'She's terrific—'

'Isn't she? I always say, a star's a star, whatever the age.'

There was a silence down the line, inexplicable as a time delay.

'What can I do for you, my love?'

'I just wanted to get a little background, about Lallie . . . '

Uh-oh. Unless it was just financial stuff, fees and precedents. 'Fire away.'

Veronica, realising her help wasn't needed, disappeared to make him his post-forty-winks cup of tea.

'Well, I met her and her mom—'

'Katrina, yes.'

'Yeah.' There was a little pause. 'Quite a lady.'

'Oh darling, if it's the mother you're worried about, I have to say you could do a lot worse, believe it or not. I mean, she's protective, but she does let Lallie just get on with it—'

'Yeah, I can see that, that's not a problem for me.' In the fractional gap before Quentin launched her next sentence, Frank's mind tumbled through the possibilities like a safe cracker: puberty? The nose (they'd fix it, why not)? The decision to go with American talent instead (despite it being an English part)? Her being too common to play a princess (elocution lessons – the kid was a mimic, for Christ's sake)?

'I just wondered . . . if, given the mom and all, she's being pressured to work.'

Fuck me, so that was it. Frank burst through. 'God, no! Have you spoken to her? She's born to it, darling, absolutely. I mean, I'm not denying Mummy has a big hand in it, you can see that for yourself, but Lallie, heavens – she loves the business, absolutely eats, sleeps and breathes it.'

Again, a little silence. Maybe there really was a delay – it was still long distance, even if it was only Yorkshire.

'She seems a little . . . joyless to me.'

Bloody hell. He'd have to have a word, pronto. What had Katrina been doing up there?

'I'm sorry about that, it doesn't sound like my girl at all. She might be tired, to be honest – she went on to the film straight off her telly job and it's been a long stretch. They do still get tired, kiddies, even though they restrict the hours. It's only natural.'

'OK.'

Frank was not used to dealing with Americans of this ambling, considered kind. Women, yes, but they tended to be hyperactive New Yorkers who condensed any conversation into its essence and shot it straight into your bloodstream. This girl sounded almost dopey.

'Maybe you saw her at the end of the day?'

'We had breakfast.'

'Ah . . . ' He chuckled. 'She's not one for the early starts, I could've told you that. Did she say she was keen?'

'She said. Mom did most of the talking. She doesn't know the book – she liked my pitch, I think.'

This sounded better. Solid ground. Veronica put his tea on the desk. Frank became brisk.

'Terrific. It's a wonderful opportunity for her, I'm sure she can see that. I've mentioned to the mother about booking a holiday once she's finished on this one, that should set her right. I'll insist, Quentin, you're quite right. She's only human.'

This was a favourite technique of his. We're all in this together, working on a problem slightly to the left of the one you thought you had before we started the conversation. He pressed his advantage.

'And are you thinking about screen tests at this stage? Might that help, to get her out at the studio, see how she looks in costume, down to action as it were? That might be a thought, if you wanted – she could do the holiday first for a week – I know she's mad to go to Disneyland, like they all are. It'd really set her up.'

'Oh. Yeah, that could work for us. I'll talk to Clancy in the office.'

He wasn't there yet, that was for sure. There was still this hesitation, this gap on the line. And he didn't buy that it was just because Lallie hadn't done a song and dance when she met her – although why the hell not, he had no idea, considering she was a song-and-dance machine whenever he saw her. Maybe she really was tired. He scribbled a curve of zeds on his notepad, next to where he had written and underlined 'holiday'.

'I hear the rushes on this one have got everyone talking.' He hadn't, but they always had.

'They look terrific.'

'What about Lallie?'

'I think she's going to be amazing.'

That, at least, sounded genuine. So what was the problem? Everyone wanted more than they should: his clients from him, the producers from the clients, it wasn't right, really. There had to be limits.

'Well, that's all that matters, isn't it, at the end of the day – what you're getting?'

'I guess so.' Pause. Frank had given up. 'She is a child. I mean, just a little kid.'

And Lassie's just a collie, darling, but it's a bit late in the day . . . which reminded him. Frank wrote 'worm medicine' next to his doodles on the pad and triple-underlined it. Kenneth had been dragging his arse along the carpet when he'd left that morning, and if he had them it was only a matter of time before Charles succumbed.

'Well, she is and she isn't. She's got a gift, that's plain as the nose on your face.' He wished he hadn't mentioned noses; it might bring Lallie's to mind, and for all he knew Quentin herself might have a problematic schnozz. 'And let me tell you, the first time I met her, she told me that the thing in the world that makes her happiest is working. This is from a nine-year-old girl. It's born in her.'

In the gap, he pencilled in the loop of the 'b' in 'tablets'. Come on, Frank. 'But can I say, I think it's wonderful to come across someone in your position who's really concerned about these things. Hand on heart, it's something I've thought about a lot, but also hand on heart, I've got to tell you that she's not one of those kiddies who's forced into it – I wouldn't be looking after her if she was, couldn't live with myself. But it's good to know that if she does go to the States, she'll have someone apart from me looking out for her.'

Quentin actually laughed at this, an unpleasant, gentle little chuckle which took him by surprise.

'Do you know Hugh Calder?'

Where was this going? He felt uneasy.

'Of course. Best in the business, Hugh.'

'Do you think he's a nice guy?'

Frank stopped doodling, banjaxed. Never for long, though.

'What can I tell you? The man's charm itself. You've met him . . .'

Now he thought he heard a sigh down the line. He amended his approach.

'I don't know about nice, but he's a true gent. Tough, mind – well, you have to be, don't you? He wouldn't be doing what he's doing if he was a pushover, but, let's say, honourable.'

That was over-egging it a bit, but you never knew what got back to people. He could hear Quentin breathing, as though she had come up a flight of stairs.

'Is he into women?'

Crikey. What had he heard? This and that, nothing to frighten the horses. He'd certainly never gleaned an atom of queerness around him. The breathing continued, awaiting his answer. If he hadn't known better, Frank would have believed that Quentin really was ringing him from what was for her the middle of the night, wanting him to keep her company. He got those calls from clients every so often, the ones he had to give his home number, although of course it was the line in the office; he wasn't mad. It still drove Lol to distraction, that interruption to sleep so Frank, dressing-gowned, could coax them through when they told him they'd taken pills, or wept for their marriages, or more usually their careers. In his experience, the pill-takers weren't repeat callers, and he didn't resent a genuine emergency, but the ramblers, the lost souls who wanted hand-holding in the sozzled small hours, they were a piece of work. And this woman wasn't even a client.

Besides, he had a meeting with bigwigs from Anglia at two. *Is he into women*, indeed.

'As far as I know,' he said maliciously, and started to wind up the call. He thanked Quentin again for her concern over Lallie, emphasizing its rarity and re-emphasizing their common values, lauded her non-existent non-brainwave about Lallie taking a holiday, and finessed the ending by pressing her to suggest a time when the studio might want Lallie to fly over. October, she proffered. Such provisional motes were all Frank needed to accrete the solid pearls of business: the next time they spoke, he would tell her that October was okay for Katrina and Lallie, and they'd be going ahead with booking tickets, unless the studio preferred to arrange it? With any luck this would be a conversation he'd have with Quentin's assistant, who more likely than not would oblige, already presuming October to be a done deal. And by then it more or less would be – Quentin's seniors would hear that Lallie was coming over, their minds would be concentrated on her as their lead and they'd want to make it work, bar her not delivering the goods. It took a stronger soul than this girl evidently was to face Frank Denny down.

'Call me any time,' he signed off. His tea was by now just on the wrong side of warm, so he asked Veronica to bring him another cup and warned her about further calls from Quentin. If she called again today, he was right, and she was a nutter. If it was tomorrow, she still probably was. By Friday, he'd be prepared to talk to her again. It was no skin off his nose. There he was with the nose again. Of course the Yanks were superb at all that malarkey – none better. That was another conversation to have with Katrina; Frank made a note.

Pauline was supposed to fill in a form. In fact, her mum was supposed to fill in a form, but even if she hadn't been in Leeds, Pauline couldn't imagine approaching Joanne with the daunting sheaf of printed pages the hard-eyed woman had given her after she left the classroom. She'd tried to explain that her mum was away working, and they'd said in that case her dad would do. Dave was the closest in the house to a dad, but he'd just tell her to fuck off if she went anywhere near him with a piece of paper. Anyway, Pauline knew better than to let him or anyone else in the house know about the film, let alone needing permission, even though she had half a mind herself to rip up the typed sheets and dump them before it all went wrong. But somehow she couldn't. Instead, she kept the form in her bedroom, flat in a drawer, and checked on it from time to time, as though writing might have germinated on the pages in her absence.

Gemma wasn't talking to her. The last day of school, she'd run away from her in the playground and told a teacher when Pauline tried to catch up. Pauline had got a keyring she'd swiped from a place in town that mended shoes and cut keys, a really good keyring with a rubbery stupid-faced doll on the end whose arms and legs you could twist into shapes, but Gemma refused to take it. It had occurred to Pauline that Gemma might be able to fill in the form, since she had far neater writing than Pauline could manage, and proper spelling. But it seemed impossible, now, to get her to do it.

The night before Pauline was supposed to turn up at school with the completed paperwork, she turned over the blank, grubbying pages and thought of money. What if she offered Gemma money, instead of things; lots of money? It was risky, but she steeled herself for it, knowing that Dave would knock seven bells out of her if he caught her going through his pockets (which she'd have to do while he slept or had passed out). She didn't care, really. Since Joanne had gone, her life had been so lonely that getting knocked about a bit would be a welcome acknowledgement of her existence. She could always kick him back, and run.

But, as it turned out, she had a stroke of luck as she crept through the unusually quiet house in the very early morning. Nan, having got her sick money and her pills the previous day, was splayed comatose in her chair downstairs in the dark. Coins had dribbled from the beige post-office envelope she obliviously proffered in her slackened hand, but it was the folded five-pound note that Pauline pincered out and escaped with under the charnel-house miasma of Nan's snoring breath. Leaving the house with the money, she doubted she'd even be blamed: anyone else passing through the living room would have taken the opportunity. Then she wavered, thinking of things she could actually buy instead of giving the five pounds to Gemma. The hair salon had taken hold in her imagination, and she thought of marching in there and making Gemma's cow of a mother wash her hair and cut it because she was paying. It would be nice to have someone brush her hair, to make her look like everyone else.

It was too early for the shops to be open. Neither Gemma nor her mother would be at the salon yet, she realized, her stupid plan atomizing. So instead Pauline got on a bus and headed for Gemma's house among the pale, suspicious shift workers. When she got there, she knocked on the door, straightforwardly. She didn't care if Gemma's mum answered; in fact, she was up for a fight. What she wasn't expecting was Gemma's dad or whoever he was, the fat man.

'Can I see Gemma?'

Pauline didn't, as a rule, look at people's faces. In her experience there was seldom much to see there that was good, and at home eye contact often flared into violence. So as he stood in front of her, it was Ian's belt that caught her memory, its sleek enamel buckle straining between his grey trousers and clean shirting, an uncommon executive rhombus in black, gilt and maroon. She remembered the look of it and her curiosity about how it came undone, with none of the usual belt-buckle mechanism visible. When they were down the alley by Wentworth Road, he had pressed it behind its display, and it had released, like a small conjuring trick. Remembering this, she darted a look upwards. There was nothing in his face she recognized – there was no exception to her habit of not looking at faces – but it was sweating and appalled. He recognized her, she could see. It had been difficult to get her hand down his trousers even with the belt and fly undone, he was so fat. That and the belt were the only things she remembered about him.

Without speaking he shut the door on her, not forcefully but firmly, as though there was logic to it. *Not today, thank you.* She knocked again and rang, but the door stayed shut. She could have stayed with her finger pressing the bell until someone came, but she knew Gemma's mum would make real trouble, worse than refusing to let her see Gemma. It almost made her want to laugh, the way the bloke had shut the door on her, pretending she wasn't there. Him and his magic belt.

So she went into town and spent the money. She bought herself two cheese rolls and a carton of orange and then, at a newsagent, a Mars bar and a copy of *Tammy*, although they'd have been easy enough to nick. The fact that she hadn't made them feel more like presents to herself. After that she marched into a hair salon – not Gemma's mum's, she knew better than that, so she went to the staider one in Silver Street – with her just over four pounds and got them to transform her. She showed them the money, because she could see they wanted to tell her to get lost, and the receptionist, who was young but hard-faced, had to give way to an older woman they called a stylist, who called Pauline 'love' and took her away to wash her hair. She'd expected it to be ace, but the hair wash wasn't, with her head strained backwards over a green sink with a dip in it for your neck, and the woman's surprisingly sharp fingers agitating her scalp. But after, as the stylist combed out her hair in front of the mirror, it was ace. She said she could put a rinse in, to get all of her hair back to its same colour, and Pauline agreed without understanding what she meant to do. The stuff smelt sharp but didn't sting like peroxide, and it was strange to see the lightness so readily stained out as the woman soused her head from the large bottle, like she was putting vinegar on a bag of chips.

'You're too young to be mucking about with your hair,' the woman admonished. 'What did your mum say?' Pauline shrugged. The stylist snipped, then blasted her with scorching air, and soon Pauline was done.

'Don't you look pretty,' the woman announced, and the other hairdressers and a couple of old ladies they were processing all murmured varieties of agreement. Pauline knew she must have been transformed, because now they were prepared to look at her. She risked a glance into the mirror – she avoided looking into her own eyes just as much as other peoples' – and caught an impression of her hair as a darkly shiny cap, so different and tended, she must now be a girl with a different life. The woman handed her a rigid plastic mask with a handle which she told Pauline to hold in front of her face as she dredged her with choking spray. Now, when Pauline shook her head, her hair stayed behind.

Progressing from the chair to the till, shedding clipped hair from the sickly pink cape that was untied and taken from her at the door, Pauline flinched from being looked at, despite the unfamiliar approval in the attention. She could feel the way the hairdresser was soaking it up, as though she'd done something fantastic. She paid the money, worrying it wouldn't be enough, or that some other disaster might befall her, born of her ignorance. But all was well.

'See you, love,' said the stylist, and squeezed Pauline's shoulder. Pauline could feel tears starting, along with the strong impulse to shout at her to fuck off, so she ran. Her hair didn't move. She touched it, its alien surface. She wasn't herself. But this was exhilarating now it was just her, instead of all those cows in the salon. She headed for the school, knowing she could brazen it out about the form, marvelling that she'd worried about it at all when she could just lie and say she'd lost it, the way she lied about everything else.

'My little brother got hold of it and tore it like,' she improvised, faced with the sharp-edged woman who had asked her a lot of questions at the audition. There was a different atmosphere at the school, lots of people hurrying around, vans parked transgressively in the playground with blokes manhandling metal poles and coils of wire out of them. She'd been found by accident as she hovered at the gates, paralysed by all the activity. A fat woman was herding a group of kids Pauline recognized from school, and added Pauline to them to be brought to Julia, which was the spiky one's name.

'We won't be able to use you if we haven't got permission from your mum and dad.'

'They're away.'

'Both of them?'

'Miss, me dad's dead, Miss, and me mum's away working.'

Julia sighed. 'Who's looking after you then?'

'Me nan, Miss.'

Julia checked her watch, which looked full of gold. She reached for a new form and handed it to Pauline.

'You'll have to ask your nan to fill it in, darling.'

'Miss, she can't read, Miss.'

As she said it, it struck Pauline that this was probably true. Julia's beringed hand hovered over the form in a stay of execution.

'What did you say your name was?'

When she told her, Julia checked a list, which made her sigh again but also persist in taking up the form. Pauline's name had, surprisingly, made a difference.

'Well, we'll fill in the form for you, and you can get your nan to sign her name or make her mark, OK?'

She further explained that making her mark meant putting a cross where her signature was supposed to be, then asked various questions whose answers she blocked out herself in neat capitals where the spaces appeared. Then she sent her away. Pauline couldn't believe her luck. Julia had told her to be quick, but she knew she'd be suspicious if she came back in five minutes, so she took a long tour of the Town Fields before coming back with the cross she'd written herself with a ballpoint lifted from one of the chaotic classrooms. Julia scrutinized the piece of paper, and her, and Pauline could see in the rake of her eyes that she'd guessed what she'd done and decided not to care. The form went with a stack of other forms, and she was chivvied into a first-year class-room which had been taken over to do make-up.

When they were told this, Pauline was hopeful that she would be given proper make-up, like Joanne wore, with pencilled eye-brows and blackened eyes. But all they seemed to be doing was sponging some stuff on to the children's faces which made them look more themselves.

'Can I have some eyeshadow?' she asked the woman who was doing her. The woman laughed, and said no.

As usual, none of the children spoke to her. It was boring in the classroom, and hot. They were provided with cups of overdiluted squash and biscuits in generous platefuls that disappeared in a

scrum for the creams and chocolate ones, which Pauline domin-
ated. She settled down with her *Tammy*, which she had been
clutching rolled up all morning. She didn't usually read comics;
it had been seeing Gemma with one, that day Gemma's mum had
screamed at her to leave Gemma alone, that had made her decide
to buy it. She flicked through the drawn pages, uncompelled.
They all seemed to be stories that had started some time before,
and Pauline found them confusing. There were girls in leotards
and on skis, or falling out with each other at posh schools. The
speech, from signs pointed from their mouths, took some getting
used to as well. But she enjoyed the act of reading the comic, of
being like Gemma, who loved them, who was recognizably like
one of the black-and-white girls being sabotaged at a gymkhana.
She turned the pages self-consciously.

'Fuck off, blackie.'

Cynthia was huddling over her, trying to nick a read. Pauline
pushed her in the face, skewing her glasses, and she immediately
shrank away. Their chaperone, the fat woman from the playground, looked up sharply, but Pauline's comic-holding gaze
was irreproachable, and Cynthia, she knew, never complained.
She didn't even move away from the range of Pauline's casually
swinging crossed leg, which repeatedly caught her on the thigh
as Pauline continued the pretence of reading.

Still, it was a relief when they finally called them to the set. This
word, 'set', was bandied about between the chaperone and the
make-up women and the bloke who came to call them. Pauline
had no idea what it meant, where they would be going, beyond
the sense of a vast and glamorously alien arena. So she didn't
realize for some minutes after they were led up to the fourth-year
classroom, noticeably altered but essentially familiar, that this
was their final destination. This was the set.

'Let's be having you, ladies and gentlemen!' said a spotty bloke
with stinking breath.

He told them to sit at the desks, ranged differently from usual at one end of the classroom. The other end was cramped with people and equipment and huge, blinding lights. The bloke glanced beyond the glare to ask where they were wanted as he led them by the arm, one by one. Squinting, Pauline could see the man who had asked her loads of questions that time before. His eyes slid past her as he indicated a desk off to the right. The arrangement didn't take long. But then there was a catch in the proceedings as the director (she remembered him being introduced as this) halted and conferred with stinky-breath bloke, who swiftly left the room. They all sat at their desks. At each place was an exercise book and a pencil. Pauline turned the pages of the book and was interested to see that it contained another child's writing and drawings for the first few pages before it went blank. The writing was sinisterly neat and appeared to have been copied from a book about the solar system, although the drawings were of plants. Before she could investigate further, a harassed-looking woman with spare pencils stuck into her shaggy hair slammed her hand on the book and told her to leave it alone. Since she then returned to chalking numbers on the blackboard, Pauline assumed she was the teacher, although her manner was unusual. The bad-breath man came back through the door, looking fraught, and went to talk to the director, whose eyes swept Pauline and the other children.

'Where is she then?'

Julia had come into the classroom. She also looked fraught. She was carrying a sheet of paper, which she consulted as she scrutinized their group, desk by desk, standing next to the director. Her thumb clamped a name as she locked on to Pauline.

'Pauline Bright?'

'Yes, Miss.'

There was a tiny power cut of relief between Julia, the director, and the man with bad breath. Julia walked up to her, followed by the men. Pauline assumed her meekest expression.

'What's happened to your hair?' asked Julia. She sounded surprisingly gentle.

'I had it done, Miss.'

Julia and the director exchanged looks, the director smiling with no amusement. He crouched down so that his head was slightly lower than Pauline's. She expected him to speak, but he just contemplated her hair. Then he stood, abruptly.

'That's a shame.' He said it to Julia, not her. She could tell that although she'd definitely done something wrong, Julia was going to be the one blamed. Pauline watched her anger tapping out of her wizened fingers and their rings, on to the desk.

'It would have been a nice moment . . . I can live without it . . . '

'Maybe hair can do something?' Julia suggested. The three of them turned back to look at Pauline again. The director shook his head.

'It's worth a try, while you set up.'

'Tony's saying ten minutes,' offered the bad-breath man, pleased to help.

'Okay then, if you tell them no more than ten.'

Julia led Pauline out of the room and downstairs towards the first-years, where she and the other children had had their disappointing make-up done. In front of one of the blinding frames of lightbulbs that had been set up, outlining mirrors, Pauline saw a policeman. She shrank back reflexively, but Julia chivvied her past him, on to the hair woman. She, as far as was possible given the spray glueing it together, pulled her fingers through Pauline's fringe in a hopeless assessment.

'What did you put on it before, lovie?'

Pauline didn't know. She told them about her mum, and the bottle that stung. The hair woman told Julia she couldn't do anything about the colour, not in ten minutes. But she would see what else she could do.

The woman led Pauline to the sink, which Pauline remembered from washing paint brushes in the first year, and soaked her head under the awkward taps. Then she towelled her off and clawed some stuff from a jar through her damp hair. Next, she inserted a couple of hair grips more or less where Pauline put them when she was taming her fringe, although now it had been cut it had to be scraped back painfully to fit under the clips. Finally, she went round the rest of Pauline's ruined hair, back-combing it and ratting it with her fingers; when she got to the crown of her head she rolled the hair briskly under her palm so that it stood up, snarled and random.

'Hedge backwards,' she smiled at Pauline through the mirror. Pauline only allowed herself one look. Bar the colour, she was back to normal, but worse. Like a witch, or some kind of mad monster. Was that what she looked like? But when Julia offered her up back in the classroom, the director just grimaced and said, 'Shame,' and Pauline knew she was wrong, that she'd changed herself for the worse, and they still hadn't been able to restore her to what he wanted. She was allowed to stay, but through the long, boring hours that followed she was in the background, like everyone else. She had no idea what they had intended for her, but the disappointment gathered in her like anger, which only found a mild release in shoving Cynthia so she came down hard among the desks and put her bottom teeth into her lip. Seeing the crew cluster round the sobbing girl, Pauline instantly regretted the attention she'd created for her. They took her away to first aid, and she came back with a plaster and a bottle of cola. Lucky bitch.

As PENANCE, QUENTIN stood under the drooling shower and suffered. Mortification of the flesh. Oh man, was she mortified. She started to scour her arms and body with the midget bar of soap, but stopped when she caught herself visualizing the shot. Norman Bates was due through the shower curtain with a big old knife any minute. Come on, babe, you can do better. Shivering, she rubbed water out of her eyes. *Shit.* When would life take over and drive this damn thing for her?

She had some calls to take, at least, once the London offices opened. The LA operations didn't open until mid-afternoon, although Quentin knew no one really gave a small damn for her field reports. Well, this time it would be different. This time she would almost certainly have something to say about the miserable idea of luring Lallie to Hollywood. Stepping out of the shower, her hungover brain careened in her skull no matter how tenderly she moved her head, a ball of pressure that flared into a sullen pain whenever it collided with its cave of bone. Who drank brandy? Not even cognac, an ascot-and-red-setter kind of enhancement of the mood, but the crap the hotel bar had to offer, which was called 'Three Barrels' – Hugh had joked about this, *Ah, I see they serve Three Barrels* – in needy double-snifters. To get out of it, so she wouldn't notice herself.

Well, it had worked. Her memory after about the third barrel was impressionistic. There had been an interlude talking to herself in the washroom cubicle, informing herself that she was drunk, as the wallpaper revolved around her. Jump cuts. The alarming hotel carpet. Same carpet on the stairs. The small surprise of Hugh's room, and the familiarity of foreplay. We're on that train now. Circumcised, which she hadn't expected, his cock as wholesome and substantial as the rest of him. The blow job, its counter-rhythm increasing hell for her spinning head, and the dawning of irritation about its longevity. *Okay, just come now, okay?* She had persisted until she could feel herself about to gag. She'd made every move in her fellatio repertoire and apart from anything else was a little insulted that he was holding out on her. What was wrong with the guy? In the end, he caught her shoulders and pulled her away, benignly. She puked in his bathroom. An unforgettable evening of sensual delights, in three barrels.

She wasn't clear how she had ended up back in her own room. Hugh must have done the gentlemanly thing, Jimmy Stewart-style, although she could find only one shoe by the bed. *There are rules about that kind of thing.* Quentin checked her memory: the rest was silence. She conjured a wishful image, almost as vivid as a memory, of sharing a bed with Hugh: the calm heat of his body, his pure, astringent smell. There would almost certainly be a really fine pair of pyjamas, navy, with a discreet lighter stripe and piping round the lapels. And now she'd never know. She sobbed a little, drily, as though the alcohol had leached all the moisture from her. And also because she was watching herself again, and it didn't play.

She really couldn't do this. Not on weak coffee and aspirin alone. And she didn't even have those yet. That would have to be rectified. What she really wanted was an espresso and a joint, with a couple of Valium humming their magic beneath. And those other pills, the ones that cute but sadly married anaesthetist from LA General had introduced her to, rounding out the strings section for that full Mantovani chord of bogus well-being. The way we were . . .

Outside, beyond the door to her room, there was a sudden shuffling. Quentin recoiled. Hugh, come to reproach her. No, to upbraid her, to remonstrate with her: take your pick of stuffy, unsympathetic verbs. A newspaper appeared, sliding under the gap at the bottom of the door. Quentin's panic subsided. Just the newspaper, then. It was one of those weird British tabloids – only Hugh contrived to get the London *Times* delivered to the hotel – and Quentin barely read it, although it was faithfully shoved under her door every morning. It had close, aggressive type, and girls bizarrely flashing their tits. Today, there was a strident headline: 'Call Girl Attack'. Quentin didn't want to know. She had her own worries. One of which, she remembered, when she had a pee and wiped herself, was that she probably had cancer. Cervical cancer, surely, despite a clear PAP test in the spring. She was diseased within. *Rotten*. It had to be working inside her, and one day a gust of wind would collapse her, like a termite mound. Maybe she could get hold of her gynaecologist and get a referral to a doctor here, just to check?

Quentin moved around the room, dressing, putting on make-up. She was supposed to be meeting with Mike and Hugh to talk about an extra location Mike felt he absolutely needed. She doubted she could make it out the door, let alone sit across a table from Hugh and hold the studio's line on the budget. Not with the cancer and all. It wasn't the sex, of course not – who hadn't done things they were a little embarrassed about in their time? Quentin carefully applied some green eyeshadow, decided it looked trashy, and removed it. It was just the cancer. They'd all cut her some slack if they knew, although it might make Hugh feel a little weird to know he'd fucked, however inconclusively, someone diseased. It would freak her out if she were him. The lipstick was more of a success. Colouring herself in often helped. She yelped when the phone by her bed rang, decided not to answer it, then on the fifth ring, did.

'Hi, darling, we're waiting for you downstairs. Everything okay?'

Hugh's voice spread solidly over the words, like butter. There were several ways she could play this.

'Small fashion problem. I'll be right down.'

She seized the moment and stepped out the door, before she could think and stop herself. Her heart rate had gone up, but she was definitely breathing. She had learned not to wait for the elevator, so she set off down the stairs, and was alarmed to be hailed, a flight before the end, by Lallie's mom, with Lallie in tow.

'We've been looking for you!'

They were craning over the banister from a floor above. Quentin formed the impression of matching outfits. She continued to flee.

'I'm running late – catch you later!'

And she was out into the lobby before Katrina could reach the end of her sentence – something about plane tickets. It was probably only a short-term escape, but if she could get going with Mike and Hugh, she might be able to fend off interruption.

They were sitting around one of the low tables near the door. Hugh looked perfect in a summer suit, Mike shifty, with his shirt unbuttoned too far. The door was propped open to circulate some air, admitting instead a block of apocalyptic light. Already, at barely nine o'clock (how late was she?), it was hot. The men rose as Quentin approached. Ordinarily, there would be social kisses, *très* European, but today Quentin sketched a wave and pre-emptively dropped into her chair, not even waiting for Hugh to pull it out for her with his customary flourish. Determined to emanate angular self-control, Quentin invoked Katharine Hepburn for a blithe couple of seconds before she crashed into *The Philadelphia Story* again. *Shit.* She reached for the coffee pot.

'Allow me.'

Hugh got there first, and poured. She couldn't tell if the fine manners were his retreat, because he was always like this, wasn't he? Taking a leaf from Hugh's book, she apologized graciously to Mike for being late. Hugh held up the cream jug, the bastard.

'I take it black.'

'Sorry to interrupt—' It was Katrina and Lallie again. Hugh popped up from his chair, obliging Mike to follow. Quentin stayed put.

'I was just saying, Quentin love, I need to have a word because I'm seeing the travel agent today, like. About flying over.'

Hugh and Mike were extremely and instantly curious. Quentin would happily have ploughed Katrina in her vampirically lipsticked kisser. *Leave me alone, bitch.*

'The LA office will take care of that, you don't need to worry.'

Quentin hadn't, in fact, said anything to LA about Lallie and her mommy visiting. Her shrink, if she still had one (now there was a badly judged blow job for you), would say she was ambivalent on the matter. Genius, childhood, a mother thing: whatever it was, it was causing her a problem. But she was definitely going to fix that, right? Definitely going to talk to Clancy and tell him what she thought, even if it was two things at once. *She's perfect for the movie. We shouldn't use her for the movie.*

'But we're booking a holiday. Like you said.'

Had she said that? She must have done. Katrina looked to Lallie, a fake appeal not to upset the kid, who cooperated and looked concerned.

'Okay, well, you go right ahead with that, and I'll talk to my office about the flights, okay? Just let me know the dates . . . '

'It's the twenty-third of September till the—'

'We kind of have to get going on this, Katrina, could I catch you later?'

'Why don't I . . . '

Hugh intervened with his handsome notebook and silver pencil, transcribed dates. *Take it away, Jeeves.* Mike smirked at her, lying low. Quentin wondered why she disliked him so much, then glimpsed his exposed chest hair and was reminded. He flourished the extra script pages at her, which she took, concentrating on the yellow paper so that Katrina would get the message.

It was a bare half page. Lallie's character, before she meets Dirk's weirdo, is exploring a derelict house. After a few rooms she happens on a teenage couple having sex. The boy catches her watching, exchanges 'a look' with her, they continue. Quentin read it twice.

'We have a fantastic location,' Mike told her. 'There's an old bomb site near the place we were shooting the car scenes.'

'Was this the writer, or you?'

'I managed to squeeze it out myself – can't you tell from the typos? No dialogue . . .'

'See you then –'

Katrina was moving off, with Lallie. Quentin was gratified to see she looked tentative. She realized Katrina had never witnessed her doing anything really connected with her job before. She probably thought she was just some chick, like her, hanging around the set and making nice.

'Bye, hon!' Quentin smiled, prepared to be friendly now they were going.

The woman and girl dissolved into the sunshine. Hugh sat. Mike continued to talk.

'I was just looking round it the other day when we wrapped, and it's so perfect. It could be such a powerful scene because we know then exactly where she's come from, that she's alone, and her milieu isn't innocent, and she's curious . . . '

'Half a day?' Quentin asked, brutally.

'At least half, I'd say.'

Mike started at Hugh's intervention. Quentin could see he'd been expecting support.

'If you're going into every room,' Hugh pointed out.

'We're not lighting it, except for the sex,' said Michael.

Quentin ignored this. 'You'll still need a second unit, unless you really want to be in on the action,' she said. 'I mean the *action* action.'

She neither looked Hugh's way nor blushed. Adults could casually refer to sex in conversations, particularly when in Europe.

'I'd prefer to do it myself,' said Mike. 'We were talking about scheduling it in on Sunday.'

'Aren't there union rules about working on days off?' Quentin asked. 'Isn't it called overtime?'

'Double bubble,' said Hugh, mysteriously. Then, to Mike, 'You've got to think about Lallie as well, Mike – they take a dim view of her working on her days off.'

Mike slumped, sulking. Where his hectic shirt gaped, Quentin got an unwelcome view of flaccid pink man-nipple.

'I just think it's a scene we're really going to miss when we get to the edit, if it's all the big bad man taking the little girl. Katrina will turn a blind eye, you know what she's like, especially if you bung her, I don't know, fifty quid.'

Hitching his trouser legs to prevent creasing, Hugh leaned forward in his chair and steepled his fingers low between his open legs, as though cradling the large, fragile sphere of Mike's ego. 'I have a suggestion.'

He'd worked it all out: they could use the school. Mike began to object, but Hugh fended him off until he'd got to the end. The fucking couple (necking and fondling perhaps, instead) could be the teacher (no extra actor fees) and another teacher used in a playground scene (non-speaking, a genuine bargain). They'd tag the scene on to the end of a day already in the schedule – no extra set-up, job done, time and money saved. Then, before Michael could voice his artistic objections, Hugh segued into his opinion that this would perhaps be a less conventional and more unexpected view of adult sexuality, compared with the humping teenagers, which he felt as though he'd seen – and he appealed to Quentin here – before. Oh, Christ, he was good. Why hadn't he come? It was the least she could do.

'I love what you've got here, Mike,' said Quentin, with maximum sincerity. 'This is just a way to build on it. Because what you gain with the teachers is the girl seeing kind of adult authority compromised by, uh, sexuality. The violation of a really crucial boundary. Which helps with the Dirk stuff, maybe.'

This took all of them by surprise. She appeared to be talking Mike's language. Fluent artistic bullshit. Who knew?

'Why would she see them,' asked Mike, as a last resort. 'In the school?'

'She drops something, leaves something, goes back for it . . . '

Hugh suggested Mike sit with it until the end of the day, when extra pages would have to be issued. Quentin admired the provision of this small pit stop for Mike's dignity. By now Mike's driver was hovering in the dazzling doorway, ready to take him to the set, so they said their goodbyes. Alone, Quentin and Hugh sat back and exchanged smiles of professional complicity.

'What a team,' said Hugh.

Then Quentin had another thought. It came on her like nausea. Three barrels.

'Wait up, hasn't he railroaded us anyway? We'll still have to pay overtime on that shooting day, even if it isn't Sunday and a whole different set-up and all.'

'Darling . . . '

Of course, what kind of schmuck was she? It was a set-up: Mike and Hugh waiting for her, the boys together. The pages were the pup they'd sold her so she'd jump at the second option, which was actually their first. She could imagine the conversation, Hugh's languid assurances that he could play her, she was crazy about him, poor girl . . . Quentin's father took over.

'We don't have room in the budget to go over, you know that, not even a couple hours. We're really not going to move on that, Hugh, I mean the guys in the studio. No deal. It happens, it's coming out of your pocket somewhere, okay? Or you can talk to the Wops and see if they're feeling generous.'

He palmed that hair of his. Had he gone into detail with Mike? Mike would love the detail, she knew. Fucking shitty bastards. You put a guy's cock in your mouth, he thinks he can put his cock in your mouth.

'Oh, absolutely. Received and understood, darling. But as long as Mike sees it's in the schedule, he's happy, and we know that makes everyone else happy. When it comes to it, I very much suspect it'll drop off the end of the day, don't you?'

God knows, she wanted to believe him. He was another producer after all, one of her tribe, on her side, the side of restraint. If it was true, she could be herself again, maybe. She ventured a look straight at him. Right here, right now, Quentin knew she needed to take something for this goddamn hangover. He gave her the old Hugh smile, the one you could eat with a spoon. She couldn't make any calls before she felt better, that was for sure.

I GO TO see my dad the day I know Pauline is meeting Lallie. I walk out of the door, telling Mum and Ian that I'm going out to play, and keep walking all the way back to our real house. I don't catch the bus. I want to feel the distance. Getting to our street, fear clenches that the house won't be there, that I'm walking in a dream that is going to turn bad, but of course the house is itself, unchanged. Dad still lives there. If everything was normal, I would have approached from the backs and gone through the garden gate and in through the kitchen door, which is the one everyone uses, but because nothing can ever be the same again I take the longer route to the official street, with its parched gardens, and knock at the front door. There is a bell, but as far as I know it has never rung.

It's Thursday afternoon, which is Dad's half day from work. Sure enough, his face appears from behind the frosted glass of the porch, sleepy and wary. He is pleased to see me, I think, although there is the briefest moment of some large and unfamiliar emotion before he builds on his usual expression and ruffles my hair and one-handedly hugs me so that I tip into his tummy, almost non-existent after Ian's.

'What's this in aid of then? Does your mum know you're here?'

Since I don't want to lie, I ignore the question.

'Can I come in?'

Inside, the house is dark and cool and, even I can see, much more untidy than it ever was before. We go towards the kitchen. Everything is the same, and everything is different. When Dad sits down I see he is wearing his usual slippers, but no socks. His cigarette is burning in a saucer, a long worm of ash. There's a nearly empty milk bottle next to his tea mug, with a sequence of slimy yellowish rings showing the bottle has been kept out of the fridge. A few old papers on the floor. A mangled packet of butter next to the empty metal dish, ordered by mum from a catalogue, whose scrape against the knife has always made him wince. I stay leaning into him as he inhales his cigarette, inhaling him. He hasn't shaved, and the stubble is grizzled white and grey. I sandpaper my fingers against it in devotion. He almost laughs. Uneasy.

'You haven't run away, have you?'

I immediately wish that I had. It's hard to speak, now. I burrow my face into his neck.

'Eh, come on. You'll start me off.'

I manage to breathe, but the end of each long breath produces a sob somewhere in my abdomen. We could stay like this forever. Dad pats my back to warn that he's going to move me away from him, but I refuse to take the cue. I burrow deeper, cling.

'It's not that bad, is it?'

I shake my head, furious with myself. I don't want to be a baby.

'Just, just wanted to see you.'

'Do you want a drink of squash?'

Glad to be busy, he makes me a cup of lemon barley from the same bottle I was drinking at the beginning of the summer. As he runs the water to get it cold, I read the paper where it's open on the table.

'What's a claw hammer?' I ask, imagining an animal claw sprouting from the metal, shredding scalp and skin. Dad moves the paper away, on the pretext of giving me the squash. But it's too late to stop me seeing the photo of the woman who's been killed, staring emptily at the camera. She has striped hair and cruel eyebrows. You can always tell in photos that someone is dead. They go blurry.

'You shouldn't be reading that.' He puts the paper on top of the dirty pots on the draining board.

'What's a vice girl?' I ask.

'Bloomin' 'eck, Missis . . . a lady who isn't very nice. How are you getting on at school then?'

'We've finished. On Friday.'

'Lucky you!'

He leans back against the sink, ankles crossed and hands spread behind him, clamping the Formica in a cowboyish way I recognize and didn't know I missed till now. We're not used to talking for its own sake.

'I saw Lallie Paluza,' I tell him.

'Oh aye?'

His lack of interest isn't sharp, like Mum's.

'She's dead small.'

'Did you get her autograph?'

I shake my head. He doesn't get it. People who ask for autographs aren't the same as people who become friends of famous people. If I asked her for an autograph, I'd always be rubbish, like a little sister but worse.

'Ooh, reminds me . . . '

He uncrosses his ankles and goes out of the room, returning quickly with a book of some kind, which he hands to me.

'They're giving them away at the garage. You collect them.'

It's not a book but an album full of empty discs that you put coins in. The coins are silver and look like money but have footballers on them, Leeds United. This is Dad's team and mine. Although I'm not really interested in football, he and I have spent many Sunday afternoons with me on his knee watching matches, drowsy with roast beef and Yorkshire pud, while Mum does the washing-up. For his sake I have learned the names of some players, and the fact that there is a goalie and a centre forward. Billy Bremner is already in the album, and handsome Norman Hunter. I only recognize them from the names printed below, because their outlines are cartoonish and not nearly as good as the Queen's on proper money.

'They give you the wotsits when you get petrol. I've got some more in the car.'

'Thanks.'

I want to cry again, but try not to for Dad's sake. He never gives me things usually. Even Christmas presents, I know because Mum has told me, are her job.

'Why don't I get them, and I'll run you back to your mum.'

He gets the little plastic bag out of the glove compartment as I sit in the passenger seat. I press the new trio of players one by one into their rightful places. The coins are oddly light.

'You're supposed to be going on holiday, aren't you?'

I'm having a bit of trouble with Gary Sprake. There's an extra bit around his rim and he keeps popping out of his circle.

'We're going to Spain.'

I don't tell him about Butlin's and the shame and sadness of my failed audition. I piggle away the spare bit and Gary Sprake goes in. Dad's got a cigarette on the go, like he always does when he drives. It's part of steering: the transfer of fag to mouth whenever he needs a full grip to go round corners, the squint against the wasted smoke. He tips ash when we stop at lights and I can feel him looking at me whenever he does it. That bit is new. He's never looked at me before.

'Will you get any more?'

'Aye, they give you them when you get petrol. I'll save them for you.'

There are six players left to get. It'll be a reason to see him. Maybe there are more teams, even. I've always liked the purple and blue of West Ham's shirts.

'Thanks.'

I slide my eyes up to him. Everyone says I've got his eyes, even Mum. She used to like that. He's got good eyes, Dad. There's usually a joke sitting in them when he does really look at you.

'Can I stay with you?'

He takes his fag back between his fingers on the wheel. In the car he smokes left-handed because of the ash tray, and it makes him awkward.

'I don't mean all the time, I mean instead of going on holiday. You wouldn't have to do anything, I could get your tea and stuff when you're at work.'

It's heady and sudden. I see myself alone in the house, making it like it used to be. Arranging chocolate mini-rolls on plates, setting the table.

'Ah, well, I don't know about that, love. You're best off with your mum.'

It's just like the way he always slides away when you hug him. If I start crying now I'll never ever stop. I hold the Leeds United album so tightly its corners dig into my palms.

These are the things I love about my dad. His cured tobacco smell; the delicate colours of the embossed sailor in its life-ring on his cigarette packet; the dip in his chest he says is there to hold the vinegar for his fish and chips; the way he says 'Hello, Gemma Barlow' whenever he sees me; the fact he has a wash and shave every night before nine o'clock telly starts; his orange summer shirt with the check; the sour lemon face he pulls, twitching one eye, if you forget to put the three sugars in his tea or even to stir them in enough.

Ian answers the door, not Mum. Dad pushes me forward. There's an invisible balloon wall between Dad and Ian, and they can't look at each other. I have to cross between them, through the balloons, to get to my new life. I'm dreading what Mum will say. Against Ian, Dad's wiriness looks puny. He nods a goodbye to me and escapes back to the car.

Inside the house, feelings swirl around like the black marks on the weather map on telly. Mum is cross with me, but also excited. Ian isn't cross, but he's upset. They tell me off for going into town without saying anything, although I can't see how it's different from me taking the bus to school like I've been doing for weeks. I try to point this out, but it goes down badly. All sorts could happen, they say. Bad men. While they have a go at me, Mum's weather front disentangles itself from Ian's, and I see that she's angry about me seeing Dad, and Ian's more angry about the bad men. As soon as I've worked this out, they collide into something new:

'It has to stop, Gemma, all this.'

All this what? I don't say it. I'd get a slap.

'Fighting at school, defying me—'

'I'm not defying you!'

'You see?'

Mum flips a what-did-I-tell-you look at Ian. Pretend helpless.

'Your mother does everything for you, young lady. You should appreciate her more. You only get one mother, let me tell you that.'

Ian's eyes, horribly, are soft with actual tears. Mum squeezes his hand.

'You see? You're upsetting Ian.'

She squeezes his hand again. 'Anyway . . . '

And then they tell me. Next year, when school starts in September, I'll be going to the private school, Hill House. Mum tells me it's hundreds of pounds a term, and Ian will be paying for it because he loves me and thinks it's important I get a good education, away from the rough children, children like Pauline Bright. Ian nods, tremendously.

There's a uniform as well, which he'll also be buying. It includes a hat and everything, like a girl in a comic. All my life I've seen those boys and girls, in their brown blazers with the yellow trim, like banana toffees, the boys in their caps and the girls in their brimmed hats. Matching brown macs if it's raining, brown socks that never fall down, heavy shoes from before there was fashion. *Hill House*, Mum has whispered, and I've known those boys and girls are better than me because they're more expensive. And now I'll be one of them. I can't work out if this is meant to be a punishment, in which case I'm not supposed to show my pleasure. At least I'm sure I'm expected to demonstrate gratitude. I cushion myself into Ian's middle and squeeze, me who so recently was cuddling up to Dad's sparseness. It feels odd.

'Nothing's too good for you and your mum,' Ian says, still tearful.

The socks are brown too, with a cuff ringed in yellow. I wonder if you play all those games in books, hockey and lacrosse, instead of netball and rounders. I know that Lallie goes to a stage school when she's not working, where she has to wear a uniform nearly as splendid.

'I'm sorry.'

'That's better,' says Mum.

I'm careful to help Mum with the washing-up after tea. When I'm scraping shepherd's pie into the pedal bin (which I enjoy operating), I see Ian's belt in there, too late to stop the slurry of mince and potato fouling its jazzy brightness. I had thought that the strangeness of our thank-you hug was in its comparison to Dad, but I realize now the missing sensation of that metal rectangle that always divides Ian's top half from his bottom, digging into you when he squeezes.

'Ian's belt's in the bin.'

'Don't be daft.'

Mum doesn't even turn round from the sink.

'It is!'

'What belt?'

I point with the fork I'm holding. Mum turns round with rubber gloves aloft, like a surgeon in a medical programme. She peers. Then she calls to Ian round the open-plan.

'What are you doing, chucking your belt out?'

'It's had it.'

'If the buckle's gone, I could get it stitched for you. It's proper leather that.'

'I've had it years, Suzanne. It's gone.'

It doesn't look old or broken, winking out from the mince. But Ian's got a lot of money to spend, on himself as well as Mum and me. Not like Dad. You can't spend the coins from the garage he gave me. When, at bedtime, I prise them from the album and heap them in a meagre pile on the pillow, it's impossible not to know they're actually plastic.

THE WALLPAPER DIDN'T match the paint on the woodwork, on the skirting. Skirting – was that right? How did she know that? Did skirting even exist where she came from? Summoning rooms from all the houses she had lived in, Quentin saw walls that ended without interruption, at the floor. These walls were usually white, the floors, wood. Maybe it was a Brit thing, this skirting? And yet, she knew the term. Go figure.

The junction she now knew intimately went like this: bobbled brown carpet, edged up against said skirting, but not fitting with exact snugness; pink skirting, with a chip the size of a baby's fingernail revealing the multi-coloured strata of previous paint jobs; wallpaper. That wallpaper, now that was a piece of work. Actually, several misaligned pieces of work. Brown, of course, but so much more. Crimson, white, beige, black. And all in flowers, vast Swinburnian blooms decadent with, well, Quentin was tempted to name it despair. Even with all the colours bleached by moonlight and street light, their busyness still hummed, like crickets in a box.

She went back to the skirting. Some time during the last long hours Quentin had made the acquaintance of two snail-trails of paint there, petrified in an unequal race to the floor. Their doomed inertia made her sad, and she enjoyed the sadness for a while. But then the drips led her to think of the man who had painted the skirting, who hadn't bothered to wipe his brush of excess paint, and that expanded into thinking of all the useless human agency implied in the room, which made her agitated rather than sad, and from that she progressed to pondering the volume of people who passed through, who slept in the bed, whose skin cells and stains were a sheet and a pillowcase away, and this freaked her out so much she had to turn on the lamp and get up.

How did Hugh sleep, if he took these things all the time? Oh, of course. One to make you bigger, one to make you small. He could have offered a Valium into the bargain. A true gentleman would have, wouldn't he? Maybe he didn't want to look too professional or something. Like a junkie. God, no. *'Is there anything I can get you, darling?'* She slaked her dry mouth with the water from the bathroom tap, which tasted as though it had been wrung out from dirty cotton wool. Quintessence of dust. More frigging skin cells. She spat the mouthful into the sink.

Quentin doubted that Hugh's little helpers exposed him to the horror of the skin cells and the failure – if they did, maybe whatever else he took cancelled that out. Unlike her, he was all action. 'Pep pills' he had called them. It was all her fault. She got back in bed and almost immediately got out again. It was rising six o'clock.

She dressed and left her room. The hotel's skeleton staff was still running from the night shift. Quentin hadn't been up this early before, so all the faces were unfamiliar. It was weird, seeing different people in the same burgundy uniform. The manager was no longer a plump middle-aged woman but a cadaverous bald man in his sixties. He had yellow skin and wore half-glasses to peer at his stale newspaper (did you save the newspaper all day if you worked the night shift?). As she came through the lobby, he nodded at her as though he knew her. Maybe they talked, him and his alter ego.

'Early bird.'

Quentin pulled up. It was Katrina. She was sitting in one of the lobby armchairs, smoking herself awake. Make-up full but fractionally awry, as though the stencil had wobbled. Or maybe her face wasn't quite up to it yet.

'Catches the worm!' Quentin heard herself say.

'Early call,' Katrina explained. 'I like to leave Lallie till the last minute, but I need a bit of time to get myself ready.'

And now Quentin was cornered. Couldn't she pretend she was on her way somewhere? Maybe, but then she'd end up completing a fake circuit by returning to her room, just her and the skirting for another couple of hours. Perhaps here, she could get away for a little. Perhaps she could be the good listener everyone assumed she was. And anyway, the car would be coming for Katrina and the kid really soon. How bad could it be?

'We booked the tickets to America.' Katrina's inhalation was famished. She wasn't going to help, then. 'Madam's so excited!' The smoke dragoned out for an inch before she sucked it back into her nostrils. Quentin had never been able to do that. It looked cool *and* grown-up. 'I've told her, nothing's settled, they're just having a look at you, hen – there's probably a lot of American girls who've done a lot more and are a lot prettier they'll be seeing and all.'

'Maybe best to see it as a holiday,' said Quentin. Katrina's make-up spasmed.

'Don't they want her then?'

'I mean, for Lallie. Take a little of the pressure off.'

'Oh, she loves all that, don't you worry.' Katrina tapped the ashless cigarette on the ashtray rim, her gaze clamped on Quentin. 'I mean, if she doesn't stand a chance I'd never have booked – it's a lot of money for us, like – but you mentioned the film and that.'

'I'm sure it'll all work out.' *Like it worked out when I fucked Hugh, who can go for ever, if that's your thing, because his dick is numb with bennies or whatever quaint Brit phrase he prefers to use. Not my fault, right?*

'Is your – is Lallie's father coming with you?'

'Aye, for a week. He can't get time off work, you see.'

Quentin caught Katrina's curious look at her arms, which she appeared to be scratching. She appeared to be embracing herself and scratching her arms so that red track marks appeared on her tan. She forced herself to stop.

'To be honest,' Katrina said, 'even if he could get the time, I don't think our Graham would come along for the audition and that. He finds it dead boring – feels like a spare part, he says.'

She rolled her eyes reflexively, the same way she did whenever she talked of Lallie feeling anything. What a bitch. Not an alpha bitch, which demanded at least some kind of energy or imagination, just your regular, cold Little League bitch. The world was full of these people, as cool and impermeable as a collection of vases. Standing together in arrangements, some sporting flowers so you thought life was there, but the flowers were cut and dead and didn't have roots. *Like Hugh.*

Quentin recognized the come-down, or even its aftermath, the disconnect after all that directionless excitement. *Greetings, old pal.* He shouldn't have given her two – what was he thinking, in fact, to have given her one, even? *In loco parentis*, didn't that count for something? I mean, he didn't know she'd chosen him to be her daddy, but still.

'Do you want a cup of coffee?'

They'd brought Katrina an extra cup with her pot: the hotel only recognized the pot-of-coffee-for-two or the inadequate lone cup. She poured for Quentin.

'It's just, you said about the book so we thought – Frank said you'd had a word with him about it as well.'

Frank?

'You know, her manager, bless him.'

Quentin kept her arms by her side and cranked herself up. It looked like there was nothing else for it, now the deed was very much done. 'Absolutely. It's a project we're very excited about. And we're very excited about Lallie. But it's all about finding a good fit, and you can't always tell that straightaway.'

That sounded okay, right? Any normal person would see the get-out clause right there. It wasn't like she'd started something she couldn't finish. And how was she to know that Katrina would be so hot to trot, would actually get off her ass and do something? Okay, that she should have known.

'I never thought – you don't, do you? Your little girl a film star.'

Quentin ached to slap her, to leave a good red mark like the marks she'd left on her own arms. Scratching would be very satisfying, clawing down past that base and blush and powder, into the flesh. Into the dumb ambition, doing it damage. That would be mighty fine.

Talk of the devil.

'Talk of the devil . . . '

Katrina stretched an arm to Lallie, who fitted herself into it, yawning.

'What's happened to your hair?'

It rose, wayward and unbrushed. Lallie palmed her eyes. 'Couldn't find the comb.'

Katrina squeezed her restraining hand to prompt Lallie into recognition of Quentin.

'Morning.'

'Hasn't woken up yet.'

Lallie dawdled, while Katrina ordered a glass of milk from Count Dracula at the desk. Some of the day staff had started to arrive. A huge porter who had once come to look at Quentin's shower (and he really had only looked, before announcing there was nothing wrong with it) hustled through the lobby, distributing fresh newspapers, whistling as he fanned them on tables. Watching Lallie watch him, Quentin saw that this was her moment: she could lay it out for the kid right now. *Get away from your mom, your life depends on it.*

Lallie picked up the nearest newspaper, one of the comic-book ones, which splashed on a hooker murder, or 'call-girl slaying', as it quaintly preferred. Katrina batted the paper from her hand as she returned to the table. It was too late.

'You don't need to be reading that.'

'Why not?'

'You just don't. It isn't nice.'

Katrina returned it, expertly, to the display. 'Here's your milk.'

'I told you, I don't want any milk.'

But the kid took it, and cleared half the glass.

'Feels sick otherwise,' Katrina told Quentin. 'Something to do with getting up so early, isn't it, hen?'

Lallie staggered, imitating someone in an old movie pretending to be shot. She was back in the room – the hit of milk had revived her. Before Katrina could reach her with a napkin, she swiped away the moustache and wiggled her eyebrows at Quentin, giving her a momentary Groucho. Katrina had to content herself with evening up one side of her daughter's T-shirt, which had caught in the waist of her jeans. Instead of pulling herself away, as Quentin had often seen her do, Lallie caught Katrina's hand and kissed it, then laid it against her cheek, finding an exact fit. It was clearly a gesture almost as old as Lallie.

'Always works, doesn't it, hen, a little bit of milk?'

It wasn't so simple, Quentin saw. *Mommy knows best.* Lallie hopped into her mother's lap, huge against her, a hermit crab on the verge of outgrowing its shell. Katrina objected, while gathering the kid into her. Whatever that meant, Quentin really did have to make the *A Little Princess* call, later that same long day. Clancy was chasing her, and it was time for her to justify her existence. Heads you win, tails you're fucked. *It won't cut it, Quentin. You've got to do something.* Didn't Hugh, now you mention it, have some stake in keeping the kid in the country? Some project he'd got brewing, with all that energy of his? 'I'm not sure we're going to let you take her away.' That's what he had said. Maybe that was a plan: she could make it all his fault, keep Lallie away from Hollywood while looking like she had given her all to get her there. Yeah, because that was the kind of girl she was – always with the moral victory, whatever the personal cost. *Loser, loser, welcome to Loserville . . .*

Quentin finished her coffee and smiled her smile. Lallie had her thumb jammed in her mouth, back to parody. Katrina twitched her hand away.

'Nutter.'

No one bothered with the papers at Adelaide Road, a world already chaotic enough with event and titillation. The TV was usually on, but the news came and went, so it wasn't until coppers visited the house that anyone knew. Dave's mate Black Baz had knocked off a lorry depot the previous night, and there was celebratory cider and weed: they'd given Gary some of the weed, and it had sent him a bit mental, in a hilarious way. Pauline herself had got the giggles, Nan had passed out. It was the closest they came to a party, although there wasn't a record player, so they'd put the TV on top volume instead for atmosphere.

It was *Playschool* when the coppers turned up. They'd been knocking and ringing for ages, but because of the noise they couldn't make themselves heard, so the first anyone knew of their arrival was when they barged into the living room, where Gary was running round with no trousers trying to bite his own willy, like a puppy snapping at its tail, encouraged by laughter. Of course, everyone thought the coppers were there for the pot, or the noise, and Black Baz made a run up the stairs, but neither of the coppers went after him. There were two of them: Taylor and Reeves. Taylor was an old hand, they all knew him. Pauline had heard him say he spent more time at theirs than at home. Reeves was younger. He had recently come from Sheffield, and looked mardy. The first thing he did was turn off the TV, while Taylor advised Dave that if there were any 'marijuana cigarettes' in the room he'd better get rid of them while he was looking the other way. This took about five years: something strange had happened to time. Pauline felt as though she was zipped into a sleeping bag, tucked up. She watched Taylor crouch to wake up

Nan, his vast arse slowly raising the vents in his uniform tunic. It was hilarious. She knelt with her face on the settee cushions, laughing herself stupid.

It all took years and years, talking to Nan, getting through to her, showing her a Polaroid picture, waking her a bit more, having to shout. In the end they looked for Dave, who had gone off. Pauline was surprised, in a dull way, when he actually came back. He looked at the photo too, shook his head in automatic denial, then he looked at it again, properly.

'Get our Pauline.'

Reeves didn't seem to think this was a good idea, but Taylor decided the other way. They showed Pauline the photo while she was still laughing in bursts, like the end of hiccups. It took her a second or two to see what it was. Not a person or a place, but a shiny mass the babyshit colour of a Caramac bar. A bag, a handbag. The strap wiggled on the flat blue surface where the picture had been taken, light flaring off it in the top corner. Beneath it were ranged its innards: a pink tail comb with teeth missing, a purse, a lipstick without a top, a single key, but Pauline didn't need to see them to know. The bag was enough.

'It's me mam's.'

Before they took the Polaroid away, she saw the dark stain down one side of the plastic, ordinary as paint. They really wanted to talk to Nan now, and tried to send everyone out of the room but her and Dave. Pauline refused to go, but in the end pissface Reeves actually made her, pulling her out by the arm and blocking the door when she tried to get back, kicking and scratching, first at him, then at the scuffed paintwork. So that's how she knew. They needed Nan to go to Leeds, but she never left the house and she wasn't going to start now. Dave went instead. It was the first time he'd ever ridden in the front of a police car.

Pauline told Cheryl that Joanne was in hospital. Nan cried for the rest of the day. Pauline ran off to the Town Fields and lay on the bare yellow grass for another five years, looking into the white sky. Eventually, she dozed. When she woke, the sleeping-bag feeling had worn off. There was almost no one else around on the Fields, bar a couple of dog walkers, and the space made her alone in the world. No one had told her anything, but she knew.

August, 1975

WHEN WE GET back from Spain, it looks like a burglar's tried to break into the dormer bungalow. That's what Ian and Mum think anyway, because there are marks on the door where someone's tried to kick it in, they say, and the small window in the back kitchen is smashed, although the catch is still fastened. After Ian's paced round the garden for a bit – the suitcases are still on the drive, where the taxi driver left them – he calls Mum, and they exclaim over something. 'Disgusting' is the word they agree on, and Mum looks like she might be sick. 'Worse than an animal,' Ian says. But I think, animals poo in gardens all the time and they don't do it in a shoebox, do they? If you wanted to be like an animal, you'd just do your business there on a flowerbed, and if you wanted to be disgusting, you'd do it right in the middle of Ian's lurid lawn. Using a shoebox you've found in the rubbish (it's the one from my new holiday sandals) means you were trying to get to the toilet and didn't manage it. Maybe even smashing the window, that was all you were trying to do. If you were Pauline Bright.

The dormer bungalow is stuffy with out-of-date air. We've been away two weeks, and it feels like our life in the hotel has become the real one and this is the holiday. When I go to my room, I'm shocked to find my nightie still puddled on the floor by the bed, next to the splayed copy of *Charlotte Sometimes* I'd been reading the night before we left. Everything else is different. Two weeks until I start at Hill House. The uniform to be bought. Downstairs, Ian and Mum are checking to see if anything's been stolen, and Mum's talking about ringing the police.

If you could tell. Suncream, and where it goes. The smell of it's nice at first, then it gives you a headache in the heat.

'They'll just file a report. Paperwork,' says Ian, discouragingly, from downstairs. Then I hear him tell Mum he'll ring them after we've got ourselves settled. I wonder if I'll get shouted at if I switch on the telly, and conclude that it's probably wiser to stay in my room for a little while, not exactly doing anything to help but not visibly relaxing in front of them while they empty suit-cases and Mum loses herself in washing. I tip out the bag I've carried on to the plane, the one that Mum bought me for the Butlin's holiday with Christina that didn't happen. The thought of Lallie and the film twinges like a bad tooth I've learned to avoid. In the different holiday world, this has been surprisingly easy. I've preferred, in the heat and the newly built white façades of the hotel, to be a secret agent, like James Bond. The daughter of a diplomat, although I'm not entirely sure what a diplomat is, called Abigail. I go to a boarding school and have adventures. If Lallie was in a film like that, I'd go a million times. I'd spend all my pocket money on tickets, probably.

At the airport, I bought Christina a Spanish flamenco doll pos-ing in a plastic tube to go with the special Spanish Pez of Hong Kong Phooey I got for her in a shop while we were out one day. I got one for myself, as well – Ian insisted on paying. Mum says he spoils me rotten, but he spoils her too. On holiday he bought her a gold necklace which sits splendidly between her newly brown bosoms. It's real gold, worth hundreds of pounds, probably. Dad never buys her presents, except at Christmas. Last year he got her a hairdrier: one with a hood that inflates with air like the bottom of a hovercraft. She gave him a funny look when she unwrapped it and asked what she needed it for, since she always does her hair at the salon, and Dad said, well, this way she'd be able to dry her hair at home from now on.

I take out the other things I've been bought on holiday, scratchy with the beach sand sugaring the bottom of the bag. There's a brace-let woven out of tiny beads with my name worked into the pattern, a diddy replica of the wine skins Mum and Ian had squirted into their mouths one riotous night at the hotel – the waiter even did it to me, although I spat out the vinegary disgusting spurt of wine; a pair of castanets painted with dancers; and best of all, a knife. It's basically a miniature version of the knife Pauline and I played with on the wall downstairs, the one Pauline and I joked Ian had used to kill his good lady. It has a curved blade and a handle that looks like it's trying to be wood but Ian says is horn. It sits in a gaudy leather sheath draped with small red tassels I'm not that keen on and have tried to pull off. Unlike the knife downstairs, it's properly sharp. I've produced a few small cuts on my hands, experimentally, and it can cut paper and even wood.

I can't believe they've let me have a knife. I spotted it really early on in the souvenir shop but knew better than to ask. I didn't even want the castanets, particularly, but I hoped a collection of Spanish things might hide the acquisition of the knife. It worked perfectly, probably because it was just Ian and me in the shop that time. Mum was lying down with a migraine from sunbath-ing too long. It was the suncream day. The night of the suncream day, actually. Night in Spain goes on for hours, it's when every-one is up and about and going to shops and having drinks and ice cream and not sending their children to bed.

Suncream and where it goes. *Let me just do your back.*

In *Famous Five*, George has a penknife, and in the first book she's ten like me. It's useful in my work as a secret agent. Mum might not exactly know I've got a knife. I might not exactly have told her, because when we got back to the rooms, hers and Ian's was pitch-black and she was asleep. My smaller dread at this was engulfed by relief that she wasn't awake to force me to take the knife back to the shop. And in the end, Ian crept into their room anyway.

By the time Mum calls me down for beans on toast, all the

clothes have been sorted into piles for washing, and Ian's spoken to the neighbours about burglars. No one else has had a break-in or seen anything funny.

'It's a rum do,' says Mum. 'What makes us so special?'

When I look up, Ian is looking at me. His eyes jump away when they see mine.

'Maybe they've got wind of what you do,' she suggests. 'Working with money.'

Ian sweated all the time on holiday. I can see that clean sweat of his gathering now on his temples like condensation on a warm window, even though the kitchen isn't actually hot.

'It's not like you keep money in the house.' Mum forks her beans neatly back onto the toast. Now she looks at me. I know she'll be able to conjure Pauline Bright's name right out of my mouth. I think of all the things I've taken from Pauline, that she's given me. Surely that will get me into bad, bad trouble? Some of them have been stolen, I bet, because she's poor and can't afford proper clothes, let alone presents. Taking things that have been stolen is practically like stealing yourself.

But Mum passes over me to Ian. A bigger look. I can see he's not sure whether to talk in front of me.

'Well, maybe it's nothing to do with that.' He mounds up the food on his plate, eats and chews. 'Maybe it's closer to home.'

Mum works this out. I don't.

'He wouldn't.'

'Wouldn't he now?'

'Course not!' Mum quells some uncomfortable words, like burps, before she allows a few smaller sour ones out. 'Wouldn't have the get-up-and-go, for a start.'

'Maybe you should give him a ring.'

They're talking about Dad. Ian is talking about Dad as though he really is a burglar, as though he's a baddie. But really, Ian's taken Mum away from Dad, and that makes him the baddie. I'm living with the baddies. And since I'm definitely a goodie, that must make me their prisoner.

Suncream.

I don't hear Mum making a phone call to Dad, or even Ian ringing the police, because I fall asleep quickly from the travelling and the early start. But next morning, I wake up early and hear Ian getting ready for work and leaving without Mum getting up with him, which is unusual. I wonder if we'll go out later to get the uniform. There's only one shop in town that sells it, Cooper and Sons. I know its window but I've never been inside. Having the uniform will turn me into someone else, more like Abigail, or even Lallie. I think that will be better. But when I hear Mum's getting-up noises after two and a half chapters of *Charlotte Sometimes* and join her in the kitchen and ask, she clatters pans and says we won't be going to Cooper and Sons today.

'Will we go on Saturday then?'

'Gemma!'

That's not nagging, asking about something twice. But her tone means I'm definitely not allowed to ask about it again. I spoon up cereal, and she does the pans with her back to me. It's funny to see her washing up wearing the same kaftan thing she wore by the pool on holiday. Her legs are really brown.

'Ian and I have had a long talk.'

I wait for ages for her to say something else, but she doesn't. So as I take my milky bowl to the sink for her to wash, I ask if I can go to Christina's today to play.

'No!'

She says it as though I'm still nagging her about the uniform, as though asking to play at Christina's is the thing I've chosen to push her over the edge of unbearable exasperation. I go upstairs and cry indignantly. I want to see Christina, I want to go back to the life I had before. I call myself a goodie but I'm a receiver of stolen goods (which is a fence, I've seen it on *Cannon*), and a betrayer of my dad.

Ian might go round and punch him if he thinks he's a burglar. He might even call the police and get them to arrest him, and then I'll have to tell them I know it's Pauline, and why, and I'll be the one the police will arrest once they know about the Kit Kat and the tights. There's the guitar charm she gave me as well: I've got it in my jewellery box. She said it was from her mum but what if she was lying and she stole that too? She lies all the time. Lies and steals.

I get the charm out of my box with the drunkenly askew ballerina that used to spin, feeling frightened even at the sight of the miniature guitar, so brightly valuable. Mum's still downstairs with the washing. I go into the bathroom and wrap the charm in loads of toilet paper and flush it down the loo, slightly surprised to see it go so easily. Flushing makes me think of the poo in the shoebox, and how Mum could have told Ian why she knew so certainly it could never have been Dad in the garden. Dad could never do a poo outside in a million years. He takes ages on the toilet, he had to have an operation when I was seven. It was for his piles, but he still has difficulties, as Mum calls them. You'd only do your business in a box if you knew it was going to be quick.

I wait for the tank to refill and give the toilet an extra flush, to be on the safe side. This is risking Mum telling me off for mucking about with the toilet and wasting paper, but she's on the phone. Even though I've just got rid of the evidence, I'm terrified she's talking to the police. I listen when I come out of the bathroom, pressed close against the corner of the landing wall so she won't look up and see me. She's using her phone voice, talking about herself as though she's her own secretary, so I know it's a call to someone important. My heart beats in my ears and throat.

'My husband and I wondered if one of your agents is available to come and value the property . . .'

I don't need to hear any more. It isn't the police she's talking to at all. Despite the lie of her pretending she and Ian are married, the relief is huge.

Call sheet: 'That Summer'
August 14th 1975.
Director: Michael Keys
Director of Photography: Anthony Williams, BSC.
First AD: Derek Powell.
6.30 a.m. call.

CAST: Dirk Bogarde [COLIN], Lallie Paluza [JUNE],
Sally Moss [MRS GREAVES], Vera Wyngate [WOMAN IN
CAR].
Scenes 74, 75, 76:
LOCATION: Town Fields, Town Moor Avenue,
Doncaster.

74. **EXT. SCHOOL PLAYING FIELDS. DAY.**
JUNE is playing rounders with her school class.
COLIN watches.

75. **EXT. SCHOOL PLAYING FIELDS. DAY.**
JUNE, at one of the rounders posts, spots COLIN.
She carries on playing, but from now on she's
aware of him watching her.

76. **EXT. SCHOOL PLAYING FIELDS. DAY.**
The rounders match is dispersing. Children,
including JUNE, gather the posts and other
equipment. COLIN goes to approach JUNE but the
TEACHER [MRS GREAVES] intervenes.

                    TEACHER
Can I help you?

                    COLIN
I just wanted a word —

                    TEACHER
What about?

                    COLIN
It's none of your business —

                    TEACHER
During school hours it certainly is — do you
know this man?

                    JUNE
No, Miss.

                    COLIN
June — she's having you on.

                    JUNE
I don't know him, Miss.

                    COLIN
What are you playing at?

                    TEACHER
I think you'd better leave her alone, don't you?

She starts to lead JUNE back towards the school,
with the other children.

                    COLIN
  June!

The children and TEACHER walk on.

                    COLIN
June! [HOPELESS] How do I know her name
then, eh?

                    194

Vera's appearance wasn't even scripted – it had come to this. But Mike had decided, at the very end of the third scene, that he'd like a look from her, a connected passer-by, at Colin's impotent rage, and they'd summoned her from London. Since they had now had to stump up for a third week (her agent always negotiated for a weekly, not a daily rate, commercials apart, bless him), Vera was more than happy to get back into her headscarf and mac and settle down for the day.

It was always strange, leaving a set and coming back, like missing school and having to find your feet again. One of the make-up girls was different; Vera's favourite had already left to start on a Hammer shooting in Wales. Hugh wasn't about, and the American girl had gone off to Italy, apparently promising to be back for the wrap party. The remaining familiar make-up girl, Julie, had told Vera that before Quentin left she had approached the grip, whose name Vera had now forgotten, for downers or uppers – pills of some sort. Apparently he'd put her on to the boom operator, as a joke, because the boom (whose name she also couldn't presently recall) was the steadiest man in the business, as he had to be occupationally, and wouldn't take so much as an aspirin in case it interfered with his professional capacities.

Vera felt sad on Quentin's behalf, hearing about all this, but hadn't she said – if only to herself – that the girl was too heart-on-sleeve? She had probably been on drugs all along. It explained her clothes, for a start.

Vera established herself with her ciggie and cup of tea in a good spot, out of the way of the crew but with a view of the action. The school playing fields were part of a larger public space, the haunt of dog walkers and idlers, and, now that it was the school holidays, children. Some of their classmates were being employed to play rounders with Lallie, and word was bound to get out. But while the shadows were long, the fields remained almost empty.

It was a shame there was no one to natter to; the girl playing
the teacher had been talkative in make-up but she was needed
now, and Dirk of course couldn't be relied upon for conversation.
Anyway, Mike had buttonholed him and was talking over something to do with the scene, Dirk nodding judiciously. Everyone
felt a tiny bit off the leash, Mike included, she thought. His stammer had relaxed, for one thing. The absence of producers may
have accounted for the change in atmosphere, or it might just
have been the demob-happy rush of the last day.

Lallie's mother – what was her bloody name? – dragged a chair
next to Vera and plonked herself down in it, juggling her own tea
and fag with all the ostentation of a music-hall turn.

'That's better. You don't mind, do you?'

Vera smiled warmly and told the woman to be her guest.

'Can't believe it, me. Last day.'

Vera agreed that it was impossible to believe. The mother hud-
dled up to her tea, as though it was cold. Perhaps there was the
faintest undertow of autumn in the air compared to the previous
weeks.

'Lallie said when I got her up, Mummy, what are we going to
do tomorrow? I said, have a lie-in for a start, hen!'

Vera laughed with her, easily. 'What are you going to be doing
next?'

The woman's face jumped. 'Now you're asking.'

'She'll be rolling in offers after this. Everyone's full of how marvellous she is. Anyway, I thought they wanted her in America.'

'Aye. Well.' The mother took a furtive drag of her cigarette and
leaned into Vera, lowering her voice. 'That's what the producer
was talking to us about, Quentin . . . '

It wasn't that much of a shocker, given the vagaries of the
business. Apparently, after Quentin had given the child and her
mother some flim-flam about flying them over for screen tests,
the mother had forked out for flights herself. Then Quentin

had turned a bit elusive, and taken off for Italy before Katrina managed to pin her down about it. Katrina had heard people thought she'd started drinking.

'You don't know what's going on,' Vera reassured her. 'Anything could happen. She could lose her job if she's got a drink problem.' Unable to resist, she added, 'I heard it was drugs.'

'I wouldn't be surprised.' Katrina sizzled her fag end into her last inch of tea. 'I can't be bothered with it, to be honest. Our kid's got a contract with LWT, they want her to start shooting a Christmas special in October. I just thought we could fit it in, since she's been so mad about the States. I mean, you do it for them, don't you?'

Vera agreed that you did.

'We can't get the money back, for the plane. I asked. Looks like we'll just go on holiday, like.'

Vera accompanied Katrina's bleak gaze to where Lallie was running about with her stand-in, both of them dressed in aertex shirts and gym skirts.

'Won't get her dad's ticket back, though. Have to ask me mam to come with us instead.'

Vera saw, as the twin figures swooped and chased, that Lallie was now very slightly taller than the adult pretending to be her.

'Doesn't your husband like flying?'

'Oh, no, he's fine with flying.' Katrina toed the polystyrene cup further under her chair. 'It's me he's not keen on.'

74. EXT. SCHOOL PLAYING FIELDS. DAY.
    JUNE is playing rounders with her school class.
    COLIN watches.

The rounders match was incidental to Dirk watching in tortured fashion, so they went close in on the girls, pick-up shots really of them running, hitting the ball, calling to each other; Lallie found and then lost among the melee. Mike left it to Tony. And then it was the reverse close on Dirk. During all this, Katrina confided that her husband, Lallie's dad, liked to put it about a bit. Katrina admitted that she'd gone right off sex after having Lallie, and gave graphic details of her episiotomy scarring. She didn't feel right, down there. And she knew how squeamish he, Graham, was; he'd told her it would have finished him off to watch her give birth, not that she was asking him to. Anyway, she knew what went on when she was away with Lallie. She put on a brave face, for her. You had to, didn't you?

75. EXT. SCHOOL PLAYING FIELDS. DAY.

> JUNE, at one of the rounders posts, spots COLIN. She carries on playing, but from now on she's aware of him watching her.

Mike wanted a little track laid hugging the rounders pitch, so the camera could mimic Colin's circling while Lallie ran, post by post, to home. It was always a fiddle, laying tracks, but the ground was flat and the grass negligible, so it was no more than an ordinary fiddle. During this, Lallie came over and asked Katrina for a drink, so Katrina resumed her brave face and Vera got on a bit with the crossword. The stand-in walked the posts so that Tony could assess timings for the camera's movement along the track. Vera looked up from a bugger of a clue and was surprised by a clutch to her gut of strong feeling for Tony, so intent on getting it right. There was no one quite like him, after all.

Lallie came back from drinking a glass of squash with an orange clown-grin at the edges of her mouth, and had to be taken to make-up to remove it, with Katrina shouting at her. Once the child was back on set, mouth restored, Katrina confided that lately, things with Graham had changed. She'd had wind that there was someone in particular, if you got her drift. No one would blame him for looking elsewhere, Katrina didn't, it was as much her fault as his, with her away so much for Lallie's sake; but there was a bit on the side and there was something more serious.

'If he's moved her in, that's that,' said Katrina. 'I'm not having it. If the papers get hold of it, it'll be all over.'

'Awful,' Vera agreed.

76. EXT. SCHOOL PLAYING FIELDS. DAY.

The rounders match is dispersing. Children, including JUNE, gather the posts and other equipment. COLIN goes to approach JUNE but the TEACHER [MRS GREAVES] intervenes.

> TEACHER
>
> Can I help you?

> COLIN
>
> I just wanted a word —

> TEACHER:
>
> What about?

> COLIN
>
> It's none of your business —

> TEACHER
>
> During school hours it certainly is — do you know this man?

> JUNE
>
> No, Miss.

> COLIN
>
> June — she's having you on.

> JUNE
>
> I don't know him, Miss.

> COLIN
>
> What are you playing at?

> TEACHER
>
> I think you'd better leave her alone, don't you?

She starts to lead JUNE back towards the school,
with the other children.

After a run-through where Mike made a few adjustments, they went quickly into a take. There was a momentum now: everyone could scent the end of the day, the end of the job. On take one, the first AD spotted one of the rounders-playing children looking straight at the camera. He was castigated, and they moved swiftly on to take two.

'What about you?' asked Vera. 'Is there anybody . . . in London?'

Katrina was taking a cigarette out of her packet. 'You're joking, aren't you? Who'd want me?'

'You're an attractive woman.' Which she almost certainly would be, if she would just put down the foundation bottle.

'When would I see a feller?' asked Katrina, watching Lallie. She was checking her position with the continuity girl, whether she'd been holding the rounders bat in two hands up against her chest as she spoke or dangling it one-handed at the side. Oh, she was a pro, that one.

'Aye, aye, it's started,' said Katrina, eyeing a knot of small girls with their mothers who jigged excitedly at the margins of the action, waiting for autographs. She liked the fans, Vera had noticed; another chance of a chat, perhaps. It was hard not to feel slightly insulted about one's own listening efforts when she got up to go and talk to them. Katrina told them they'd been lucky to catch Lallie, it being the last day. Big party tonight, then back to London. Yes, lovely thank you. The Barrington. Spoiled us rotten. A real home away from home. All the time, Katrina was assessing when she could extract Lallie from the action and get her to sign the little girls' bits of paper. She was hushed by Derek as they went for a take. The mums watched, rapt. As soon as 'cut' was shouted, Vera heard one of the women point at Dirk and ask, 'Wasn't he in those films?'

To Katrina's annoyance, Mike was firm about going straight on without taking time for autographs.

'This is the end of the story they're doing then,' said the Dirk woman, disappointed.

'The end of the filming,' Katrina corrected. 'They do it all out of order. Does your head in!'

```
            COLIN
    June!
```

```
The children and TEACHER walk on.
```

```
            COLIN
    June! [HOPELESS] How do I know her name
    then, eh?
```

They did Lallie walking away first, so she could knock off for her tutor.

```
            COLIN
    June!
```

Dirk howled, which Mike didn't go for. He asked for restraint, and the next time it was like a wounded old dog someone had trodden on in its sleep. The concentration moved on to the girl, and her walking away. Too fast. The fans, bored by all the stop-start, had wandered off.

```
            COLIN
    June!
```

She made more of a meal of it, this time. A little laugh with her friends, not too much.

```
            COLIN
    June! [HOPELESS] How do I know her name
    then, eh?
```

Lallie gave a look back, on the second cry, a taunt and a challenge. Take it down, Mike encouraged, maybe this time just stop and don't *quite* turn. Keep rolling. Turn over. The pace was quickening. They had so much to do.

```
                    COLIN
        June! [HOPELESS] How do I know her name
        then, eh?
```

Oh, and that worked perfectly, Vera could see. The decision not to turn, the contempt in that – I'm not even going to turn, you pathetic old bastard. Devastating, it would be, with Dirk's anguish cut against it. So no wonder he'd do what he was going to, the scene they'd already got in the can. Come with me, little girl . . . They went one more time, for good luck, but she'd lay money that was the take they used.

Katrina had finally run out of chat. In any case, it was Vera's turn now, once they'd cleared the shot of clutter. It had taken Mike's fancy that Dirk/Colin might turn out of his last line to the teacher and there would be Vera/Woman watching him, some distance away, for a single (but Vera hoped quite long) conscience-lancing moment.

'You see – that point of contact, it'd be nice, I think – you become the audience,' Mike told her. His stammer hovered, almost landing on the 'p' in 'point'. 'Tis all one, darling, she didn't say. Put me wherever you like, tell me which face to pull. You've got me for the day and you've paid for me for the week. As Mike moved away from her, Tony winked, deadpan. Oh, she loved the man.

Derek came to get her into position, breathing his foulness upon her. Wide wide wide, Mike wanted, then bang in on her: the very last shot they had time for. Vera trotted up to the top of the field with Derek, he and Mike semaphoring back and forth to light on the exact place. Once there, Vera could see where Mike had got the idea from. The field formed a natural bowl with her perched on the lip, near the road. As flies to wanton dirty old men and what have you. Derek plodded back and Vera started breathing through her nose again. Poor boy. When would anyone ever tell him?

Vera felt like the outfielder in a game of village cricket. Eventually, she would get the thumbs up and spring into life. But for now they were back crowded round Tony and the camera. Two little girls were passing her. They'd come down from the road, one an absolute urchin with fierce eyes and a thatch of odd dark hair, the other blonde. It was the blonde one who spoke, politely.

'Excuse me, is Lallie Paluza down there?'

Vera told the girl that she had been but that now Lallie was in one of the trailers parked up by the road, 'doing lessons'.

'What kind of lessons?'

Vera explained about tutors, and missing school.

'It's the holidays,' the dark one objected. 'Ey, there she is!'

She back-handed her friend, pointing to Sue the stand-in, who was having a fag with some of the crew. She still had her wig on, ready for the wide shot. From the distance they were, it was genuinely hard to tell she wasn't Lallie, although to Vera her demeanour seemed entirely adult. The blonde girl's eyes were perfect saucers of shock and disapproval.

'She's smoking.'

They were already heading off. A funny pair; certainly not sisters, and hard to put them together as friends. They'd soon see for themselves it wasn't Lallie, if they got close enough before they were chivvied away. Maybe the real thing would appear and make their day.

Vera stood, alone once more, waiting for the sign. When the camera came close enough, she would be all judgement and wisdom, but for now, it was enough just to stand, hands on hips. She watched Tony, the dip of his head, the command of his fingers. Maybe that was why she was alone in her old age: all the men she had felt closest to loving were the ones who were absorbed by something else. She doubted that the men themselves knew this – either that she'd loved them, or the lack of threat her love posed to their greater concerns. Not that it mattered, in the end. Even if you did wear your heart on your sleeve, more often than not it all went to the bad. Like Quentin and Hugh, if she wasn't mistaken. And look at the girl's parents. Vera was sure the poor child would work out the lie of the land fairly soon, even if Katrina wasn't telling her. That was, if she didn't come across it in the papers first.

It HADN'T BEEN Pauline's idea to go and see the stupid fucking filming. She had been stood there, outside Gemma's house, like so many days since she had found out about her mam, waiting to see her. She had worked out they must be away, which was why she had only been going off and on. But that morning, the curtains were open, and Gemma's bike was out propped by the garage, so she knew they must be back. There was a sign, as well, on a post hammered into the lawn: 'For Sale'. Pauline, excited by Gemma's reappearance, didn't consider the implications of this. There was no point ringing the doorbell, so she settled herself on the kerb a few houses off and waited. Sure enough, Gemma got sent out to the shop – the milkman must have forgotten to start delivering again. Pauline hid at the mouth of the alley and jumped out at her. Gemma screamed. Good job she wasn't on the way back from getting the milk or she'd have smashed it. She tried to run off, but Pauline grabbed her arm.

'Let go of me, you gyppo!'

Pauline knew she was much stronger than Gemma. She hung on till Gemma realized she was getting a Chinese burn from twisting so much.

'I just want to talk to yer!'

'What about?'

Gemma had stopped thrashing, but Pauline was now unsure what she wanted. 'Just talking.'

Of course she wanted to tell her about her mam, of course she did, but if she told her, it would happen again.

'Just wanted to, thought we could walk around or summat.'

Gemma told her that she had to go to the shop, but allowed

Pauline to come, on the understanding that she'd wait outside, like a dog. But when she came out with two bottles of milk, she'd bought them both a chew with the change. She'd got brown from her holiday. As Gemma was unwrapping her chew, Pauline smeared her finger along the top of her bare arm, half wondering if the new colour would come off, like paint. Gemma flinched away theatrically, as though Pauline had hurt her.

'What you doing?'

Heading back, Gemma warned her that she wasn't allowed to come near the house or she'd get done, but she said she'd come back after she'd dropped off the milk, so Pauline hovered by the alley, watching her go in. The chew shocked a bad bit on one of Pauline's teeth, and she switched it to the other side of her mouth. She was hungry, she realized. Being back at school would be worth it for the dinners.

The chew was just a splinter of sweetness by the time Gemma came out again. Pauline had started to wonder if Gemma had been stringing her along by saying she was coming back out, but finally there she was, carrying a cardigan her mum had made her bring out, she explained, and her library ticket so that she could go to the library and come straight back.

'What's that doing there?'

Waiting, Pauline had considered the 'For Sale' sign. Gemma stalked away, convulsed in exasperation. 'Some sort of mistake or something, I don't know. They came yesterday and put it up.'

'Are you moving away then?'

'I don't know, do I? We don't even live there, not really.'

'Where do you live then?'

'Shut up!'

They really did go to the library, to begin with, because Gemma said otherwise her mum would know, and she'd get done. Pauline had never been inside it before. She'd always assumed the red-brick Edwardian building was some kind of church, another category of building closed to her. Inside, Pauline breathed in the respectable stink and closed her eyes while Gemma scanned the shelves. She prayed for her mam. She was actually praying for her to come back, something she'd never allowed herself to do while Joanne was still alive. The trick of the prayer was pretending that Joanne was still just in Leeds, and that prayer magic was being called on only to summon her quicker. That night, Pauline would get home, and there she'd be, drinks and food laid on, a trip to the launderette, calling her gyppo like Gemma did, charging the place with her danger.

You couldn't spend much time with your eyes closed, which was why Pauline hadn't been sleeping at night since it happened. The worst was when she saw a picture, more real than a dream, more like a film come to life there in her bedroom, but you knew if you touched it it would be solid: it was Joanne, but Joanne melded with the bag in the picture the police had shown them, flayed, boneless and terrible with blood. The blood was dark, like the stain she'd seen on the bag, but liquid and pouring. Even there in the library, her nodding at a table, it lurked. She snapped her head back. Gemma loomed, holding a couple of books, their dull covers loosely wrapped in protective plastic.

'Come on then.'

She was so wholesomely like herself, Gemma, socks pulled up, books one on top of the other, fringe exact. Pauline had started to think that if you put your finger out you might poke a hole in people or tear them, but not Gemma, standing there with her cardigan folded over her forearm, her hair bobbles aligned. There was always a smell about her, clean, from her clothes. Suddenly, Pauline wanted to hit her with a hammer. She followed her out of the library.

They walked on to the Town Fields. Gemma was asking her about meeting Lallie when they'd done the filming at the school, and Pauline was telling her all sorts, because the thing she remembered most was the drama of her own hair and what they'd done to it. Lallie or whatever she was called had come in near the end, after they'd already been in a class with an empty desk, where they had to look serious because she'd been killed in the story. After that they were having to be noisy and stuff with Lallie at the desk, nicking a pencil from the nig-nog's table. She looked older than them, even in the same uniform (Pauline had been given a newish one for the day and had managed to walk off in it at the end without anyone stopping her). Lallie hadn't bothered talking to them really, but Pauline invented a conversation which expanded to fit the many questions Gemma was then driven to ask about it, starting with what Lallie had been wearing ('School uniform' – 'Did you see what she was wearing before?' 'Erm, yeah, sort of jeans and that' – 'Not dungarees?' – 'What's them?' – 'You know, with a bib and braces' – 'Oh aye, them, with like flowers on' – 'What colour?' – 'Purple') and progressing to her invitation to Pauline to go on holiday with her to America ('She never!' – 'She did and all, they've got a swimming pool and she was supposed to be taking a friend but she got really poorly so she couldn't come so she said I could come instead.').

That was when Gemma noticed the cameras and the people down in the bowl of the field and got all excited. She asked a lady who was stood at the top ridge if Lallie was around, and she seemed to know what she was talking about, although Pauline caught her out on saying she had lessons during the holidays.

There was no stopping Gemma then. She started to go on about how Pauline might be able to get Lallie to invite her on holiday as well, if they managed to find her. Or Gemma could talk to her mum and dad and they'd arrange to be on holiday at the same place, even though they'd just got back from Spain, because Ian was an accountant and was rich. It was a relief to Pauline when they saw Lallie smoking and Gemma went mental about it, even though she barrelled down to the middle of the field to see properly and goggle at the outrageous sight. They got

stopped before they could get too close, headed off by a mardy-
looking bloke in a T-shirt.

'We're busy here, girls, if you don't mind not interrupting.'

He hadn't been around the school the day Pauline had joined
in the filming, but he sounded like a southerner, like all the rest
of them. Beyond him, the back of Lallie's head blew an insolent,
perfect smoke-ring as she laughed with another couple of blokes
in T-shirts. One of them, one of the shirts that is, looked familiar
to Pauline. She remembered then, its block of striped green and
white, like a spearmint chew, seeing it as she ran towards town
the day she'd bought her mam the guitar charm, thinking she'd
get in trouble for disturbing the filming. The stripes had flashed
out at her, along with his white bum poking out of his slackened trousers and the motion of the girl's little hand on his cock,
through the trees as she ran.

'I saw her with him before, wanking him off.'

She could see Gemma, scandalized by the smoking, didn't have
a clue what she meant. Pauline pumped her hand.

'Down his kecks.'

Gemma stared as what's-her-name toed her cigarette end into
the grass. Pauline thought Gemma was going to cry. Her face had
that disintegrating look, and she'd turned a bit red.

'Liar.'

'I did! Down Hexthorpe Flats. They was in the trees.'

Gemma set her mouth. 'D'you think her mum knows she's
smoking?'

Why did that matter? Pauline shoved her. 'I'm not lying!'

'You're a liar, you!'

Unusually, Gemma pushed her back, taking her by surprise.
And then they were grabbing at each other, hitting, clawing,
tumbled to the ground. Pauline was stronger, but Gemma was
heavier and using her advantage. Pauline knew she was bound
to win, because unlike Gemma she didn't care if she got hit. But

Gemma wasn't hitting, she scratched, which hurt in a different way.

'You lie! You're that mucky, you! Say you lie!'

'I'm not lying, you fat cow!'

The shock of being clawed in the face made Pauline lose her grip, allowing Gemma to roll partly on top of her, pinning her down. She squirmed astride her, legs near her neck.

'Say you're lying.'

'I saw it!'

All Gemma's weight was on her chest, making it hard to breathe. She tried to snake out from beneath her, but Gemma just bore down harder. And now she gouged her nails into Pauline's cheeks, threatening.

'Say it.'

'It's true, I saw it, you can ask her.'

Gemma dug her nails in, but Pauline was determined now. She could kill her if she liked, she didn't care. Truly. So it was weird that the tears were coming to her eyes and spilling, that her chest was trying to force them out despite Gemma pressing down on her.

'I can't breathe.'

'Just say you're a liar.'

Pauline sobbed. 'I'm not.'

Gemma roared, and scratched. Pauline screamed, thrashed a leg enough to knock Gemma off balance for a moment and writhed free. When she held her cheek, blood came off on her hand.

'You've hurt me, you fucking cow!'

Gemma looked shocked by what she'd done.

'I'm bleeding!'

Gemma offered her something from her dress pocket, as though that was going to help. It was a folded pad of white cloth, yellow-edged. At one corner there was a matching yellow flower embroidered on it, with a sky-blue middle.

'What the fuck's that?'

Gemma shook it out so Pauline could see it was a handkerchief, offered for the bleeding. She took it and clamped it to her stinging cheek, spotting the white with her uncopious blood. There was only one deepish scratch where the nails had pierced her skin. Holding the handkerchief so close to her face suffused her with Gemma's washing-powder smell. The material had creases in it from where someone had ironed it. Her mum, of course. Pauline balled up the cloth and chucked it back at Gemma. She picked the hanky up from the grass as Pauline wiped her full nose on her arm.

'I've got nearly a pound,' Gemma cajoled. It wasn't what Pauline was expecting. 'We can get lollies. Or chips.'

Pauline was so hungry that even the word, *chips*, had salt and vinegar on it.

'Aren't you going to talk to her?'

But what's-her-name, Lallie, had gone off to the bus parked up at the ridge on the main road. The people and their camera had moved up as well, where they seemed to be concentrating on the lady with the headscarf they'd asked about Lallie in the first place. So the lady wasn't a real person at all. The surprise of this suited Pauline. Maybe most people weren't real, just pretending to be. It helped when you knew that, that they might be ghosts, like you. Unless that meant the people you only had a chance of meeting as ghosts, like Joanne, were less likely to be ghosts themselves.

She and Gemma ambled to the road, almost friends.

'I'll get done,' Gemma said. 'I was supposed to come straight back, me mum'll be really worried about me.'

And then she looked down at herself. She saw the grass juice staining her knees and hem, which led to her discovering a tear under the sleeve of her bright dress.

'Oh, God,' she said, and this time she wasn't playing. 'She'll kill me.' Pauline could see she meant it. She was terrified. She definitely couldn't go home.

FRANK DIDN'T TAKE a holiday, as a rule. In his opinion, holidays were overrated, unless you could afford to stay somewhere in the lap of luxury, which was beyond his means. The crotch of luxury, as Lol called it. Fortunately he did quite well with invitations to the country, weekend jollies which made a nice change, although there was still so much talking to do to earn his keep, and after a week of yapping, what Frank craved was peace and quiet, emphasis on the quiet. Sometimes he thought that was why he and Lol rubbed along so well, because God knows it hadn't been for the sex since nineteen ought dumpty. Lol knew when to be quiet. If he didn't actually soothe, he certainly didn't agitate.

The one concession Frank made during the August exodus was to work the odd day from home, since Veronica insisted on her two weeks, and he couldn't get on with breaking in temps, except for typing letters. Inducting an eighteen-year-old into the arcana of which clients to put through to him and under what circumstances, let alone in a fortnight, was plain impossible. So Frank resigned himself to the modest difficulties of a stretch of doing his own phone work, which was lighter in any case because most people were away. And on the days he was at home, he knew that only the chosen few had the number to the hotline in the study.

Which is how Katrina got him, on an afternoon when he was putting his house in order, appraising the contents of his sock drawer. He didn't even hear the phone. As usual, it was the boys – as Lol said, Jack Russells were traditionally agents' dogs, bred to alert you to the phone ringing even through walls. They trotted in to find him, then both accompanied him, weaving eagerly through his short stride, to the study.

'Have you spoken to her?'

It was left to Frank to work out who was on the line. Quite a few of his clients did this, as though the unique umbilical connection meant it could be only one person. But Katrina had been phoning a lot recently, so he had no difficulty.

'We've left messages,' he soothed. 'The Yanks say they don't know anything about it, and the Italian lot don't seem to know where she's got to.'

'Never mind that, she's supposed to be coming to the party. What about the plane fares?'

Frank put the unpaired socks he was holding down on the arm of a desk chair. He never sat during calls, but paced, as far as the telephone cord would allow, which was almost as far along the corridor as the bedroom, the boys running shotgun all the while. Lol was out, and he was their best chance for a doubleyew ay ell kay. These bloody plane fares. Katrina really didn't seem to care anymore about the kid's screen test, or the film, so long as she got the money back, which you might reasonably say was holiday money, which the family could in any case well afford from what he happened to know Lallie had earned last year, however much they claimed it was all salted away for her until she was eighteen.

'I'll talk to the studio direct, my love, go over the producer's head. She's not really the producer anyway, it's the way they are over there, all chiefs and no ruddy Indians.'

It might be worth a try. He knew that girl had been off-kilter when she'd rung him to ask which team Hugh played for. Although evading her financial responsibilities was pure producer. Professional enough really, if a bit on the cheap side for a studio boss. At the stretched limit of the cord, Frank and the boys began the route back to the study. 'But while I've got you . . .'

He had been sent a script which was top of the pending pile there on his desk. LWT were punting a comedy, what the Yanks called a sit-com, Lallie as a kid living with her dad and vetting his

213

new girlfriend, who was a zany girl-about-town, working title 'Me Himself and Her'. The title you could take or leave, but it was a cute premise. He pitched it to Katrina, along with the fact that it had come from Dennis Morel, who practically had a clause in his contract obliging you to put 'best in the business' after his name whenever it was mentioned. Frank also touched on the possibility that Richard O'Sullivan might play the dad, which was more a notion of his than a possibility. But that's how he, Frank Denny, made things happen.

'What about the specials?' was Katrina's first, suspicious response. But he could tell he'd got her attention.

'This is additional to the specials,' Frank reassured her. That, at least, went down well.

'How many episodes?'

There was talk of six, to begin with – of course they'd have to get the scripts ready, but from the look of the pilot it wouldn't take them long. It wasn't his cup of tea, but then left to his own devices the only thing he'd willingly watch on TV was *Crossroads*, if he was back in time before supper. And according to Lol that might as well have been radio, since his eyes closed as soon as the theme music started up.

Frank flicked the pages of the script against his thumb.

'We'll get you a copy.'

It would be decent money, on top of the whack for the specials, and taking it all into consideration, nobody would lose out on Lallie not going to the States. Of course that would have been silly money to begin with, but if he was honest Frank knew she was never going to have the profile over there, even if the film was a smash. Here, even his ten per cent of her personal appearances and panto was something to write home about. And the thing about telly was it went on and on; another couple of seasons and she'd be a national treasure. As long as they could get her through the terrible teens, who needed a pension? It was as plain as the nose on your face. Which reminded him. He'd had a nasty jolt the other day, glancing through a consignment of cuttings. He'd only met Lallie's dad once, back when she did the audition at Tyne Tees, but seeing a shot of him with Lallie and Katrina taken months before at some charity beano, Frank had stopped short. Lallie's facial future was there, bar some five o'clock shadow (please God), and the future had a massive conk.

It would be money well spent, sorting that out now, and not the shock it might be if they let things get out of hand. Of course Cilla had been very upfront about her nose job, and everyone had loved her for it. It might play differently in a pre-teen though.

When he said this, Katrina, as he had hoped, wasn't offended in the least.

'I've always worried she'd end up with our Graham's nose,' she confided. 'It's bad enough on him like, but can you imagine on a girl?'

As far as she was concerned, the sooner they could do something about it, the better. The thought seemed to lift Katrina as much as the prospect of the comedy show, and finally prised her away from her preoccupation with the thwarted journey to America. Mission very much accomplished.

Frank promised to have a dip into Harley Street to investigate ways and means. Not out of his way, given his recent trips to the specialist. He didn't mention this, of course. As far as clients were concerned, he was immortal. He'd always followed that line himself more or less, so it had been a bit of a blow to discover they were all mistaken. Only Lol knew, although Veronica must have suspected, since she kept his appointments diary and had seen the entries spreading over the last couple of weeks. Heigh-ho. She'd never ask until he told her, but she must be curious. After all, it was her future too, in a less essential way.

He wasn't in any pain that a couple of aspirin couldn't dull, the same echo in his waterworks that had finally impelled him to make a doctor's appointment, but from the way the specialist had promised future discussion of pain relief, Frank knew there was worse to come. Well, there was worse to come anyway, pain or no pain. Finishing the call, he dropped into the desk chair, dislodging the orphan socks. One of them, a burgundy Jermyn Street cashmere Lol had treated him to one Christmas, had a hole worn in the ball of the foot, where he always wore his socks and even shoes through – probably from pacing, from appearing so light on his feet. He chucked the sock in the bin. Frank allowed himself one moment to close his eyes and feel sorry for himself before he snapped out of the chair to find a manila envelope and put the comedy script into it for the afternoon post. Onward and onward. What else could you do?

Now that Quentin was back in England, it was tough to grasp why being there had seemed so urgent when she was in Rome. Despite a great deal of what she'd been hankering for ever since she'd landed in Europe, including mind-clearing coke and real coffee – although of course no decent shower – Italy just hadn't done it for her in the way that Poland West seemed to. It was Hugh, of course, that damned elusive Hugh. Particularly as she hadn't seen him before she took the Italian trip, ha ha. In his absence, well, her absence, Quentin had gone through quite a lot of scenes where she expressed to him just how uniquely she understood him and he, in return, noted her private sorrow. It was good stuff. It was shit, of course. And now she was back in the grey, the singed yellow-brown, she was going to see him really, which sucked. A verb to be avoided. Perhaps he'd been out of it, the night of the three barrels? Of course he hadn't. And she mustn't take *on* so. It was unsophisticated.

She had fucked two guys successfully while she had been away, if you counted success as humping to orgasm – theirs, obviously. And there was no more than the lightest dusting of self-loathing about fuck number one, a fleshy but well-tailored studio executive from Cinecittà in his fifties, and absolutely none about fuck number two, a grip of god-like beauty who had fixed her up with the coke and some joyful grass and had the muscle definition of a Renaissance statue or a Santa Barbara porn star. So that was all fine. She should be getting back here like a girl in a perfume ad, hair swinging, stride co-ordinated, the world at her command. It was just a wrap party, for God's sake, and having seen how they did everything else round here, and given the start time of six

217

thirty, she was guessing it wasn't going to give Truman Capote a run for his money. In the Black-and-White-Ball sense, that was, although it might veer a little more in the direction of *In Cold Blood*. Oh, wasn't she the snippy one.

They put her right back in her old room at the hotel. Quentin assumed no one else had stayed there in her absence, which helped with the whole skin-cell thing. She'd barely arrived when Bri, the antisocial projectionist who had run the first dailies for her the night she'd met Hugh, turned up with a muttered injunction for her to see the final batch. In case Hugh was part of the deal, she brushed her hair and spritzed a little Cristalle (she truly was that girl), and followed Bri to the suite. But it was just the two of them, in the unsuccessful dark. She sat down. The thin drapes could only tranquillize the glare of the day into a woozy dimness, bisected, where the fabric didn't meet, by a brutal sliver of sun that sliced into her eyes. Bri adjusted the drapes until she stopped squinting, then started the projector.

'They're not in order,' he told her, grudging the words. 'Well, just in the order we got them back from the lab.'

So the first shot she saw was possibly the last of the movie. A classroom, kids at desks solemnly regarding the camera, which would be the POV of the cop, she guessed, as it roamed among them, hand-held. The kids were unromantically plain and tousled. The camera cherished their scabs and surfaces, then stopped among them at the empty desk, the empty chair.

After this came a double run of a more stately pan, close in over the desk and chair, marking out the kid's absence for any numbnuts who hadn't got it yet. Maybe they wouldn't use that, maybe it'd be beautiful and essential in the assembly, maybe she and her bosses would be yakking on about cuts and it would go in the end.

Suddenly, at the end of the slow journey, Lallie's face reared, hijacking the end of the shot in a real-life cameo, home-movie style. Huge and partial and unfocused in the frame, she roared mutely, exposing her fillings, then was consumed to black. Never out of the picture for long – she must have turned up from make-up just as they were finishing the shot. The contrast when she appeared in the next sequence gave Quentin a drop in the stomach. So real, when she was pretending. Restored to life for a scene that would come right at the beginning of the film, before all the bad stuff started, there she was, among her snaggle-toothed classmates, lifting a pencil from her pal at the next desk, just one of the gang, although you knew to look at her. And again, and again. She'd break their hearts, if they had hearts left to break. How did the kid know to be ordinary in her pretending, when in truth she fought every moment of her life to stand out from the crowd?

But hey. Dead kid sad. Let's all agree that on the whole, killing children is a bad thing. It was an entertainment, a fake constructed of glued-together sequences, whatever Mike's solemn pronouncements about the ending offering 'no consolation' (and those certainly made Hugh and her and all the studio guys prone to conversations behind his back). The rushes were finished. What was she, Quentin Montpellier, even doing here? Pretending to have a job which pretended to help to make pretend shit. A butterfly who dreamed she was a producer. A botch job.

Quentin plucked at the secret sore places on her arms. She needed something. The party should at least be good for that. Even Hugh should be good for that, if there was nothing else on offer but his magic beans. There was something wrong with her, that's what people didn't realize, although you'd think they could see it, the way her skin didn't hang right. Everyone else's seemed to, even Bri's, whose one scampering glance at her tits as he tweaked the curtains had been underlyingly furious. She wondered if she could play chicken with her self-love to the extent of screwing him, an old game of hers. It could be dangerous, and not just for the ego, and was really only possible drunk or stoned.

'That's it, unless you want to see the last batch as well.'

Quentin declined, saying she had to get ready for the party. Was Bri coming to the party? He was, unenthusiastically. She left him, diverted by film cans, and headed back to her room. Had Hugh set up their little session to keep her out of his way? Would have served him right if she had screwed the little jerk. As. If. He. Cared. Oh God, how she dully, truly hated her own company. It was like a holiday in hell. An unending cruise with a nagging, overweight country cousin, whose polyester gingham wardrobe gave her BO which permeated their tiny, shared cabin.

She stuck on false eyelashes for the party. Why not? When Quentin looked in the mirror she didn't recognize herself, which was always a bonus. Why hadn't she got hold of something in Rome, instead of freaking out about being stopped at Customs? Prescription medicine, after all, wasn't illegal. She was even shambolic about self-abuse. OK, if she devoted herself to acquiring a stash of some kind she would become a professional pill-head, but the amateurism was getting her down. And the hotel room. And her cancer was troubling her.

It was just a trip down the stairs to the party. Straightaway, to be on the safe side, she stopped at the bar and downed some warm vodka. The function room was packed with people Quentin didn't recognize, or not enough to speak to. Just as the vodka was stroking her nerve endings, there he was.

'No Dirk, I'm afraid. He hit the M1 the moment they called it a wrap. He'll be somewhere near London by now.'

Midnight-blue suit, white shirt, close shave. A good smell. Bay rum? Or maybe she was fantasizing that he was a cocktail.

'Lucky Dirk.'

'Indeed.'

He gave her the smile. She saw the trademark flash of wrist and cuff as he smoothed his hand over his hair. Maybe she'd been in love with his watch all along. Maybe it was a translation issue. Because if you took away the accent, and the suit, and the way

he held himself, Hugh was just like every guy who'd left her staring at the complicated reality of her shoes as she took a leak in
his bathroom in the small hours, wondering if this really, truly,
could be all there was.

'Don't you look wonderful.' Hugh cradled her elbow and kissed
her. That good smell. That thick shirting. Bastard. An intimate
squeeze for the elbow, that well-known erogenous zone. But
then, suggesting she say hello to Mike, Hugh's hand moved to
the small of her back, where her dress wasn't, and the confident
pressure of his dry fingers went straight to her cunt. Better than
shoes. Realler than shoes. It wasn't nothing, when all was said
and done.

They reached Mike, who leched her formulaically, although his
actual interest, as ever, was himself. 'Have you seen the rushes?'

'I cried,' Quentin claimed. 'Real fucking tears. The chair . . . '

Mike's teeth showed, which was his version of a genuine smile.
He swigged some gin and tonic. 'Oh, I was pleased with the chair.'

Hugh tossed her a look. They were in it together. She liked
that. Just at that moment, Quentin felt fine. Not as in OK, as in
the full Katharine-Hepburn-*Philadelphia-Story*-CK-Dexter-Haven
fine. As fine as Hugh. *Yar.*

Mike looked even shiftier than usual. 'I was just saying to
Hugh, if there was any chance of doing a few pick-ups—'

For once, being hijacked by Lallie's Groucho Marx was a
relief. Quentin had no desire to try and hold a line with Mike.
It was a goddamn party. And Lallie seemed momentarily to be
Katrina-less. Quentin saw that the kid hadn't gotten over her
little warmie for Hugh. Hey, who could blame her. She was
capering, doing the voices. In a few years she'd learn that she
was on the wrong track – as far as men were concerned, per-
sonality was never a bonus. Hugh was sweet with her, though:
Quentin recognized the trick. He made you feel like he was
paying attention. He insisted on getting the fat teenager behind

the bar to mix Lallie a 'cocktail' out of Coke and stunted bottles of fruit juice. Quentin followed his lead and pretended she was into it too, while Mike dropped away. Nobody had heard of a Shirley Temple, and in any case Quentin was pretty sure it contained things like ginger ale and grenadine that didn't exist here. She told Lallie and Hugh about how her dad used to order them for her whenever they went out for dinner on custody weekends.

'This was actually at the Brown Derby, you know.' They didn't. 'Where all the big movie stars used to hang out.'

Her dad had wanted it to be a thrill for her and got annoyed when she, silent with devotion, didn't deliver the goods. She didn't say that, obviously, the way his disappointment and irritation invoked his better, shadow daughter to sit beside them: blonder, thinner, more vivacious and appreciative – a sort of Skipper to her new stepmom's Barbie. She just mentioned the Shirley Temple as companion to his highball, a cute little father–daughter vignette.

'My dad's coming,' said Lallie. 'He's getting the train after work.'

'Don't get drunk then,' said Hugh.

Lallie beamed and giggled. It was hard not to feel jealous of such simple happiness. Her tutor, blotto of course, waylaid the kid with a maudlin hug. The woman had a peninsula of zits along her jawline, despite being middle-aged. How did that happen to people? The two of them bounced off to check out the jukebox, Lallie leading the way. Quentin couldn't say she was sorry to see them go.

'Is your dad still around?' she asked Hugh. He slicked his hair one-handed as he knocked back his drink with the other.

'Alas, no.' She waited. 'This'll be the first time he's been down, you know, since we started shooting.' It took her a second to work out the diversion to Lallie's father. She ignored it.

'When did he pass away?'

'Nearly ten years ago.' Hugh and his glass of whatever communed, antsy. 'He was a remarkable man.'

'I've heard a little about him. From Vera.'

Who was there, somewhere, in the throng – Quentin had glimpsed her, suddenly striking with her own hair and clothes.

'Ah yes, of course.' Hugh focused on some invisible screen. Quentin tried to work out if his pupils were unusually contracted. 'He had this amazing energy, drive, always. On the go from morning until night, everyone always said Sidney Calder could get more done in a day than most people managed in a week. Quite hard to live up to, actually.' He finished his drink.

'It wasn't until he popped his clogs . . . He used to have shots, vitamin injections, you know. Pure amphetamine, as it turned out. I was rather devastated about that, stupid, actually, but I'd spent so bloody long trying to keep up with him. It was *exhausting*.'

So now she knew. Oedipal substance abuse. Oh God, now she loved him again, offering her his confidence with his pristine smile. She would have lain at his feet like a dog, right there. Was this a good time to ask him for a little something to make the evening go faster than the vodka?

'Cooee,' Katrina trilled, clamping Quentin by the waist, her nails making escape a hazard. *Always a pleasure*. Quentin could see Hugh was immediately on the front foot to go. Traitor.

'Has Katrina seen the rushes?' she asked. Desperate.

'The what, pet?' Katrina was drunk.

'Any of the, er, you know, footage.' Hugh ducked an admonitory glance at Quentin. 'We thought it was best not to let Lallie see anything along the way. Makes you horribly self-conscious. It's bad enough with older actors!'

But Katrina had other things on her mind. Her nails indented Quentin's side.

'Anything from the studio, pet?' she asked. 'About the *Princess* film, like?'

Quentin wasn't drunk, but she wasn't sober either. She was tired of running, that was the truth, bone-tired, like Hugh keeping up with his old man. Italy hadn't solved anything. Removing herself from the equation still left a whole page of algebra. *This is why you should never try to do anything, Quentin, ever.* What did it matter, if Lallie had the meeting or didn't have the meeting? Who was she kidding, thinking she could protect the kid from her mom's ambition, in America or out of it? Wasn't it even possible that America, and the brutality of the studio system, might even *dilute* Katrina? *Yeah, right, we're actually doing you a favour, kid.* If she'd been at home, at an industry party in the Hills, with ice in the drinks and lines on the glass-topped table, maybe she'd have been able to summon a little backbone. But here, in this nowhere place (the wallpaper was furred, that had to be wrong, and Lallie's dwarf double had her hand on Mike's ass, which was probably also furred), who could blame her? *Get used to it, baby. Producers are phoneys. Hollywood is a cesspool. How d'you like them unsurprising apples.*

'You must give me your travel details, we can fix something up before I go.'

I landed her for you, Clancy.

Katrina's nails spasmed into her back in delight. Hugh had shimmied away, mouthing 'drink'. Lallie had caught him again on the way to the bar, she and her tutor attempting a conga. Seemed the tutor had the hots for Hugh as well. Form an orderly conga line, ladies.

'Oh, she'll be made up when I tell her,' said Katrina, in that exaggerated way that made everything she said seem as fake as the stripes of blush on her cheek. 'She's been on at me about it non-stop! Not a wink of sleep for either of us, I tell you. I've aged ten years, me.'

With a final pinch, she detached her nails. 'Lallie, love! We're going to America!'

The last thing Quentin was expecting to see was the unguarded confusion invading Lallie's face.

'But what about the other show, the comedy? You said Frank said—'

'Never mind about that—'

Katrina shovelled Lallie close, wielding those claws to silence her. Hugh turned, curious.

'Hollywood, here we come!' Katrina crowed.

'A toast,' said Hugh, and nodded for more drinks.

'You'll be able to tell your dad when he arrives,' said Quentin, amazed to find herself cheerleading. At the very least she'd been expecting to give Lallie what she wanted, however badly it turned out for her. Hugh was pissed too, which wasn't so surprising. 'He'll be excited.'

'Oh, he's not coming tonight,' said Katrina, reaching for a new glass. 'He couldn't get away. We'll tell him on the phone, eh, pet? Maybe in the morning.'

Lallie's face curdled into tears. She pulled away from her mother and ran for the door. It took Katrina a second or two of gin-delay to register what had happened. Then she ran after her. 'Lallie!'

Hugh, fielding a surplus glass, grimaced.

'She'll be all right. She's a trouper.'

Quentin took the drink. 'It's all they've talked about. The mom's practically turned into a travel agent.'

'I'm sure she's thrilled. Just disappointed Daddy's not coming for the party.' He left a moment, clear-eyed. 'And since you rather left them dangling, darling, I think Lallie had got it in her head that she was going to do something over here, closer to home. Closer to Dad. She talks to me, you know. Father figure.'

She was damned if she was going to take that one sitting down.

'Weren't you thinking of signing her up for something, Hugh?'

He warded her off with his glass. 'I wouldn't dream of treading on your toes.'

You'd cast him like a shot as the trusty family doctor, his hand in his pocket like that, the other with his drink but confident enough for a pipe, radiating wholesome energy. Not just as good as the real thing, but better. Quentin could feel herself weakening. Unchilled, the oily vodka entered your body intimately, formaldehyde in a corpse. Then it opened up a little space, high in your skull behind your eyes. Hugh leaned close, that intimate, devastating invasion. If it had been a movie . . .

'Although it does strike me as odd that you want her to go to America to film an English part in an English book. Why not shoot it here? Cheaper all round, for a start. I could handle it at this end. We'd be a team. Licence to print money.'

She was Wile E Coyote, pedalling the air before the fact that she'd run out of cliff caught up with her.

'We're both adults,' he insisted.

She plummeted. 'You know what? You are so fucking wrong about that.'

And she launched herself off, landing near Mike, who had been abandoned by the dwarf. When she saw Hugh again, towards the end of the night, he had gathered in both Lallie and Katrina. Lallie was back doing impressions, urged on by cast and crew. Personally, Quentin was truly beyond caring. Until next time, she wasn't going to care about anything ever again.

IT'S ALL PAULINE'S idea. I can't go home because I'll get done. If there's one thing that sends Mum mental, it's me not looking after my clothes. Getting them dirty's bad enough, and the dress is certainly dirty, but there's the big hole I've torn under the arm as well because of Pauline. I can't even blame Pauline either, because Mum'll go even more mental if I say I've been playing with her. I feel sick just thinking about it. Ever since she's been with Ian, Mum's temper has been scarier. It's always been scary, but now you can tell she likes staying angry, and it's usually with me. And Ian always joins in as well, not angry but sad, because as far as he's concerned I should be looking after my mother since she's precious and I only get the one. The second time he said that to me, I nearly said that that might not be true as I seemed to have ended up with two dads, but Mum was in the room, and it would have been a guaranteed slap to the back of the legs. At least. Pointing out that the proper arrangement was her looking after me would also have earned me a slap, but that was true too. Ian's mad on Mum being looked after, as though she's fragile, like the sad clown with balloons at Nana's I'm not allowed to get down from the mantelpiece. Maybe Mum seems like that to him because she's so much thinner than his good lady. For saying that I'd probably have been killed.

But now I'm going to get done, properly done. Not just for the dress, but for staying out so long without permission. It's later than teatime already, hours past it. On top of that, probably when Pauline and I were rolling around fighting on the Town Fields, I've managed to lose my library ticket. I can't begin to imagine what lies in store: thinking about it, I reach the door and Mum's face, and my imagination faints. The later it gets, the more trouble I know I'm in. I want tomorrow to come, and for it all to be over, but it gets harder to think of going back with every minute that runs out of the day. I want to run away, but I don't know where to. I know after the last time that Dad won't let me run away to him but, just in case, we go down our old road to the house, and I make Pauline wait by the gate while I try ringing the bell. There's no one there. It's too late now for Dad still to be at work. He always comes straight home, usually for his tea and his wash and shave and telly. The bell rings on, into emptiness. It's no good. There's no one to help me.

'I thought you said we'd get chips.'

Pauline and I walk round and round, and sit and eat chips and walk again, and nothing we think of makes it any better, until she suggests the launderette.

That's what comes first. Why don't we go in there and wash my dress, Pauline says, and I can recognize that's a good idea. Some of the shops have closed, but the launderette stays open late, I've seen it from the bus on winter nights. But when we get there of course the 12p I've got left isn't enough; to wash and dry the dress will take 30p. Pauline suggests we just wash it, which is 20p, and then I tell Mum I was walking underneath a window-cleaner's ladder while he was emptying his bucket to explain why it's wet. I know this isn't going to work, and besides, we're short even for the wash. Pauline doesn't care. While I watch, terrified, she unclasps the purse left on one of the orange chairs by a lady who is distracted by wrestling her sopping sheets into the drier. It's the same lady we've asked about the prices, which makes it worse, but Pauline palms the silver like she's been given permission. A 10p and two fives – enough for the drier as well. She'd take more if she could, I can see, but I'm frowning furious disapproval, although I don't dare say anything, because the lady will hear, and we'll get caught, and I'll be in as much trouble as Pauline. We might even go to prison. I feel hot inside and out, with the desert air from the driers blowing over my skin and the sickly heat of my own fear deep within. It's clear to me that Pauline will do anything bad, and that I'll let her.

Next, we have to ask the woman we've stolen the money from for powder, because we can't afford any. Pauline does this because she isn't as shy as me, although I smile a lot, pleadingly. The lady gives us the powder, although she doesn't return the smiles. Her unfriendliness makes me feel better about taking the money. We put the dress in the machine and wait, and I don't even care that I'm sitting in the launderette in just my pants and vest for all the world to see. Well, not as much as everything else that's bad about the day and the general run of days up to now. In the chair next to me, Pauline seems to be dozing, in that weird way she has. For the first time since we saw her on the Town Fields, I think of Lallie. I feel very far away from her. I don't think ever in her life she's had to sit in a launderette in her vest and pants, unless for some funny skit with Marmaduke that turned into a big song-and-dance routine. I don't want to think about what Pauline has said Lallie does, what we fought about. I put it in the same place I put Mum's angry face, and Ian and the suncream, and Dad's absence, a sci-fi blank, like a pit someone gets thrown in through a door in *Doctor Who*. 'For Sale' is in there too, now. I prefer to think instead of my version of what Lallie's doing now, a life on the set of the TV show, without parents, but looked after. The trick, like squinting with one eye and then the other so your focus hops between them, is to see her in my life, sleeping in a version of my bed, eating versions of my meals, wearing the clothes I'd prefer to be wearing, me, but better: me as Lallie. Telling myself about this usually comforts me, but now I can't get it to stick, and I'm left sweating in my underwear, staring at Pauline. She has grey grooves under her sliding eyes, and grease from the chips we ate earlier slicks her chin. Her head jerks back brutally every time she falls asleep, so that her hair shakes and releases its sour smell, but it doesn't stop her nodding back off. I don't want her to go to sleep and leave me on my own. I prod her awake.

'Mam,' she says, her eyes still roaming. Then she realizes who I am and kicks me sharply on the side of my leg. I kick her back, just to show her. She's already crying, though; she started in her half-sleep.

'What are you crying for?' I ask her.

She tells me to eff-word off, although real tears clump her eyelashes. There's no point in insisting. And anyway, I'm now thinking that my dress will still have the tear in it, leading, with my lateness – later than ever now – to my still getting done. I point this out to her. Pauline thinks, one knee up, contorting her hand to chew the fleshy bit at the bottom of her palm. Or I think she's thinking, since she seems to have gone away again. At least she's not falling asleep.

Just after we've put the dress into the drier, and I feel as though I've lived my whole life in the launderette, like I did in the airport when our flight was delayed in Spain, a girl and a woman come in to do their washing. The woman Pauline stole from has left, and for some time we've been alone except for the launderette manager, who is only a muffled stream of Radio Two from the room at the back. The mother and daughter are coloured, the woman with a baggy wool coat and a hat which have nothing to do with the weather. The girl is wearing a Brownie uniform, but it's the cardigan slipping off her domed shoulders that I recognize first as belonging to Cynthia, my bullied charge at the school dinner table. There is something very different about her. It takes me some staring to realize it's nothing to do with her change of outfit. It's because she's talking to her mum and her mum is talking back to her, and she's smiling – not the appeasing, frightened smile she produces at school, but a real smile with a giggle bubbling from it. It's as shocking as realizing teachers have first names.

Cynthia's mum is neither young nor old in her strange clothes.

Like Cynthia, she wears cartoonishly thick glasses. I feel like a spy. The two of them, talking, laughing, unload their washing from the mum's maroon wheeled shopper and a blue mesh bag. Cynthia is too busy and happy to notice us. Pauline is as interested as I am to begin with, then she goes back to chewing her hand. Once the washing is in the machine, Cynthia settles back in a chair at the end of our row (there are two rows of plastic chairs, back to back) and her mum hands her something from the shopper. It looks like a book. Then she gives her a yellow apple, which Cynthia puts on the chair next to her, and then, surprisingly, her mum turns and wheels the shopper off out of the launderette, leaving her alone. Cynthia swings her bare, calfless legs and sees us for the first time. She jerks her old familiar smile and caves her chest, as though we've already hit her. Just like that. My hello makes a point of being matter-of-fact and friendly, despite me being in my vest and pants. Very quickly, Cynthia ducks and picks up her book, which isn't a book at all but something limp made of felt which she's sewing. I stare at the absolutely straight white parting, like a perfect road, that divides her black hair into two stubby bunches. She doesn't look up. Her fingers crest in and out, making stitches as her legs swing.

'Can we have a lend of that?' says Pauline, loud enough for me and Cynthia both to jump. Cynthia is already cowering as Pauline gets off her chair and snatches the sewing from her. It's shaped like a small book, with white felt inside and a purple felt cover, stitched with an incomplete bouquet.

'What's it for?' asks Pauline.

Cynthia mutters, glasses downcast.

'You what?' Whatever she says, I can see Pauline will be inclined to disbelieve her.

'It's a needle case,' I explain. 'You keep needles in it, so you don't lose them.'

'Can we lend it?' Pauline says, taking it. Cynthia's slack fingers acknowledge that this isn't a request. I wonder what Pauline is going to do. As she pulls the needle free of its thread she briefly admires the embroidery, which is much better than the lumpy cross-stitch we occasionally produce at school.

'You can sew your dress,' she points out to me, and then to Cynthia, 'Got any more cotton?'

Cynthia shakes her head. Unbothered, Pauline hands me the needle and begins to tug at the woven yellow thread attached to the buttercup petal Cynthia is stitching. The surrounding fabric buckles and bunches, but the embroidery silk doesn't give, even when Pauline uses her teeth. It'll be hard to smooth out what she's done. I stand there, holding the needle, as Pauline glares at Cynthia, ready to blame her for thwarting her brainwave.

'Nig-nog,' she says.

I know it's hopeless, really. I know Mum will find the hole beneath the sleeve, if not tonight, when I'll be in enough trouble for being out so late, then another day, dealing me a double portion for my attempts at deception. But the force of Pauline's determination blunts this knowledge. She chucks the soft booklet at Cynthia's face, making her flinch.

'It's no good!'

Taking the sewing on to her lap, Cynthia's fingers attempt to smooth the clotted stitches. 'Sorry,' she says, keeping her remote eyes in their bottle lenses turned away from us. She's saying it to make us leave her alone.

'We just need to get some cotton,' I reassure Pauline. And then for Cynthia, in the same spirit in which I give her big portions at school dinners, 'Embroidery stuff's probably too thick anyway.'

But Pauline isn't about to let go. 'Was that yer mam?' she demands. Cynthia nods. Suddenly, Pauline shunts forward hard on both legs so that she rams Cynthia's shins with her own, making her slam back in her chair. Pauline's face denies what she's just done. 'When's she coming back?'

Cynthia attempts to shrug, but it isn't good enough, and

Pauline rams her again so that she gestures at the machines and says, 'When it's dry,' in her almost voiceless voice.

'Fucking nig-nog!' Pauline grabs the sewing from her and chucks it across the row of chairs. I go to rescue it. It's probably a present for someone, like a grandma. I wonder if I'll ever make a present again for my grandma, since she belongs to Dad. I feel sick and tired and excited. No one comes from the back room where the radio chunters on, playing 'The Most Beautiful Girl in the World' by Charlie Rich. No one comes in to do their washing. Cynthia is crying, which she sometimes does at school, the type of hopeless crying you usually cry only at the end, when you've been crying a long time, the way Pauline was crying in her sleep.

When I pick up the needle case, I start unpicking the petal Cynthia was working on, reversing the smooth official stitches to decode the back of the felt square where the connecting lines are chaotic and random, in search of a starting knot.

'We can just undo this bit,' I reassure them both. Pauline is interested. She wants to do it, but I won't let her. Her filthy hands have already greyed the white pages meant for the future needles. Once I've started, it's enjoyable to undo Cynthia's embroidery. I'm being nice to her really. It could be much worse. After all, I only need one bit of cotton to repair the hole in my dress.

As I thread the needle with the wrinkled, freed cotton, Pauline gets my dress out from the drier. It's puckered around its seams and I realize it might have shrunk from the heat. I try to smooth it, panicked again. Everything gets worse, whatever you do. Looking up from the mess I've made, I see Cynthia staring out of the window, probably wondering where her mum is, and I realize that's another mess. She might be a blackie but Cynthia's mum is still a grown-up, and if she gets back before we've gone, Cynthia will dob us in. Her mum's anger will be another route to my own mum and the final reckoning of my crimes, which now includes conclusively ruining my clothes.

'We'll get done if her mum comes back,' I tell Pauline, and hoist the dress back over my head. Sure enough, it feels newly snug and comes further up my legs than before. Pauline doesn't notice, though, so maybe it's not as bad as I think. And at least it's clean.

'What about the sewing?'

'We'll take it with us.'

I pincer the needle and then, since I need to carry my library books, give it to Pauline. Cynthia is holding herself tense, waiting for us to go. Pauline pricks the top of her arm with the needle as we pass. Two more effortless tears crawl from beneath Cynthia's glasses. They make me feel bad.

'Listen,' I say, about the needle and thread, 'we'll give it back.'

She doesn't make any response at all. I may as well not have bothered to speak.

'Promise,' I say. 'Swear to God.' Which is a promise I have never in my life broken. But she doesn't know that, does she?

'You're really good at sewing,' I proffer. Pauline's nodding me out of the door, but it feels essential to get Cynthia to know that I'm not horrible, like Pauline.

'Tell you what, why don't you come with us and you can sew my dress? It's got a hole.'

I lift my arm to show her, but her glasses don't angle up to take it in. She's beginning to nark me.

'I'm rubbish at sewing,' I tell her, which isn't even true. I make a last attempt. 'If you sew it for us I'll get you something. A lolly, sweets.' Even though we don't have any money left. She won't know that though, will she, until after she's finished? And it's true that she might do a better job than me, better than Pauline certainly, and if I sew it myself, wherever we go to I'll have to take the dress off again outside and parade my underwear. In any case it feels very important now not to leave her alone, unconsoled, before her mum gets back. It feels important that she can't resist us.

'Go on,' says Pauline, wheedling. I'm surprised she's so instantly keen for Cynthia to come with us, but I'm grateful for the help. I pick up the needle case from where it's slipped to the floor, square its soft pages.

'It's really nice.'

Patiently, I hold it in front of her and in the end she stands to take it. Then she shuffles with me to the door, as though she has no choice. I feel like I've won. She must believe I'm not horrible.

'Is it a present?'

She nods.

'Who for?'

Outside, the low sun is about to be swallowed by buildings. I wonder if my dad is at home yet, having his wash and shave. Pauline and I both seem to know we need to be somewhere where there are no people. We walk for a bit, and although Cynthia casts a look back a couple of times as streets grow between us and the launderette, she doesn't say anything. She could say something, and if she did, I would listen to her, but she chooses not to. I know she can speak up, now I've seen her with her mum, so it's her own fault. There's no pushing even, now she's walking with us.

Once we reach the Town Fields, I lead the way to the back of the pavilion. It's boarded up and shabby and is the only destination, apart from our school, in the whole space. It's never been used by the school, as far as I know. As far as I know, it's never been used by anyone, although it must have been built for a reason. It has Tudor beams and pebble-dashed gables at the top and powdered glass and cigarette ends at the bottom. The rubbish accumulates on the side away from the road, screened from both the wind and a human view. Standing there, I raise my arm, ready for Cynthia to sew up the tear. She's nervous about it, because of my skin being so close to the material, especially now the dress has shrunk.

'Don't prick me,' I warn her.

If she told me to take the dress off, I would, but if she won't tell me and she hurts me with the needle then it's her lookout. Of course when she approaches with the needle and thread it tickles so much that my arm clamps down of its own accord and refuses to lift again. Cynthia blinks, head bobbling, unsure what to do. She holds the needle out again, and I twitch away before it can even touch me. I'll have to take the dress off, which I don't want to do, here where anyone could come round the corner and see.

'You're not doing it properly.'

She can't do anything properly, that's clear enough. She stands there, holding the large needle as though she's been told to play pin the tail on the donkey and no one's explained the rules. She lurches towards me again, but I push her away. Not hard, but it's enough to make her sit down suddenly on the grass. She has no ballast. It's like batting away a balloon.

Behind us, Pauline laughs.

'It's not funny,' I tell her. 'I'm going to get done!' The self-pity that our trip to the launderette has delayed arrives in knots at the back of my throat. It's night-time. I want to be at home. Real home, with Mum and Dad, watching Lallie on the telly, just that. That's all I want, and it will never happen again, ever. *For Sale.*

There's a wrenching sound. I turn and see that Pauline is pulling at one of the damaged, ancient boards nailed over the pavilion's empty windows.

'You want to be careful, there's glass,' I warn her.

'Stinks,' she observes, poking her head through the gap she's exposed. 'Like you, blackie.'

Cynthia's getting up. I can't say I've noticed she smells, and anyway Pauline's not exactly one to talk, as my mum would say. Getting stuck in, Pauline wrenches a larger piece of wood away, rusty nails and all, and waves the studded plank around like a club, grunting caveman sounds. It makes me laugh. She and Cynthia are about the same size, but the fight that's in Pauline, you never think about her being small. She makes a mock-lunge at me with her new weapon, and I dodge away, even though there's far too much space between us for her to hit me.

'You'll get splinters!'

Pauline runs down the pavilion steps to get me, and we dodge and chase, giggling, until I see that Cynthia has taken advantage of our distraction to start running away. She's a rubbish runner, I know from the disaster of school rounders matches, but she's already managed to cover quite a lot of ground despite her knock-kneed shamble. I exclaim, and Pauline and I chase after her. If we weren't already chasing each other, we might not bother, but it adds to the momentum of our game. Pauline gets to her first, and since she's still holding her makeshift club, swings it. The wood makes contact with Cynthia's side, down at the back near her bum, and she goes down hard. Much harder than Pauline was expecting, I can see. When I catch up, Cynthia's writhing on the grass, clutching the bit where she was hit.

'That's got nails in!' I admonish. I can't see any blood but I don't want to look. Pauline nudges Cynthia with her foot.

'Gerrup then. You're a right fucking crybaby, you. I didn't even touch yer.'

Surprisingly quickly, Cynthia does what she says. Pauline back-swings the piece of wood again, threatening, playing really, and Cynthia jerks back, cradling her head, the sudden movement making her back foot slip and bringing her down again on the grass. It looks really funny, like something in a cartoon, the way her feet lift before she falls and the dismay on her face. The impact dislodges her glasses and for the first time ever I see her eyes, which are large and horrified. Somehow, this is even funnier. I pick the glasses up for her, but before I give them back I can't resist trying them on.

'Aw, don't,' says Pauline, doubled over now at the sight of me instead. 'You look a right spaz.' Everything is a colourful fog, and my eyes strain as though I'm crossing them. Pauline snatches the glasses off me and tries them on herself. She looks hilarious. Instantly lost and useless, like Cynthia.

'Speccy four-eyes,' I laugh. And then to Cynthia, 'Don't worry, she'll give you them back.'

But Pauline takes off the glasses and chucks them in a high arc. They land far away, on the grass.

'Fetch, doggy!'

Cynthia stands, frozen, until Pauline swings the piece of wood back, threateningly. Then her legs stutter off after the glasses. When she puts them back on they're skew-whiff – one of the pink plastic armpieces won't sit flat on her ears any more. Pauline doesn't let herself stop laughing.

'Look at you, you're that bloody ugly.'

Cynthia keeps her body kinked where Pauline hit her. She puts her hand there, and from the way she dabs at her side I know she must have seen some blood, although it's invisible to me on the Brownie uniform. I'd been promised Brownies myself, but since we moved to Ian's, Mum has made excuses about not being able to take me because of work. Seeing the few pathetic badges sewn on Cynthia's sleeve makes me indignant. I know my own sleeve would be crowded with them if I were allowed to go.

'What badges have you got?'

I approach to have a look. Cynthia flinches, which makes me want to get the bit of wood from Pauline and hit her hard. I don't, obviously. I just want her to talk normally. The black badges have emblems stitched with green and yellow and the names at the bottom of each: housekeeping, music, sport. The last one sounds extremely unlikely. It has a sewn tennis racquet crossed with something I think is supposed to be a golf club.

'Sport?' Hearing this, Pauline comes to have a look.

'What did you have to do?'

'I don't know.' She's stupid to be so terrified of me. And she must know.

'You've only got three, you must be able to remember.' I make my voice like Mrs Bream's. Cynthia twitches more obligingly.

'Running,' she admits.

'Running?'

Pauline produces more laughter. I don't blame Cynthia for not liking it, it's getting on my nerves even though it's not directed at me. Although the thought of Cynthia getting any kind of badge for running is ridiculous. It isn't fair, either. Pauline twists the sleeve of the uniform, pretending to get a better look at the badge and pinching Cynthia's arm as she does it.

'Go on, show us then.' She releases the sleeve. 'Run.'

Cynthia's head jerks between us, to check she's understood. 'She wants you to show her your running,' I reassure her, still being Mrs Bream.

She's careening and aimless, like a daddy-long-legs released from a jam-jar. Even by her standards, it's rubbish. Her body's still arched at one side where Pauline hit her, as though she has a stitch. Pauline gives her yards and yards of head start, then takes off after her and catches up in about two seconds flat. This time she aims the plank more, square between her shoulders. I'm expecting Cynthia to go down like she did before, weight-lessly, uselessly, but there's an odd moment as she and Pauline stagger forward together and then fall, Pauline more or less on top of her. This time Cynthia's squeal is thin and high, and there's no apology in it, only pain. It gets louder as Pauline wrestles herself away, and the struggle as she pulls her weapon free makes delayed sense of their dance to the ground: one of the old nails has stuck into Cynthia's back, and it's hurting her more as Pauline tries to pull the wood away.

After that she does what we say even if she isn't up to much. We don't need to hit her to get her into the pavilion. Pauline breaks more of the boards off and we climb through the low window, with a bit of contemptuous coaxing from Pauline because

I'm worried about the broken glass I can see framing the gap like shark's teeth, its danger disguised by the ancient muck inside. Going in feels wrong and exciting. The air smells old and pissy. I think of Howard Carter and the tomb of Tutankhamen, with its curse. As I climb in, the dusty tunnel of light from the window illuminates something heaped on the floor, further back by a wall. It can only be clothes over a skeleton. I shriek. While I back up to the window, careless now of the hidden glass, Pauline strides up and kicks it. The body's mound shifts, and I see it's a torn badminton net, rolled around metal poles.

'Give me heart attack!'

Cynthia plays no part in either the fear or the laughter. She cries on, huddling her wounds, snot and tears coating her chin. I'm sick of her now. I hate her now. It's all too late. Because of her, I'm going to get done.

'Shut up!'

I push her, forgetting it'll make her fall. My hand comes away with blood on it, and I'm curious to see, in the light from the window gap, that it's standard red. We're all the same under the skin, as Mr Scott has told us. The blood is a smear, not drops, and to get rid of it I wipe my palm on Cynthia's Brownie dress. As she lies there, a sudden hot stink makes me jump back, just in time to avoid the tide of wee spreading from under her thighs. I yelp with disgust, and Pauline laughs again. There are no words for what I feel, seeing Cynthia douse herself with her own urine. It isn't something to watch. All I did was push her to shut her up.

'Shurrup, pisspants.' Pauline knees her in the face. She is more interested in the pavilion, though, than in Cynthia. She wanders off to explore the dim corner beyond the badminton net, where a door hangs askew. I don't know what her plans are. I only know that coming to this place is the end of the world for me. Suncream. Lallie. For Sale. I want to close my eyes and never open them, but I try and I can still smell the sweet vinegary piss stink, new and old. I wish Cynthia would stop crying. She's got the worst cry ever, like a donkey or some other old animal, but it doesn't sound real. It sounds like she's trying to imitate a donkey, just to be annoying. A deliberate *ee* as she pulls in a breath and a long exhaled *aw* of involuntary distress.

'Shut up!'

And this time, I mean to hurt her. I punch and kick, not aiming, just hurting. To get to what. To make her stop. To make everything stop. I do stop, in the end. She isn't trying to kick or scratch or grab my hands. She's balled in on herself, rigid, moving only with the impact of my hurting her. I haven't got anywhere. I hate her more.

'Pauline.' She's over in the corner, poking around in a cupboard with the wonky door. 'Come and hold her.'

Because that's what will make a difference. Being able to get to her. Pauline ambles over, striped with dust and carrying a half-strung badminton racquet. Between us, we uncurl Cynthia, pulling faces at the wee, so that Pauline can kneel by her head, pinning back her arms. We take off her glasses. Cynthia's knees double up to protect her stomach but I'm much stronger than her and pull them down and sit on them so she can't do that any more. I know what I'm going to do. I've got the knife, the one I got in Spain. I put it in my pocket this morning, along with the library ticket.

'Get her fanny,' urges Pauline.

'You what?'

'Sambos' fannies are different. I've seen.'

'What d'you mean?'

'I've seen pictures. Have a look.'

I can see the sodden navy crutch of Cynthia's knickers.

'She's wet herself.'

Pauline shifts, business-like, releasing Cynthia's arms.

'Take your pants off,' she commands.

It seems that Cynthia has stopped being able to understand us, even when we shout, so in the end Pauline gets hold of the sturdy waistband, loose around Cynthia's narrow belly, and pulls. Gingerly I take the wet pants as they twist round her legs, leaving them to shackle her ankles as I push her knees apart to get a better look. Cynthia's donkey sounds continue, softly. I don't know exactly what I'm looking for. I'm not going to tell Pauline, but I've never taken a really good look at my own privates. Cynthia's fanny is like a surprising pinkish ear hidden in the brown skin. I don't want to get too close in case she does another wee.

'Told yer,' says Pauline. 'Can you see the hole?'

Not really.

'Oh yes!' I exclaim.

Pauline arches over from where she's holding Cynthia's hands. She grins at me.

'Dare you to touch it.'

I refuse, until she calls me nesh. I've got the Spanish knife in my hand now from my pocket, and I use the plastic bone handle to prod, glancingly. Pauline claims it doesn't count. Cynthia has started to writhe like a hooked fish, so Pauline knees her head back against the concrete floor and she stops, wailing.

'Go on, properly.'

I'm not nesh. It's not disgusting anyway. But Pauline thinks it's the most hilarious thing she's ever seen, in that unhilarious way she's keen on. She says I'm a lezzer because that's what lezzers do, touch each other's fannies. She says they lick fannies as well, and dares me to do that. I refuse. Then she starts saying 'jam rags'. I tell her to shut up. I wave the knife. She dodges back but she doesn't stop saying it. She swoops her badminton racquet like a sword, like we're having a fight. She's enjoying herself more than me, even though all her laughter is like hitting someone. It makes me frightened.

'Eww, Grimsby docks!' she says about my hands, which I don't even understand, but has something to do with the smell from touching Cynthia's fanny. I wish I was brave enough to make her shut up.

'You know you can put things up her. Where willies go. And jam rags.'

Pauline flourishes the racquet. Its handle is bound with faded black tape which has unravelled at the bottom, mummy-like.

'Go on then,' I say.

It isn't me. It's definitely her. I don't even use the knife, except for when I cut the three Brownie badges off Cynthia's dress. Pauline hasn't even asked to borrow the knife, she just grabs, as usual. I grab it back and wipe it off on my own dress so I can cut off the badges. I don't care about the state of my dress any more. Pauline says I'm mad for getting the badges, but I can tell she's just jealous she hasn't thought of it herself. It's true I haven't got a Brownie uniform of my own to sew them on to, but that doesn't matter. You could unpick the stitching, done so carefully in green to match by Cynthia or her mum, but it's too late now to bother. I saw at the thick nylon, leaving three ragged holes. After that there isn't anything left to do. Pauline and I roll her in what we can unwind of the tangled badminton net, like a huge caught fish that's stopped trying to flip itself back in the water. The last thing I see is Cynthia's eye, alive and ordinary through the dirty grey mesh. At least I think it's alive, but it's almost too dark now to tell.

Before we climb back out into the world, I bring the heel of my Clarks sandals down on the glasses that have skidded near the window, one, two, so that the lenses are smashed. Of all the things we've done today, it's the best.

NOT LONG AFTER they'd put the light out, the phone went in the office. The boys yapped him along the corridor after Lol had mumbled him out of bed. Frank had already been so deeply asleep that he didn't even think to put his glasses on; his reach for the receiver was a fuzzy guess. For a second or two there was just breathing at the other end, delicate and young and distressed.

'It's me, Lallie.'

'Lallie. What can I do for you, my love?'

The boys quivered. Frank sat. He didn't feel too clever on his legs. The noises at the other end, hesitations and breaths and swallowings, suggested that he needed to draw it out of her. This wasn't the time. He wasn't up to it.

'Sorry,' she said in the end, and hung up. He fell asleep in the chair until Lol came to get him. Then he did one of his miserly pees and got back into bed. It wasn't until the next morning, when he was loading his briefcase, that he saw he'd left the receiver off the cradle. He'd call her mother once he was in the office, sort everything out.

July, 1977

IF THERE HAD ever been an invitation to a screening, it didn't reach her letterbox, so in the end Vera paid eighty new pence of her own money to see the film, a few days after Virginia Wade's glorious Jubilee Wimbledon victory. There were very few other people in the cinema in Swiss Cottage, which was as it should be on the kind of bright day it was. *That Summer* wasn't much of a title, in her opinion, but then no one was asking.

The crits had been tepid. Well, *The Stage* and *The Times*, which were the ones Vera didn't have to go out of her way to read. Both had praised the girl, and Dirk, but *The Times* chap had pronounced Mike's direction to be dated. It wasn't the sort of thing she could tell, herself. It all seemed to trot along well enough, and they were right about the performances. There was the familiar shock of seeing herself not looking like herself, then wondering if this was in fact how she looked. Already two years younger than she was now, of course. Where did the time go, people said, and films showed you, ten times as large as life. Mind you, the two years showed most on the girl, whom Vera had caught a few times gurning away in a dreadful comedy programme on the box. Well, perhaps it wasn't dreadful; she was unreliable about those sort of things. Never got it. Anyway, she had watched enough of the show to register the spots matted out by pancake and the new breasts. They'd even tried to give her a bit of glamour, which she would never have. Apart from adolescence, there was something different about her face, although it might have just been the strain of trying to make the script funny.

The girl in the film was something and someone else entirely. In the film, Vera forgot who she was watching. She believed everything Lallie did, so that the girl you saw was an ignorant, cunning little pain in the arse, but transparently compelling. It was an awful waste, really. When she'd encountered Dougie at a crammed Christmas drinks party in Earls Court, he'd mooed about Lallie going to America, and the scandal of her getting kicked off a film for not being pretty enough, or for behaving unprofessionally, or for being caught pleasuring members of the crew. The third purely bilious and mainly alcoholic theory reminded Vera of the stand-in on their shoot – what was her name, Sue? Lou? – the lascivious 25-year-old midget. It would be an easy mistake to make, blaming Lallie for those escapades, always assuming she'd taken her stand-in across the pond with her. But really, what did she know? As for unprofessional behaviour, if you were giving them everything else they wanted, it meant sweet Fanny Adams. Plainness was a much more believable lapse. All the talent in the world didn't make you a star, and stars had to shine. Of course, since Vera herself had come at it from the opposite angle, smouldering in her small way, she wasn't about to deny you needed a bit of talent as well.

On screen, Dirk was gearing up to no good, and then there she was herself, hatchet-faced and disapproving. She'd not done badly for herself, considering. Only that morning, after a very lean period, she'd got a call-up for an episode of an awful action-spy-series thing. Apparently Hugh was one of the producers, bless him. She'd heard about him taking the telly shilling, and good luck to him really. It hadn't come to anything with the other producer, the American girl. In fact, Dougie had sworn blind she'd had some sort of a fling with Mike, of all people, and got him on another film in the States. Anyway, as far as Hugh was concerned, it had obviously not done Vera any harm to be nice. Seeing the film was her little treat to herself, a celebration of employment. She could write it off on her tax, as well.

79. EXT. HEXTHORPE FLATS LOCATION. DAY.

COLIN leads JUNE towards a derelict building,
once a bomb site.

> JUNE
> It doesn't look special to me.

> COLIN
> Well, you can't always tell, can you, from
> the outside?

In front of Vera, to the right of the screen, was a pair of canoodling teenagers, very clearly not there for the film. The boy – it had taken her some time to establish that he was a boy – had pink cockatoo hair, shaved at the sides in that way she'd started to spot doing the rounds. Sitting behind him would have been as bad as being trapped behind a hat-wearer. The girl, on the other hand, judging from her silhouette, didn't have any hair at all. They were odd, those youths that had bloomed in the heat, vivid and hostile, like troglodyte teddy boys. Their choice of nappy pins to adorn themselves baffled her: did they want to be babies? One she'd seen near Leicester Square had appeared to be wearing a Nazi armband, of all things.

The two in the cinema were keen for an audience. As soon as a jacketed fellow in the row behind them coughed reproval, they started acting up, the boy straddling the girl and extending his tongue, to which the girl responded ostentatiously, in a reptilian French kiss. It was annoying, but on the whole ignorable. Vera decided to ignore it.

The girl Lallie was playing walked her lonely way past the school. The scene forced the grimness of real events into Vera's mind, although at the time she had made a point of not reading anything beyond the first few newspaper reports. Certainly nothing to do with the trial. They'd had to recut some of the school scenes, apparently, as both the children involved, the victim and the other one, had been extras, and there were sensitivities to be observed. Still, justice had been done and there was enough in the papers every day to top it. There had been another girl as well, from a better home; what had happened to her? It was an awful, awful business. Better not to dwell. It certainly made you glad not to have children.

80. INT. DERELICT HOUSE LOCATION. DAY.
JUNE is unafraid, defiant even.

> JUNE
> There's nothing special about you.

> COLIN
> Shut up!

> JUNE
> Everyone knows about you, you know, you're just a—

> COLIN
> I said shut up!!

The wrench is already in his hand. JUNE screams.

Watching June meet her fate, its framing tastefully askew, Vera realized that what had happened was almost certainly the reason for the delay in releasing the film. It pursued the story, a ghost at the edge of a mirror. When, in the final moments, the camera lingered on the empty desk and the dutifully innocent faces that flanked it, Vera's tears of artistic empathy were amplified by a nearly enjoyable frisson of the real. All such a bloody waste, really. The time it took to make a film. It seemed like the be-all and end-all, and then it came to this. A July afternoon with ten people in the audience, two of them practically copulating.

She stayed long enough to catch her name, just to be sure. She always did. There it was, large as life, although not as large as some. She was the only one left to see it.

WHAT THEY DO
IN THE DARK

Amanda Coe

WHAT THEY DO
IN THE DARK

Amanda Coe

AMANDA COE ON WRITING HER NOVEL

I started writing *What They Do in the Dark* by exploring the lives of the three main characters: Gemma, Pauline and Lallie, the child TV star. Remembering my own fascination with child celebrities when I was the same age as the girls in the book, I was intrigued by the way that a child uses popular culture as a way to read the world, whereas in adulthood you realize it's a reading of us – and a wishfully inaccurate one at that. This melded with the date, 1975, a period nostalgically invoked in British culture as the last gasp of childhood innocence, but at the same time, very oddly, mythologized in the north of England as the period when the serial killer Peter Sutcliffe began to be active. (Sutcliffe, known as the 'Yorkshire Ripper' targeted sex workers.) It was a socially volatile and economically depressed era, and one in which the feelings of children were not – to put it mildly – widely considered.

I think the motor for many writers is a relationship between certain characters, or even a mood – and that was certainly the case with me: the desire to re-enter a place and time and see it through the lenses of Gemma and Pauline, and the more refracted image of Lallie. I became compelled by the developing bond between Gemma and Pauline, which is less a friendship than them holding each other in their thrall. At its outset, the relationship appears to be that between victim and bully, but the path they take together is far more complex. Charting the highs and lows of daily existence as a child became a way through the darker undertow of the narrative, and often a comic one. It was totally absorbing and strangely enjoyable to re-enter the world of ten-year-old girls, where the smallest things have entrancing, absolute importance.

DISCUSSION QUESTIONS

1. Gemma and Pauline are two very different ten-year-old girls from opposite ends of the economic spectrum. Are there similarities between the two girls?

2. The book is set in the north of England during the 1970s, a socially volatile and economically depressed time. How would the plot change if the book were set in the present? How would it stay the same?

3. When the childhood television star Lallie Paulza shoots a movie in their hometown, Gemma and Pauline jump at the opportunity to meet Lallie and audition to be in the movie. How are their motives similar? How are their motives different?

4. One major theme of the book is the relationship between parents and their children. Is the age of ten significant? How would the plot change if Gemma and Pauline were younger or older?

5. Throughout the novel, the points of view alternate from the major characters, Gemma and Pauline, to the minor players, Vera, Frank, and Quentin. Why do you think the author chose to tell this story from multiple perspectives? What are the advantages and disadvantages?

6. The reader does not hear Lallie's voice throughout the book. How does this affect your interpretation of her character? Is Lallie fully developed? How would the novel be different if Lallie's point of view were represented?

7. Why do you think that Pauline is chosen for the guest role in Lallie's movie? Do you think that the novel's climactic and devastating conclusion would unfold in a similar fashion if Pauline were not selected?

8. What does the subplot involving the cast and crew of Lallie's production company add to the story? Are there thematic paral-

lels between this subplot and the primary plot of Gemma and Pauline?

9. Juxtaposition is a major trope used throughout the book. What examples of juxtaposition can you find? What do these juxtapositions achieve?

10. Do you identify with Gemma? Does your opinion of Gemma change as the novel progresses? Why or why not?

11. Why do you think that the book opens with Lallie's obituary? How does this frame your reading of the rest of the novel?

12. Why do you think that the book ends with Vera watching Lallie's movie in the theater? How does Vera's point of view shape the conclusion?

*Available only on the Norton Web site: www.wwnorton.com/guides